D1116133

MARRY IN HASTE

AN ENDURANCE MYSTERY

MARRY IN HASTE

SUSAN VAN KIRK

FIVE STAR
A part of Gale, Cengage Learning

GALE
CENGAGE Learning®

Farmington Hills, Mich • San Francisco • New York • Waterville, Maine
Meriden, Conn • Mason, Ohio • Chicago

Copyright © 2016 by Susan Van Kirk
Five Star™ Publishing, a part of Cengage Learning, Inc.

ALL RIGHTS RESERVED.
This novel is a work of fiction. Names, characters, places, and incidents are either the product of the author's imagination, or, if real, used fictitiously.

No part of this work covered by the copyright herein may be reproduced, transmitted, stored, or used in any form or by any means graphic, electronic, or mechanical, including but not limited to photocopying, recording, scanning, digitizing, taping, Web distribution, information networks, or information storage and retrieval systems, except as permitted under Section 107 or 108 of the 1976 United State Copyright Act, without the prior written permission of the publisher.

The publisher bears no responsibility for the quality of information provided through author or third-party Web sites and does not have any control over, nor assume any responsibility for, information contained in these sites. Providing these sites should not be construed as an endorsement or approval by the publisher of these organizations or of the positions they may take on various issues.

LIBRARY OF CONGRESS CATALOGING-IN-PUBLICATION DATA

Names: Van Kirk, Susan, 1946– author.
Title: Marry in haste / Susan Van Kirk.
Description: First edition. | Waterville, Maine : Five Star Publishing, a part of Cengage Learning, Inc. 2016. | Series: An Endurance mystery
Identifiers: LCCN 2016007118 (print) | LCCN 2016012670 (ebook) | ISBN 9781432832339 (hardcover) | ISBN 1432832336 (hardcover) | ISBN 9781432832377 (ebook) | ISBN 1432832379 (ebook) | ISBN 9781432834821 (ebook) | ISBN 1432834827 (ebook)
Subjects: LCSH: Man-woman relationships—Fiction. | Murder—Investigation—Fiction. | Abused wives—Fiction. | BISAC: FICTION / Mystery & Detective / General. | GSAFD: Mystery fiction.
Classification: LCC PS3622.A5854938 M37 2016 (print) | LCC PS3622.A5854938 (ebook) | DDC 813/.6—dc23
LC record available at http://lccn.loc.gov/2016007118

Find us on Facebook– https://www.facebook.com/FiveStarCengage
Visit our website– http://www.gale.cengage.com/fivestar/
Contact Five Star™ Publishing at FiveStar@cengage.com

Printed in the United States of America
2 3 4 5 6 7 20 19 18 17 16

For my mom and dad, who taught me about kindness, love, and courage. Lucky enough to meet in this huge world and fall in love, they were never parted except by death.

ACKNOWLEDGMENTS

Bringing Grace Kimball, her friends, and the tiny town of Endurance to life was a labor of love, and it was also helped along by many other friends and experts through multiple stages of development.

Research was the first phase. Doug and Jeff Rankin, former students and later colleagues, gave me advice about old-house renovation, copyright questions, and the history of our small town. I'd like to think I taught them those things, but I fear they learned them on their own. Lockwood House is based on memories of a Victorian home I shared with a number of people living in various apartments. I am thankful to Dale Unverferth for his accurate memory of this house, right down to the mahogany woodwork.

Stan Jenks, President and CEO of Security Savings Bank in Monmouth, was very patient in explaining bank policies and practices and answering questions, sometimes more than once. While I promised him a banker in my novel, I don't think my fictional banker, Conrad Folger, was quite what he had in mind.

As always, I am grateful to Bill Feithen, Monmouth Police Chief, and Suzy Owens, Ames, Iowa, police detective, who helped me on many occasions with questions about police procedures and crime scenes. I believe Detective Owens took gleeful pleasure in telling her former English teacher, "No, it isn't right. Rewrite. Again." Marcum Spears, attorney, helped me with town history, legal questions, and the interpretation of old property notations. Thank you, Marcum.

Libraries have always occupied an acre of my heart. In researching this book, I used the facilities and helpful people in these places: the Warren County Public Library, Hewes Library at Monmouth College, the Galesburg Public Library, the Seymour Library Special Collections and Archives at Knox College, the Warren County Courthouse, and the Warren County Genealogical Society.

Four beta readers gave me feedback and helped in the first draft stage. All are senior citizens, and they provided advice about my plot. Thank you to Dorothy Behnke, Hallie Lemon, Christie Meldrum, and Marilyn Van Hoozer. Ageless brainpower and experience win.

In the next stage, I worked with Lourdes Venard, my freelance editor. She has been far more than an editor to me. She smoothed the rough edges, asked the right questions, and kept me in focus. She has also been my "chief encourager." It was a very fortunate day for me the first time she turned up at the other end of my email program.

A special thank you to my proofreaders, Hallie Lemon and Jan DeYoung. Former educators and lifelong readers, they did the close reading because we all hate typos.

I would like to thank all the people at Five Star/Cengage who have worked on or helped with my Endurance series so far. This would include Tiffany Schofield, Nivette Jackaway, Alice Duncan, Tracey Matthews, Erin Bealmear, and Deirdre Wait. And thank you to all others who work tirelessly behind the scenes, setting up the printing, compiling the catalogue, and dealing with legalities. I appreciate your help in making my books a reality.

Throughout this process I had my cohort of friends—Judy Brinkmann, Jan Gebauer, Hallie Lemon, Dee Long, and Eileen Owens—who often tolerated my absence from our adventures because I was writing. And thank you to the kind people in our small town of Monmouth. Many of you encouraged my writing and kept me going. You know who you are.

CHAPTER ONE

The heavy glass and metal doors of the Second National Bank of Endurance swung open silently, and Grace Kimball nudged her way in, checking each footstep. Her scarf hung lopsidedly, mostly to the left, and her purse strap dangled at an odd angle from her right arm. One hand was mittened, the other was bare, and her coat was covered in snow and slush, some of which dripped from her hem and onto the floor. As Grace tried to catch her balance, her boots slid unpredictably. She watched out for people brushing past her, maneuvered right along, and concentrated on her footing. Anyone familiar with her usually composed face would have been surprised to see it so flustered.

The receptionist rose from her chair and rushed over. "Oh, Ms. Kimball, what happened? Are you all right?" Frantically, she brushed snow off Grace's coat, all the while clutching her arm as if both women might end up in a pile on the floor.

"Nothing a little cleaning won't fix," she said. She struggled to unbutton her coat with frozen fingers. "I hate to be late." Grace shook her head in frustration. "I slipped on the ice as I got out of my car, and fell down." She sighed. "My dignity is all that's hurt." She shrugged off her coat and held it out and away from her clothes in disgust. Then she looked at the receptionist, and asked, "What's going on? Why are so many people out and about?"

"I suppose they're still taking back Christmas rejects and using gift cards," the receptionist answered. "By January third

11

you'd think that would be over, but the weather's kept most people inside."

"Whew! Well, I'm here, I guess. Finally." She checked the hands of the grandfather clock near the front door, and her eyes scanned the bank. "Any idea where Jeff Maitlin might be?"

"He's over in the loan department waiting for Mr. Folger. I'll walk over with you. We have coffee and hot chocolate to warm you up."

"Sounds wonderful." Grace followed her, shaking off snow as she went. She remembered the receptionist. *Sylvia Lansing. Years ago in high school she played a main role in the class play,* How to Succeed in Business without Really Trying. *Guess she's made it this far. If she can work so long for a man like Conrad Folger, she's quite a successful woman.*

That was the thing about Endurance. Grace had taught high school English in the small Illinois town of 15,000 for twenty-five years. And even though she had retired last year when she was fifty-six, she often ran into former students who still lived and worked in the area. She supposed it was good those students-now-adults couldn't read her thoughts because Grace remembered ridiculous, trivial details from their shared high school histories. It was her curse—the high school teacher curse—that those details stuck in her head as if they had a direct line to the "door of yesterday" part of her brain. At the same time, current details she needed to remember eluded her, often returning at two in the morning.

"Here's Mr. Maitlin." Sylvia pointed Grace to an attractive man sitting in a brown leather chair. Jeff Maitlin stood up, his six-foot frame unfolding at a slow pace, and he grasped Grace's cold hands, a warm smile spreading across his face. His graying brown hair fell back in a gentle wave behind his ears. She, of course, noticed his blue eyes immediately—cornflower blue. He had moved to Endurance the previous year to take up a part-time, semi-retirement job as editor of the *Endurance Register,* and only recently had he and Grace begun to date. He grinned like a snowman, and Grace gave him a quick hug. As always, she almost came up to his chin.

"I'm sure it won't be long now," Sylvia promised, and she smiled at their hug. Then she turned and left.

"How long have you been waiting?" Grace asked. She shook her brown hair back into place and finger-combed it after its snowy beating.

"Not long. You look like you've been through a blizzard. You have a cute—but red—nose. Can I get you some coffee? Hot chocolate?"

"Ah, hot chocolate would be grand." She sat down in the chair next to Jeff's and looked ruefully at her wet boots. "Why does it keep snowing?"

"Because it's January in the Midwest. When I spent all those years in New York City, I was simply preparing to survive Midwest winters. Obviously, some universal plan is at work." Jeff turned and wandered a few steps to a round table filled with coffee, tea, hot chocolate, and cookies, and he came back with a paper cup of hot chocolate. "Here you go. Say, I had several people in for a meeting this morning—town advisory members—and they raved about your latest history article. We should put more of those pieces in the newspaper."

Grace sipped her hot chocolate. "I already have in mind an article about the Victorian house you've almost bought. I'm going over to the courthouse to trace its owners. After all, 'Newspaper Editor Decides to Stay in Small Town' is such big news. At the least it would fit on page three, wouldn't you say?"

"More like back in the 'Bits and Pieces' section. Maybe you should wait until I sign the loan papers for sure. Who knows? The bank might pull out."

"I'm glad you invited me along. Coming with you gives me a chance to grill Conrad Folger about the old Lockwood house you're buying. I'm sure he knows a great deal about its history since his family goes back several generations in town."

Jeff smiled and put his hand on hers. "I missed you while you were in the desert."

"Good to be back from seeing my kids, but it's sure an enormous change from sixty-five degrees and sunshine to twenty-five degrees and snow. It's as if people in Arizona live in a parallel universe, and when I was out there, the Midwest weather was often the lead story on the evening news. I began to wonder if my plane would be able to get me back here with so many flight cancellations." She sipped her hot chocolate and glanced up at him. "Any big news while I was away?"

Jeff took a last drink of his coffee and said, "A new restaurant debuted downtown—The Depot—but you knew it was opening before you left. Your former students—I forget their names for the moment—started the place a week ago, but I think they're waiting to have a grand opening. Oh, and the Christmas tree lighting was an unmitigated disaster, but quite humorous. It was Mayor Blandford's big moment to shine, and he was primed and ready to deliver the spectacular tree lighting on the public square to kick off the Christmas season. After a few chosen words about the pioneers and the town, he pulled the switch, and several bulbs didn't light at all, but a few other bulbs exploded with a glass-shattering bang, and the breaking bulbs spooked at least five dogs in the crowd. They got loose, made a frenzied leap at the tree, and knocked it over, pinning Emily Dunsworthy against the historic fountain the mayor had so eloquently just described. But after we brushed Emily and the tree off and stood them back up, all was forgiven, and the crowd sang, 'We Wish You a Merry Christmas.' " He shook his head and chuckled at the remembered sight of the elderly former postmistress pinned against the fountain.

Grace was laughing at the Christmas disaster when suddenly

a voice exploded from behind the closed door of Conrad Folger IV's office. A second angry voice rose in disagreement—*a woman's voice*, Grace thought. Then it grew very quiet again, as if the arguers realized people might hear them. She looked at Jeff, barely able to conceal her concern, and he smiled and patted her hand. "That must be why he's running late. I deduced from people's reactions that an unplanned appointment is in my time slot. Must be a loud, disagreeable, unplanned appointment." His eyes softened, his shoulders relaxed, and he changed the subject. "So, tell me about Phoenix. How are your kids? Still dropping huge hints you should be out there full time?"

"Roger Junior wants me to move there and be a nanny to my granddaughter, Natalie. He calls her 'Little Pumpkin' because she loves eating plain pumpkin pie filling. Crazy kid. And said granddaughter, who is only four, has decided I am at least ten years old and can't be trusted. Daughter Katherine wants me there because I think she misses me, and James hasn't rendered his reasons. Now that I've retired from teaching, they think I can pull up stakes and move. I must admit I'm torn." She paused and collected her thoughts. "But I enjoy the newspaper, and I like to write and research, as long as it doesn't get me into another life-or-death situation. Last summer's murders are still fresh in my mind. After that happened, my kids decided I should stick with 'safe' topics, so I explained I'd be researching the historic old house you are about to buy and fix up. It should be safe enough."

She searched Jeff's eyes for several seconds, and then she said, "Isn't that what the guy says in the movie before he's squashed by a giant, flame-breathing lizard? On the other hand, the town's murder quota should be met for another hundred years after last summer. Maybe two hundred." She looked down at her hot chocolate, cradled in her hands on her lap. Then she turned, relief in her voice, and said, "The decision about where to live has been temporarily tabled."

Grace had just stuffed a dropped mitten into her coat pocket when, again, passionate voices rose behind the bank president's door. Both Jeff and Grace listened intently. She caught a word or two like, "can't" and "regret it," and they were quickly followed by the sound of a heavy object falling hard on the floor. Then silence. Folger's assistant, shocked, started to rise from her chair, thought about it, and sat down again. Grace turned to Jeff as they both heard the sound of glass crashing and breaking.

"Oh, dear," said Andrea Dunning. This time she rose from behind her desk and took a few tentative steps toward the office door. As if the door sensed her anxiety, it opened, and a furious Conrad Folger motioned her over. He focused on her and ignored the other inquisitive faces, and Grace watched him whisper something. Andrea left and returned with a broom and dust pan. The door closed. A few minutes later the executive assistant came out, broom at her side and dust pan horizontally squared. Focusing on the dust pan, she marched past Grace and Jeff and disappeared through a door near the back of the reception area.

Jeff looked at Grace, his expression puzzled. "Well. Maybe this isn't such a good day to sign loan papers." Then they were both silent for a moment. Jeff spoke first, asking, "So, teacher lady, what do you know about Conrad Folger IV, bank president?"

Grace thought for a moment. "I heard he had quite a temper in high school, but I doubt that he throws objects at his customers. You understand, I never had him or his brother Will as students, but I hear things. I try to be fair, but I'd have to say he wasn't terribly likable. He was smart enough, but not a genius. He was a bit arrogant—well, more than 'a bit'—and usually got his way. And if he didn't, his father made sure he did. Went to an Ivy League school." She lowered her voice. "Though he hardly had the grades to get in. My guess would be his father arranged that also. And, of course, he had the bank waiting for him if he managed to graduate, which, somehow, he did. But you must understand I heard much of this secondhand. Roger, my husband, had dealings with Folger's father and certainly heard a great deal about his son's temper. Folger married Emily Petersen. Never could figure out how that happened. But he must have some good qualities for Emily to marry him. Maybe he's changed."

"Why? What was so puzzling about his wife?"

"Emily? She was a clever girl who found her footing when she left for college. Don't get me wrong. In high school she was quiet, but she had friends and graduated near the top of her class. I worked with her closely on class plays, and I got to know her well. She was wonderful—I thought of her as my other daughter. College was where she gained her self-confidence. Can't think why she married someone like Conrad. Maybe it's that 'bad boy' syndrome—you know, nice girl attracted to bad boy."

Just as Jeff was about to reply, the door to Folger's office tore open, slammed against the wall with a shattering crash, and a blond woman, swearing loudly, her face flushed, stormed out of the office. She adjusted her sunglasses, stalked toward the front door, and anyone in her path quickly moved back, giving her considerable space.

"Who was that?" Jeff asked, and his gaze followed the woman out the door.

"Got me. I've never seen her before," Grace replied.

"Probably someone we shouldn't invite to our loan-signing open house?"

Grace paused and turned to Jeff. "Really? You've planned a party?"

"Well, the guest list only has one. Thought I'd stop there. No need to have the house too crowded." His fingers grazed the collar of her blouse, and he gave her his most charming smile.

"I'll have to check my calendar, Mr. Maitlin, and see if I'm too busy."

"Thought you might. Hope you won't be . . . too busy."

She raised her eyebrows and gave him a bemused look.

Just then, Andrea Dunning returned, wiped her hands as if that situation were over, and stood before Jeff and Grace. Her usually assured voice was flustered. "Sorry for all the noise. I can promise you those events rarely happen here. Well, not always . . . I mean, never . . . but, actually, I guess 'never' doesn't work after this morning." Shaking her head in confusion, she picked up some files from her desk and delivered them to Folger's office, knocking on his door. Grace heard a muffled reply.

Andrea disappeared inside and closed the door momentarily. Next, the door opened and Conrad Folger walked out, turned down a hallway, and disappeared. Then Andrea returned, her equilibrium restored, and said, "Mr. Folger will see you shortly. Follow me, and you can wait in his office."

"Is it safe?" Jeff asked.

She turned and looked at him to gauge if he were joking. Seeing the smile on his face, she answered, "Oh, yes. He didn't throw the vase. He seldom throws glassware at customers. Maybe only twice a month." Then she smiled.

CHAPTER TWO

They followed Andrea Dunning into the bank president's office. "Mr. Folger will be back in a moment. He just stepped out. Make yourselves comfortable." And, with that, she left.

Grace gazed around the lavish office. She saw an entire wall of bookshelves, possibly solid walnut, which held bank regulations and official-looking document boxes. On the opposite side of the room were shelves of leather-bound books, many of which appeared to be first editions. A white leather sofa and chairs sat in the middle of the room, and the hardwood floor was topped by an expensive Persian area rug. Conrad's massive desk occupied the corner farthest from the door, with a library lamp and gold nameplate. The desk was immaculately clean. No paper piles or folders sitting at various angles. It was quite the impressive office.

The wall behind Folger's desk displayed old pictures of the bank from when Conrad's father and his predecessors ruled over their empire from this office. Grace wandered over and scrutinized the photographs. One grainy photo showed the first Conrad Folger laying a cornerstone in 1852. It appeared to be the oldest picture and had probably been restored from an original. Grace stared at his face and studied his hard eyes, thin mouth, and square jaw. Standing behind him, back a few steps, was Folger's wife. She was dressed for the occasion in a black skirt with matching black gloves. The plain skirt was topped by a standard white blouse with a corset under it and a dark jacket over it. Her hat covered a severe hairstyle, and her eyes stared at the camera as if she wasn't sure what it did.

Grace studied another black and white portrait next to the first one. This photo appeared to be a later, better-quality picture, and was labeled "Conrad Folger II." She almost gasped at the similarity. He was the mirror image of his father, with comparable, stark features that announced "frugal." As if guarding the vaults, he, too, stood in front of the bank doors. He must have been president of the bank in the twentieth century, since Grace could see the edge of a Depression-era car near the side of the photo.

Finally, she studied a more present-day picture; judging from the people's clothes, she guessed the scene was from the 1980s. This must be the current Conrad's father. His pinched mouth and hard-eyed look were copied by three children who stood in front of him. Next to Folger, his wife—dressed in a conservative, old-fashioned suit with the large shoulder pads of the early 1980s—looked on unhappily. The tallest child was the Conrad Grace recognized. His brother, Will, was the oldest, and his sister, Jessalynn, stood between them, ill at ease. Grace speculated their father was a "spare the rod, spoil the child" kind of parent. Glancing back at the group of pictures, she thought about the four generations of discontented, glum faces. Could it be a genetic inheritance? Scattered nearby the historic photos were framed certificates and awards. She turned and joined Jeff, who was looking at the family photos on the credenza.

Grace followed his eyes to the photo of Emily and her two children. The boy looked a little older than the girl, and he smiled with an engaging look, directly into the camera. "He has Conrad's eyes," Grace said. The girl's hair was neatly brushed back from her face and gathered into cascading ringlets. She stared off to the side of the camera lens, her mouth and eyes expressing discomfort at having her picture taken. Grace smiled at the resemblance to her mother. Emily had been the student assistant for several plays Grace directed at the high school, and the two had spent long hours together. Of course, that had been years ago. More recently, Grace had seen Emily from a distance in the drug store, and before she could catch her attention to say "hello," Emily scurried out of the store by a different exit. It was obvious she had wanted to avoid speaking.

"Well," said Jeff. "Quite a nice-looking family."

"Emily looks much as I remember her, but a little older, more brittle, and hardened at the edges by life, I suppose. She was my student, along with Jessalynn Folger, the first year I taught. Her family owned a store and was the epitome of middle-class. Conrad's brother, Will, is a vice president at the bank. I always thought he was considerably smarter than Conrad and definitely more human. I've talked with him several times at the bank. But Emily is the one I knew best." She stood in front of the photo a moment, silently. Then she turned and glanced at the fireplace. "I wonder if it's a good idea to have a fireplace in a bank. All that paper."

"Another satisfied customer," a voice boomed. Conrad Folger smiled as he walked in the door with his executive assistant following a few steps behind. "Sorry about the fracas." He shook his head. "It can be a scary world out there, and sometimes people who are, shall we say, 'a little confused' walk in."

At that moment, Andrea Dunning stepped around Folger and adjusted his tie.

"Ah, thank you, Ms. Dunning. Guess I am still a little tense." She patted the tie in place—gave it a satisfied look—turned, and left the office, quietly closing the door. "Don't know what I'd do without that woman. Of course, Emily chooses my secretaries. Never too young or too good-looking. Well, you remember Emily from high school, don't you, Ms. Kimball?"

"Oh, please, call me Grace," she said. "And you're right. Emily was a student of mine." She put her hand on Jeff's arm and said, "This is Jeff Maitlin, Conrad, and he's the one you actually want to speak with—I'm just along for the ride."

Grace still remembered Folger's eyes after speaking with him on several occasions. They were gray, almost a hard, steel color. Even now, he had a look of aggressiveness about him—the muscles in his shoulders strained the material of his pale beige shirt. *How could Emily have married him?* she wondered.

Folger turned to the editor. "Jeff. What a great job you've done reviving the newspaper. You've breathed new life into the old rag." He shook Jeff's hand. "Please, both of you come over and have a seat on the sofa. I'll pull up a chair. My loan officer, Gus Hart, is putting the finishing touches on your papers, and he'll be in with them soon."

"I don't know who that young woman was," began Jeff, "but are you all right?"

"Sure. All in a day's work. People think anyone can borrow money—like that young woman. Fact is, I turn down a lot of loans to people who don't qualify, and, believe me, I can tell on the spot. As someone important once said, 'The poor will always be with us.' " He laughed quietly. "Not with me, however. Lots of changes in rules about lending money. After the recent hard economic times, the government regulators are breathing down our necks." He turned and indicated all the heavy files along one of the walls. "Way too much to read and learn." Then he walked to the bookcase and slowly ran his fingers across several of the book spines absent-mindedly.

Grace decided to turn the conversation to a more personal note. She said, "I was admiring your historical photographs of your family on the wall. Who are those people?"

Conrad came back across the room and a satisfied smile came over his face. He glanced at the photographs and then walked over toward them, pointing at the first one. "This one is the oldest. My great-grandfather began the Second National in 1852. Quite a man of foresight. Anyway, he left it to his son, Conrad II, in 1901. That's his picture with his wife over there. He was an amazing man, my grandfather. Guided the bank through the Depression and both world wars, and he never closed its doors. I'm told he was instrumental in bringing job-saving industry to the town, and while he might have been a bit aggressive in his tactics, he helped restore the economy of Endurance in a financially shaky time. Then," he said, as he moved to the photo with the three children, "this is my father, Conrad III, and my mother, Gertrude Folger. Of course, they're gone now. I think this must have been taken sometime in the eighties, because I would have been about ten. That's my brother Will and my sister Jessalynn. She doesn't live here anymore. Moved away after she finished high school. Probably married by now to some beer-swilling construction guy who keeps her knocked up and in line."

Before Grace could close her astonished mouth, which was hanging open at that thought, Conrad abruptly changed subjects. "Where is Gus Hart?" he asked, as he glanced impatiently at his watch. Walking over to the desk, he touched a button and called Ms. Dunning to remind the loan officer to bring the Maitlin papers immediately. Then he returned to his chair, his charming smile appeared once again, and, glancing at Jeff, he said, "I always wondered what the old Lockwood house looks like on the inside. You know it was built when my great-grandfather was alive, and he knew the old judge quite well. Used to play poker with him at one of the saloons downtown, I've been told. So many people have owned that house. Too bad they turned it into apartments." He glanced at his watch. "What do you plan to do with it, Jeff?"

"Thinking about restoring it to its late 1800s specifications, and perhaps turn it eventually into a bed and breakfast. Actually, I thought it might be a good place for folks to stay when they come back for various occasions at Endurance College."

"Sounds like a clever idea. Does this mean you'll have to consult the National Register about how to do that?"

"No, it's not on the Register, but I am going to get some help from Todd Janicke, who, I'm told, is an expert at restoration. The newspaper's going well right now, and I figure our circulation has gone up considerably. I can use some of my time on the weekends to work on the house, but it will be a hobby for a while."

"I remember my dad talking about old Judge Lockwood. I think he'd heard tales from his father. Lockwood owned a great deal of the town back in the late 1800s. One business was a lumberyard, so that's probably what he used to build the house. Quite a showplace in its day. Even had a huge ballroom on the third floor. I'm not sure what happened to the house after his death."

"Speaking of history, how many generations of your family have run this bank, Conrad? I'm relatively new in town so I don't know the history like Grace does," Jeff asked.

"Four so far, and my son, Conrad, will be the fifth generation. We just had his eleventh birthday last week." He glanced at the photo behind his desk. "That's a great picture of Emily, don't you think?"

"She is an awfully special woman," Grace responded. "And your daughter? What's her name?"

"Caitlin."

"She looks like her mother." Grace glanced at the photo and wondered once again how Emily could have married Conrad. Then she looked at the bank president and, remembering why she came, decided to bring up a new idea.

"What you mentioned about the judge interests me. I'm planning to research the history of his house, and I'll have to check out the judge, too. I don't imagine your great-grandfather would have left any papers mentioning Judge Lockwood?"

"Not really. Anything he left generally had something to do with the bank." He shifted in his seat and brushed an imaginary piece of thread off his pant leg. The room was silent for a moment. Then Folger said, "Grace is a great addition to the paper, Jeff. She would have been horribly tough on me in high school— all those commas and dangling modifiers. I never was much of a writer. Numbers were more my thing. But I know she and Emily were thick as thieves. Emily often talks about you, Grace, always in reverent tones."

Grace rolled her eyes. "Exactly how I need to be remembered—in 'reverent tones.' "

Folger was about to reply when they heard a knock at the door and a dark-haired, rotund man entered, carrying a brown folder. Grace judged him to be in his forties, and he handed the folder to Conrad without a word.

"Ah, good. Jeff Maitlin and Grace Kimball, this is Augustin Hart, one of my loan officers. Oh, you already met Gus, didn't you, Jeff?" He turned to Hart. "Always a few minutes late."

Grace saw Hart glance at Folger with a dark look, but then he quickly changed his expression, greeted them, and shook hands, forcing a smile. After he turned and left, an awkward silence settled on the room.

Conrad dropped the file on his desk and rubbed his hands together. "Well, let's get to it. You sit here, Jeff, and Grace you can relax on the sofa if you'd like. We'll get these signed in no time." He reached for a pen in his desk drawer while Jeff moved over to a chair next to Conrad's desk. As Grace watched, they began turning pages and writing initials and names. Every so often the banker would explain a clause or a paragraph. Grace glanced out the window and thought about how much work

Lockwood House would be. *Lots of long and expensive work,* she thought. She observed people walking down the sidewalk out in front of the bank, helped by the salt on the concrete. Suddenly, the sound of Peter, Paul, and Mary's "If I Had a Hammer" filled the air. Both men looked up at her, Folger's face a study in irritation.

"Oh, no. Sorry," she said, as she fished through her purse for her cell phone. "I thought I'd turned the sound off. Guess when I nearly broke into pieces on the ice this morning, I totally forgot." She punched a button to decline the call. "It's my contractor. Excuse me."

The men went back to their business, and Grace tiptoed out of the office and quickly called Del Novak's phone.

"Hi, Del. What's up?"

"Well, 'what's up' is that a crazy woman is standing in your kitchen with an iron skillet in her hand, ready to use it on my head at any moment. I thought I was supposed to come over and do some measurements in the kitchen this morning."

Grace blew out a long breath. "You're right, Del. I forgot to tell my sister-in-law, Lettie, you were coming. In fact, I hadn't mentioned the renovation plans to her yet. I figured she'd have a heart attack. She considers the kitchen hers. Sorry about this. Please, put her on the phone, and I'll straighten it out."

"Thanks, Grace." Then she heard him explain to Lettisha Kimball that Grace wanted to speak with her.

"Who is this man?" Lettie nearly blasted Grace's ear as she yelled into the phone. "This guy is over here saying he's supposed to measure stuff in *my* kitchen. Say the word, Gracie, and I'll throw him out. I was about ready to start some lunch, and he just knocks on the door, says he's here to measure something, and walks right in, free as you please. What's going on, Gracie? He looks suspicious to me. Want me to run him off?"

Grace decided not to chastise her, as usual, because Lettie

had called her "Gracie," a habit of Lettie's that drove Grace crazy. "First of all, it's 'my' kitchen, even though I appreciate everything you do to help me. Second, I am going to make some changes. Modernize a bit. It will actually be easier on you, Lettie. The gentleman with the measuring tape is a contractor named Del Novak. I've hired him."

Silence at the other end of the phone. Then, "Hmph! Well, I never. You know you can't be too careful these days. I haven't seen this guy before. What should he look like?"

"Lettie, Del doesn't look familiar because he recently moved here from Massachusetts. His daughter and grandchild are here, and he's retired, but doing some carpentry to keep busy. I met him at the newspaper when he stopped in to start a subscription." Silence at the other end of the phone. *Lettie seems to be at a loss for words, a highly unusual circumstance,* thought Grace.

After the long pause, Lettie said, "Well, all right. But I will stay right here and keep an eye on him."

Grace looked up at the ceiling, counted to five, and said, "Thanks, Lettie. I promise we'll discuss this when I get home. For now, please just let him do his work, and give him the phone so I can talk to him."

Then Del Novak's voice came over the phone, surprisingly calm. "Grace, it's fine. I hadn't met your sister-in-law, but she certainly looks out for your interests. I'll do the measurements, and you can explain."

"Thank you, Del. I'm sorry she's so blunt. Lettie lived with me after my husband died, years ago, and she helped with the children. Even though she doesn't live with me these days, she does come over and cook. She considers my kitchen her territory. This may be a bit of a problem, but I'll get it sorted out."

"Great. I figure I'll start next week."

"Sounds good. By then the kitchen should be peaceful." *I hope,* she thought.

Will Folger, Conrad's brother, brushed past Grace, smiled, and walked into Conrad's office. Grace followed him in, glancing up at his slightly stooped shoulders. He walked in a jittery manner, as if his nerves were tightly wired. Curly, light-brown hair fell slightly over the collar of his shirt, and Grace saw he was carrying some folders. Looking past him, she watched Jeff and Conrad shake hands, the official signing over.

"Conrad, when you're finished here, I need to see you on an urgent matter," Will said.

"Jeff, this is my brother, Will, who is a vice president at the bank. Will, Jeff Maitlin, the editor of the *Endurance Register,* and now a happy loan recipient of the bank."

After another round of handshakes, Grace and Jeff turned to leave, but not before Grace noticed Will whisper something to Conrad that caused the bank president's face to darken.

Conrad broke away from the conversation quickly to say, "Oh, Jeff. By the way, I'm having a dinner for several couples and a poker party for some of the bank managers and a few men friends. Just a small group. Why don't you and Grace stop over too? It'll be on the sixth around seven. You do play poker, don't you?"

"Sure. Love to. Maybe I can win enough to make a payment on this loan. But we can't make dinner. We have some plans earlier in the evening. Thanks for the dinner invitation. I'd like to stop by for poker, though. Around nine or so?"

"I'd say make it nine-thirty. It's a friendly game, right, Will?"

"Sure," his brother said, smiling. "Mostly Conrad and I try to best each other and not do too much collateral damage."

As Jeff and Grace left, he closed the door, but not before they both heard a gruff urgency in Will's voice. Jeff turned to her and whispered, "Is it my imagination, or should I be worried about borrowing money from a bank full of anxious people?"

CHAPTER THREE

Emily Folger stepped into the warm, scented water, tentatively at first. Biting her scarred lip, she immersed herself in her bath, relieved Conrad and the children were gone for the day. She sat perfectly still and listened. Silence. Conrad had hustled the children off to school, dropping them on his way to work. She could hear her pulse pound at the thought of her husband. Looking down at her arms, she examined the bruises that were healing just in time for the new ones. This time what was it? Oh, the dishes weren't in the right place in the dishwasher. *If only I could do things better,* she thought. *If only I could remember and think about what I'm supposed to do.* She winced as the warm water washed over her arms and lower back. This time he'd used his belt, the first object that came to hand. Her chin trembled, and she clasped her hands.

Carefully, she straightened her back. *I need to get dinner ready early tonight, as soon as he gets home. Cook something special, something he likes. Maybe veal cutlets. He's had a lot of stress lately.* She passed her hand over her forehead as if it would help her think better. *And I have to plan and shop for his poker game and dinner. I need to ask him for more money for the alcohol.* Emily's pulse raced faster, and her stomach knotted. *How to get him to see that?* She stared out the window into the backyard and a single tear slid down her face. She grimaced and clenched her jaw at the thought of asking for the money.

Flinching, she gently washed the purplish bruises on her

arms. *I didn't read his face right this time. How could I be so dumb?* She squeezed her eyes shut, then opened them again. *I can't seem to focus these days. Stupid me.* She heard a noise, and, startled, looked up at the window, but she didn't hear anything else. No car door. No footsteps on the gravel. He'd stop by the house at various times of day, and she knew the sound of his car door closing. When she heard that door shut, she'd try to stop shaking and look like she was cleaning the kitchen or folding laundry. Anything to use her hands so he wouldn't notice her trembling. He hated weakness. This time she must have imagined the door. Letting out a slow, deep breath, she tried to control her anxiety, slow her breathing.

"Go ahead. Call the police," he'd said, in his scary, deadly quiet voice she had grown to fear. "Who would believe you?" Conrad crossed his arms, and his face broke into its usual belittling smirk. He was right, of course, like always. Then she remembered the time they talked about her getting a part-time job. "Why do you think you need money? I'm a bank president, for God's sake. How would it look in the community to have people see my wife working? If you need money, just ask me for it." Then he swept all her perfume bottles off her vanity and glared at her as they fell to the floor, breaking into jagged pieces, their sharp, fragrant odors a stark contrast to the dark silence.

She leaned down, groaned slightly, and began washing her legs, ankles, feet. Sometimes it was harder to bend, but today her lower back was feeling not too bad. *What day is it?* she thought. *Thursday? Friday? The poker party and dinner. Which day was that? Is this a day Conrad comes home for lunch?* She bit her lip. At such a fearful thought, she cautiously pulled herself out of the tub and slouched into her bathrobe. Her chest tightened, and she rubbed her forehead.

Sitting down at her vanity, she brushed her hair and cringed as her hairbrush stroked the soft spot where he had pulled out a handful of hair. Her head still hurt a little, but she could comb some hair over so the bald spot wouldn't be noticeable. She stared at her blue eyes. Her eyelashes looked thinner than they used to. Was she imagining it? She blinked her eyes several times and stared again. She stopped her hairbrush in mid-air. Her hair—the shiny, gold, thick tresses—was now thin, drooping, and dry. Maybe she should go see Judy, her beautician. No. It had been so long since she'd had her hair done, and Judy would wonder why her hair was in such disarray. She couldn't think of what else she could do.

She stared down at the pale-pink hairbrush—a gift from her mother. Emily brooded about her parents. They'd been married fifty years. Never had there been a divorce in the Petersen family. Never. Her parents were only a few hours away, but it might as well be continents. She thought about her mother's advice: "You marry, you stay married, through thick and thin. If your marriage is not working right, you figure out a way to change it." Emily stared in the mirror without seeing. *Change it,* she thought. She knew it must be her fault—the bruises, and the sore back. She forgot so many things lately. *I'll call my sister-in-law and get her to tell me the date of the dinner,* she thought. *Darlene will know.*

Perhaps Conrad's day at work would go well, and he'd be happier tonight. Maybe she could get him to forgive her for her stupidity. He was right, of course. He was better at making the decisions. She kept forgetting.

Suddenly her brush stopped as if it had remembered something. *The poker party. Alcohol.* She involuntarily shuddered. She knew what that meant. One time when he drank too much, she heard all about how she had to quit her volunteer job at the hospital because she needed to be home for him and the kids. She quit, despite the pleas of her mentor to stay. The patients loved her and looked forward to her volunteer day each week. She discarded the thought and moved on to a volunteer job as room mother in Caitlin's class at school. It lasted a month before Conrad heard in town about his wife and told her to stop. That night he went through half a bottle of whiskey and, well, she didn't want to think about it. After that he was more careful and didn't break any bones resulting in a trip to the emergency room and awkward questions.

Maybe he'll be happier when he comes home tonight, she thought, trying to fortify herself.

She jumped at the peal of the front doorbell. Carefully slipping down the upstairs hallway, she stole a peek out the corner of the living room window, and recognized the van from the local flower shop in the driveway. She slumped and sagged against the wall in relief. Then she lurched to the bedroom and tugged on a sweater and sweatpants. Moving down the stairs as quickly as her bruises would allow, she cautiously opened the front door.

"Hi, Ms. Folger. Got a delivery here. Man, the guy must love you a lot."

"Thanks, Jim," she said. She took the roses and added, "Yes, Conrad certainly is thoughtful, isn't he?"

Chapter Four

Grace Kimball stared at the façade of The Depot, a restaurant her former students had opened while she was in Arizona. Endurance had always been a railroad town, and the brick building on south Main Street was perfect for a restaurant. Some of the brick came from the old depot, saved by quite a few people in town when the historic building closed and was eventually razed. A vintage clock stood on the sidewalk in front of the restaurant, as well as an old-time lamp with three globes. The restaurant's name, in gold, old-fashioned letters, was painted on an oval-shaped wooden sign, and a wooden handcart, used to move passengers' luggage, leaned against the wall. Her former students, Abbey and Camilla, had been working on this project since late summer.

She walked into the restaurant, spotting her friends immediately, but before going over to them, she studied the new décor. Recessed lighting was easy on the eyes and it was aided by skylights, which helped the plants in the hanging pots. One whole wall was comprised of original brick from a building that had seen over a hundred years of history. The predominant colors were dark green and white throughout the room, contrasting nicely with the faded red brick. Booths lined the walls, and tables sat through the middle of the space. An old-style wooden bench from the train station sat at the front of the room where people could sit while waiting for tables. All along the walls were signs from railroad stations in various locations.

Jeff had told her Abbey and Camilla planned to hire some college art students to paint a train mural with historical events from the town's history on the back wall. The kitchen must be in the back, Grace thought, because she could see flames rise from the far side of the room through the window in the kitchen door.

She hung up her coat and scarf and went over to a table where her friends were waiting as they silently studied menus. TJ Sweeney, Deb O'Hara, and Jill Cunningham often met Grace for lunch, and all of them agreed this might be their new "go to" place. Grace had studied the new restaurant's menu in the newspaper ads. She thought the house salad with candied pecans, apples, and crumbled goat cheese would be a good start. But the menu also included historical references to The Ties that Bind (French fries), a Santa Fe Salad, the Burlington Northern Quesadilla, the Depot Steak, a Train Wreck Burger, a Porter's Delight, and a Conductor's Special. Deb O'Hara had mentioned to Grace that the owners planned to have a wild mushroom celebration in April.

"This should keep ya happy," Abbey Parker said, as she placed multiple dishes in front of TJ Sweeney, Endurance's only female police detective. TJ pulled in her chair, grabbed a fork, and dug in like she hadn't eaten in three days. Her dark, shiny hair glowed, reflecting the light just above their table. She had olive skin, which turned the head of more than one guy as she walked down the street—a gift from her white father and black mother. "And here are your extra fries, Detective Sweeney."

"Sorry, Grace. Had to order early because I'm due back at the office soon."

Grace smiled at TJ, her best pal. The detective had been in Grace's high school English class, and Grace had mentored her and convinced her to go to college. TJ not only graduated from the state university with honors, but she also blew away the

Endurance police exam and forced the male power structure to hire her. By last summer, TJ had moved up the ranks to detective and solved several murders. Because Grace had become involved in the whole ghastly situation, the harrowing experience had also proved TJ and Grace had each other's backs.

The rest of them ordered their lunches from Abbey while TJ worked on hers.

"How did the big paper signing go this morning?" TJ asked, before she shoved a sweet potato fry in her mouth.

"Very uneventful," Grace replied. Then she remembered, and her voice became animated. "Oh, no. Not uneventful. We heard some sort of big skirmish in Folger's office just before we went in, and some blond woman came out ready to take the place down. I have no idea what that was about."

They caught up on news and then Abbey brought their food, placing multiple dishes on the table, and left in a hurry. "I'll come back and talk in a minute, Ms. Kimball. Right now I'm just rushed." Then TJ returned to the story from the bank.

"We didn't get any calls at the police department from the bank."

"Conrad played it down," said Grace. "Said she didn't qualify for a loan."

"Did you know this blond woman?" asked Deb O'Hara. She leaned in toward her friends and said, "I do occasionally hear whispers and rumors about Conrad Folger."

"Speak of the devil," Grace murmured. She looked over Jill Cunningham's shoulder toward the open doorway, as Folger, his brother, Will, and two other bank employees walked in, allowing a stream of cold air to whip over the tables. Grace watched them swagger past her and her friends, laughing loudly at something one of them had said, and navigating toward a table near the back of the restaurant. She also looked across the room at Abbey and was surprised to see her eyes glaring at

Folger, her hands balled up into fists. Then the men pulled out chairs and hung up coats and hats on a coat tree in a corner. As quickly as the noisy entrance began, it ended on a quieter note: they sat down and sorted through table mats, silverware, and menus.

"That's quite a group," Jill ventured. "They have the strut down perfectly that says 'boys' club' and 'we own the place.' "

"Maybe they do," answered Grace. "It's likely Abbey and Camilla borrowed money from Folger's bank to get their restaurant started. I think Jeff told me they plan to have an official grand opening in a couple of weeks. I'm glad the two of them managed to pull this off. Abbey has always wanted a restaurant of her own, and Camilla is an amazing cook. I hope they can make a go of it." She continued to observe Abbey, who had turned and stomped back to the kitchen, thrusting the door open so hard she nearly struck one of the waitresses.

"If these sweet potato fries are any indication of their new menu, they won't have any problem," Deb added. "Here, Grace, try one," she said, pulling it from her plate. "Yum. Now I need a margarita to go with them."

"Fantastic," Grace replied, and watched as Abbey brought more plates. "You know, I've noticed, since I came back from Arizona, that everyone looks so pale and depressed," Grace ventured, taking a bite of Deb's sweet potato fry. "Mmmm. Those are good!"

"You have to remember winter in the Midwest—gray skies, seasonal affective disorder, and disgust with the wind, cold, and ice," Jill answered crisply. Jill Cunningham was an accountant, and her world was a black and white, factual place. She ran two miles every morning, snow, rain, or shine, and her red, curly hair bounced as she walked. Fishing a piece of chicken out of her noodle soup with her spoon, she scooped it into her mouth, closed her eyes, and whispered, "Mmm."

"Not everyone has hibernated because of the weather," said TJ. "Just before Christmas break, five of the frat guys from Endurance College were out racing on the lake ice north of town, and a piece of the ice broke off and stranded them in the middle of the lake. The thermometer said ten degrees. It's good one of them could find his cell phone and still have the wits and unfrozen fingers to dial for help. Put quite a few people out since a helicopter from Woodbury had to rescue them. Evidently, they were still full of 'anti-freeze' and thought they were on some television reality show. Their interview on WHOC was hilarious because they were still drunk, and all they wanted to know was if they'd been voted off the island."

"Geez. To be that young and stupid," Jill said. She waved a hand and dismissed the college generation.

"Who's the waitress over there? I don't recognize her, and I thought I knew most of the people in town. Grace? Was she one of your students?" Deb asked.

Grace turned around and took a surreptitious look at the waitress. She was in profile, taking an order from a table a few yards away. Quite a stunner, she had dark red hair and, despite her standard issue waitress uniform, a voluptuous look about her. Grace also noted a decidedly competent air to her mannerisms. Slowly, she turned back around. "I don't know her."

"My, my," said TJ. "The guys in the place are sure eyeing her." She glanced around the room at the admiring looks directed toward the newcomer.

"No wonder. In a town the size of Endurance we don't see new faces often. And she is quite attractive," Deb answered. "That red hair is gorgeous."

Grace studied the restaurant. Abbey scurried back and forth with plates, and another young woman, whom Grace remembered from high school, carried trays and glasses. Across the room, the red-haired waitress finished up an order and headed toward the back to place it with the kitchen. Grace guessed Camilla was in the back, cooking, with at least two of her henchwomen, and she could see tops of heads moving behind the window in the door separating the kitchen from the eating area. Occasionally, the cooks placed plates of steaming food on the top of the counter just outside the kitchen door, waiting for the waitresses to scoop them up. Grace noticed Janice Binderson picking up plates to deliver to customers. *Janice. I remember her speech on how to make hand-tossed pizza dough. Cynthia Moore, self-crowned queen of the cheerleading squad, was in the front row. Just as Janice was tossing the dough into the air, the fire alarm went off, the pizza dough went flying, and it landed in Cynthia's blond, perfectly coiffed hair. Janice never had much sense of focus.* Suddenly, Grace was called back from her memories by Jill's voice.

"I like the menu and the theme they came up with for the place," said Jill. "The Depot." Her voice turned quiet and she sighed. "Too bad it isn't there anymore."

"You're so right," said Deb, and sighed also. She brushed a hand through her curly, blond hair, looked off into the distance, and did her dramatic long-ago-and-far-away impression. "When I went to Endurance College, we'd go to the train depot on the first morning of finals. Blueberry pancakes. They'd melt in your mouth. I've never eaten any better, and the memory of them is stored in my taste buds. We would walk in the front door and see a group of shoeshine stands—guys would be sitting in the high chairs with their feet up, and youngsters would be shining shoes, whipping those cleaning rags across the shiny surfaces and twisting them around. It was such a grand old station. The porter and ticket agents would have on snazzy uniforms. Hard to forget. Now it would be as if you had walked into another time."

"Strangely enough, the station was already there when the Lockwoods lived in the huge house Jeff is buying. They might have taken a train from that station," Grace said.

"Must have been nice to get on the train, go to Chicago for the day, and come right back to this little town. And that depot was an architectural gem—all black stone, tile floors, high ceilings, and huge spaces. Most of the small town depots have been phased out in favor of speed, ugly architecture, and less overhead," TJ said, and she yawned. "Man, I must have been hungry. I'm done while you all are about halfway through."

"I can never figure out how you eat so much food, TJ, and still stay in such amazing shape," snapped Jill. "I have to run miles and miles just to keep even."

TJ leaned back in her chair and patted her firm belly. "Good genes, Jill. And, every so often I get a good workout . . . at night."

"Oh, honestly," said Grace, her voice feigning exasperation. "We haven't heard anything about the latest boy toy to grace your nocturnal hours."

"Let's say I'm between relationships. What is it they say these days? 'It's complicated.' "

"Well, not to change the subject, but this should be a celebration," Deb said. "After all, we haven't been together for a while, and Grace has finally returned from Arizona. Now that all our kids have gone back to where they live, we finally have a little time together. How was Arizona, by the way, Grace?"

Before she could answer, Grace noted a small but growing problem at the back table with the bankers. The red-haired waitress had delivered food and coffee, and just as she was leaving, Conrad Folger pulled the belt ties on her apron so it came loose. She turned, gave him an exaggerated smile, and spilled some coffee on his pant leg. Folger immediately stood up and grabbed his napkin and his leg where the hot coffee hit. Grace could barely hear their conversation in the buzz of voices in the room.

"Why, you little—I'll have you fired. You did that on purpose."

The waitress looked at him with mock concern and said, "Oh, I'm so sorry, sir. My clumsiness. Just a second and I'll get a wet cloth to fix the damage." She turned and went through the door to the kitchen. Will smirked at his brother as only a competitive sibling could.

"Grace? Arizona?"

"Oh. Sorry. I was watching the bankers. Arizona. Yes. It was wonderful. Lower sixties and seventies instead of twenties like it is here, and gorgeous, blue skies every day. But I had to come back to my besties, my best friends, that is."

"And the children?" asked Deb, a solicitous look on her face.

"Oh, they're fine. Very busy. You know, when you're retired, you forget how busy you were all those years you worked and raised kids. It's wonderful to go out and see them, but they have crazy, over-scheduled lives, and I don't really fit into those schedules well. Reminds me of those years when I raised my own three, and we'd go see my parents in Indianapolis. It was lovely to visit, but the older my parents got and the busier I became, the less our worlds had in common." She paused and looked at each of them. "Kind of sad when you think about it."

"All right. Enough 'sad'," TJ cut in. "We're celebrating. Remember?"

Camilla Sites came out of the kitchen and walked over to their table. Grace could see she was perspiring from the hot ovens. She had a bandanna over her black hair, and drops of sweat glistened on her forehead. Camilla smiled, a beautiful smile with white, straight teeth, framed by mauve lipstick. Grace remembered Camilla and Abbey from their high school days, and they were best friends then, too. From what Grace had heard, they were evidently a couple and partners in the restaurant as well.

"Ms. Kimball. Abbey said you were out here, and I just had to come and say hi. Was lunch okay?" She wiped her forehead with the hem of her apron, and Grace could see she was exhausted.

"Wonderful, Camilla," said Grace. "You've done it up big here. I love the restaurant, the décor, the menu. My food was fantastic."

"That's what we like to hear. It's been a dream of ours, Ms. Kimball, ever since we were both waitresses ourselves. But we're hard workers, and we plan to stick around. I'm so glad you and your friends came. Abbey's fixing you a special dessert, and it's on the house. You always told us to dream big, and we followed your advice."

Laughter from the Folger table drifted across the room, and Camilla looked in their direction, a frown on her face. "I wish we could refuse those jackasses service." Turning to Grace, she covered her mouth and said, "Oh, sorry, Ms. Kimball. Sometimes my mouth gets away from me."

"I figured you got your loan from them," Grace said.

"No. He refused to loan us money because of 'our sexual orientation.' It seems lesbians aren't welcome at his bank."

"What? He can't do that. Not in this day and age."

Camilla shrugged. "We know. We've already contacted a lawyer and filed discrimination charges against him and his bank. He's a despicable man, and the world would be better off without him."

"I'm sorry to hear that," said Grace, shocked by Folger's prejudice. Even as she watched Camilla watching Folger, she could physically feel the anger bleeding from Camilla's body language.

Then Camilla relaxed and said, "It's all right. Abbey keeps me calm. She says the courts will handle him."

Grace, too, took a deep breath because she remembered Camilla in high school. Abbey was a slow smolder, but Camilla had quite a temper, and she was one strong woman.

"We'll be back again, I'm sure," said Grace. "By the way, the planters with the gorgeous greenery are perfect. Who's the one with the green thumb?"

"That would be Camilla," said Abbey, advancing on their conversation. Unlike the tall, willowy Camilla, Abbey was short, somewhat stout, and had blond hair hanging straight down from the center of her head. Her dark eyes twinkled as she patted Camilla on the shoulder. "She can grow anything. I can't even get a philodendron to stay alive." As if to prove her statement, she looked up at the ceiling where large pots of plants hung from a metal bar, and their greenery spilled over the edges and dangled down like forest vines. "Yup, she is amazing with plants. And the décor was her idea too. Thought the train history would be a good connection with the town. Paint, wallpapering, signs, plumbing. She can do anything."

"Electricity. I don't do that," said Camilla, with a grin. Then she headed back to the kitchen.

"Don't believe her," said Abbey. "She put in our alarm system. It even works."

The redhead came up to Abbey and waited.

"This is Sandra Lansky," Abbey said, by way of introduction. "She's new in town, and we hired her on the spot. Had lots of experience waiting tables in Chicago, so we thought she'd be a great asset here."

Sandra smiled at them and added, "I'm so glad to get away from the hustle and bustle. This seems to be a nice little town. My cousin lives here and told me to come visit her. I hope to stay for a while, and The Depot seems to work just fine for me." Her red hair almost tumbled out of the clip holding it back.

TJ chimed in with a grin on her face. "I see you've learned to handle the guys over there."

Sandra glared across the room at the Folgers, disdain on her face. She put her hand on one hip, leaned over closer, and cracked, "I've had my share of groping, pickup lines, and unwanted attention while waitressing. Not much I can't handle. Been on my own for quite a while." She turned her head and looked across the room. "Those guys are child's play."

"Oops. We'd better get back to work. Enjoy," Abbey said.

Camilla came back about the time they left for the kitchen, and placed four plates of brownies and ice cream in front of Grace and her friends. "Compliments of the house, ladies. Come back soon!"

"Oh, my," said Grace, as she counted the calories in her head. "These look great. Thanks, Camilla." They all dug into the dessert with many *ooh*s and *ahh*s.

Then TJ managed to say to Grace, between bites of chocolate, "Are you back at the newspaper again?"

"Yes. Now that Jeff has bought Lockwood House, I'm going to research the house and the historical district. According to Jeff, people liked the history articles, and he definitely wants to know about his house. He thinks it might be haunted."

"So will he live in the house?" Jill asked, cutting her brownie in half and putting one of the halves on TJ's plate.

"Well, not yet. It's a mess. He calls it a fixer-upper, but I think it may be a project for life. Once he gets some of the rooms in order, I'm sure he'll move in. But I hope he finishes it before he's too old to climb all the stairs. Wants to make a bed and breakfast out of it, but also put it back in order the way it used to be when the Lockwoods lived there—plus modern appliances in the kitchen, I hope. He'll never get back what he put into it, but I don't think it bothers him."

"And?" TJ looked at her with one of those inquiring, detective faces.

"And what?" Grace said.

"And how are things with Mr. Maitlin?" Deb finished.

Grace tried to hold back a wide grin. "Well, *things* are fine, if it's any of your business."

"Of course it's our business," Deb said. "But we don't know much about him. He's still 'Mr. Mystery Man.' I think we'd better get on top of that." She looked around the table, and everyone nodded.

"*We?* 'We' will not do that. I will grill him when the time is right," Grace said.

The Folger brothers and their banker friends pushed in their chairs, grabbed coats and hats, and left as loudly as they had arrived. As they passed Grace's table, they said hellos. Then the restaurant was quiet once again. As if filling the void, Grace's friends began to make leaving noises.

"I have to get back to the Historical Society," Deb said.

"Me too. That is, I have to get back to work. No rest for us accountants. Tax time will be here soon," Jill added. They each rose, took their bills, and headed for coats and the cash register.

"See you guys," Deb turned and added, as she followed Jill.

TJ's cell phone rang and she grabbed it quickly. "Sweeney." She listened briefly. "Yeah." She listened with more concentration, her lips pressed into a fine line, and then replied, "Okay. I'll be right there." She looked at Grace and shook her head. "I knew I should have left sooner. We hired a couple of guys at the police department while you were in Arizona. Alex Durdle is fine, but Zach Gray is a bit difficult to handle. Has a real chip on his shoulder. It's like herding cats." TJ gave Grace a playful grin and rose with an easy manner.

"Well, shape them up," Grace replied, as TJ pocketed her phone and left.

Grace finished a couple swallows of her coffee, pulled on her coat, and paid her bill. She pressed the door open with her shoulder, and the wind ripped at her face and hair, forcing her to wrap her scarf tighter around her head. *And this is only January,* she thought, *and early January at that.* She walked around the corner of the restaurant to the parking lot. As she was about to get in her car, she noticed Will Folger at the other end of the lot. Grace was surprised to see he was talking to Sandra Lansky. They both smoked cigarettes, and Will was angry. Occasionally, his voice carried on the wind, but Grace couldn't make out the words. The tone, however, was unmistakable. He stood back from the red-haired waitress and gestured furiously. The Lansky woman appeared to simply take it all in, smoking and looking bored, her arms folded across her chest. Frigid winds whipped around them too, and Grace wondered what they were saying.

I suppose he's still mad about the spilled coffee on his brother. Or is it more than that? She strained to hear their words, but the wind made it impossible. Still, their body language said they were more than casual acquaintances.

CHAPTER FIVE

Grace stepped out of her car and felt a gust of wind clutch her scarf. She was meeting Jeff Wednesday morning at Lockwood House on Grove Avenue. She grabbed her scarf just before it blew into the air and glanced up at the gray sky and clouds promising more snow. The bitter cold was a little better today— all of twenty-five degrees—but the wind still buffeted the trees and made her pull her collar up tighter. It almost took her breath away. According to the weather forecast, tomorrow would be even colder. *Why, oh why, did I leave Arizona?*

She glanced up at Lockwood House dominating the corner lot of Grove and Second Street and noted the torn curtains in a third-floor turret. The entire mansion had a neglected, forlorn look, as if no one had paid it much attention in years. The vacant windows stared at Grace, and the bare wooden siding resembled a wrinkled face, abandoned by time and neglect. Jeff was just getting out of his car on Second Street, which ran north and south past the Lockwood lot, and he waved at Grace and waded through the snow to meet her.

He looked up at the Victorian mansion. "After yesterday, it's all mine—all four thousand, four hundred, and ten square feet— well, except for the eighty percent currently owned by the bank. So that probably means a piece of wood in the ballroom on the third floor is mine." The vapor from his breath disappeared into the wind.

"Ah yes, the ballroom," Grace repeated, and she shaded her

eyes and studied the third-floor tower, starting with the tattered roof and moving down. It was three stories high with gables and a pointed tower over a third-floor window. She and Jeff stood near the front porch stairs, which led up to what used to be an impressive entrance. Now, however, the wood was splintered and uneven. Wooden spindles—a few missing and others at odd angles—enclosed the porch, and three pillars—their paint chipped and neglected—held up the porch roof. A dark picture window brooded over the snow cover just to the right of the porch. The upper floor had five windows on the front side of the house. The wooden siding was rough and splintered in places, and the roof looked like it would need to be replaced completely. Grace couldn't help but shiver as she noticed the dark windows and the general atmosphere of decay and neglect. *I'd better be cheerful and optimistic,* she thought, seeing Jeff's animated face, *but I truly think it resembles the doomed house in Poe's* The Fall of the House of Usher. *All it needs is a moat in which to sink until it disappears.*

"It looks . . . really impressive. Am I wrong in thinking this may be more than a weekend fixer-upper?" she asked. Then, wanting to be supportive, she suggested, "Let's walk around the outside, but quickly because it's so cold." She pulled her scarf tighter. "How many doors are there?"

Jeff counted doors under his breath, and then he said, "The east side has a door that probably went into a dining room, and the north side has a door into the kitchen." They waded through the snow. "I think the original house had an entrance on the west side, but it's something you might research. If it did, it's been closed off for a long time." He pointed toward the door they were passing. "I believe another door on the northwest goes up the back stairway. I think it was the servants' staircase, and the outside door was added when they divided the house into apartments. Just wait. We'll whip it into shape in no time."

"We?" Grace asked, raising one eyebrow.

"Well, the royal 'we.' Come on." He grabbed her hand and led her around the last corner of the house, emerging again at the front door.

"Did you get the keys from the realtor?"

"Got it—well, the main key—right here."

Grace looked up, marveling at the size of the house. "Just one family lived in this whole house when it was built?"

"Yes. Judge Lockwood was evidently expecting lots of kids because there were six bedrooms on the second floor, and the third floor had, besides a ballroom, a few small rooms for servants. Of course, whoever owned it somewhere down the line partitioned the second and third floors into apartments."

"Please tell me they added inside plumbing."

"Of course. Lots of people have lived in the house since the late 1800s. I'm depending on you to do the research so you can tell me who all those ghosts are."

"Ghosts? Really?"

"Nah. I just figure someone must have been unhappy in this house. Look at it. Can you imagine creaky, rusty hinges—I do know how to use WD-40—and dark, secret passages?" He glanced at Grace, his eyes shining and his voice buoyant. "I'm hoping to make it a much lighter, sun-filled place. Research—your project, Grace. I can't wait to hear what you find out, and if I meet a ghost some night on the second floor, I'd like to know who he or she is."

"I'm freezing, Jeff. Can we go inside?"

"Sure. Right this way. The key to the front door is huge." Grace looked at Jeff's hand, which held a large, antique skeleton key. "This could be the original," he laughed. They walked carefully up the front steps, and he turned the key easily, opening the door. "I had the furnace guy come over yesterday, and he decided the furnace wouldn't blow up. We turned it on, and it started right away, so we should have heat."

Grace peeked in. "This looks kind of spooky. It's so dark. Are you sure it isn't haunted?"

"Just follow me." They walked into an entrance hallway and stopped, closing the door against the frigid outside. Jeff flipped a switch and coaxed dim lights to come on, which caused Grace to look up at the chandelier suspended from the second-floor ceiling. A wide stairway, its dull carpet threadbare, rose right in front of them. Grace viewed the distant ceiling and the leaded glass windows high up on the walls. *Probably to let light in,* she thought.

"That's the main stairway leading up to the third-floor ballroom. But there's the servants' stairway at the back, too." Jeff turned to their right and opened a set of pocket doors into a spacious room, which was probably a front parlor. "I'm anxious to take the paint off the woodwork and see what's under it. From the looks of the pocket doors, it might be mahogany. I can't wait. I imagine this was the front parlor for guests. Huge. High ceilings. Let's go upstairs and check out the bedrooms."

"Really, Mr. Maitlin, when we hardly know each other?"

He moved closer and put his arms around Grace's waist. "No time like the present to get more acquainted."

"Mmmm," she said, as his lips met hers, and lingered in a soft, but convincing, kiss. Then she pulled back and said, "I think you've had some practice."

"I'm working on the 'getting better acquainted' part."

"So do we call this 'dating'?"

"Do we have to call it something?"

"I'm a retired English teacher. Remember? We like descriptive words. I have to confess, however, I haven't been on the dating circuit since my husband, Roger, died. Does it take some practice?"

"I think so. We should get started. Soon. No time like the

present." He moved his hand up her neck to her hair and pulled her in for another kiss. Then, looking closely into her eyes, he added, "I love those dark-brown eyes."

"I think I could get used to this," she whispered. Then she swallowed, flustered, and moved back a step. "I believe we have plenty of time to practice." She turned, looked up the staircase, and announced, "Let's check out the second floor."

Jeff reluctantly moved to the entranceway and started up the main staircase, grabbing Grace's hand. She climbed the stairs, looked back, and said, "I'm beginning to catch your enthusiasm."

"For us or the house?"

"Ha, ha. The house," she said, laughing. "This must have been really something in its day. Can you imagine the lovely couples—women dressed in elegant ball gowns and men in fashionable waistcoats, frock coats, and trousers—walking arm and arm up these stairs to the ballroom? I've read that the wealthy actually imported ball gowns from Paris, even here in little Endurance."

"Grace, I get crazed with excitement when I think about putting this back together the way it was in its grand days. Think about it. It's, well, a piece of living history. Just imagine the people who walked through these rooms." He paused at the top of the stairs, noting the hallway leading from the front to the back of the house. "Here's the front bedroom, which would have been—" The floor squeaked loudly. "Think I need to make sure that gets fixed. Anyway, this would have been the master bedroom looking out over the street—huge windows, lace curtains, and handmade shades."

The squeaky board complained as Grace followed him over to the window. "You're right. But a loud board means no ghosts can sneak up on you when you're asleep, if ghosts walk on floorboards. Hmmm . . . actually, they probably don't." She stood beside him and gazed out the windows. "They would have had a lovely view. I'm sure the park across the street had its share of events and genteel sports long before television and video games, and you can see out the east window all the way to the square." She turned toward Jeff, her eyes shining with enthusiasm.

He put his arms around her again and said, "I know this isn't easy for you. Me either. You don't know much about me, and I haven't exactly been forthcoming—"

"Oh, geez. Please tell me you're not married," said Grace, a look of alarm on her face.

"No," he laughed. "Nothing like that. I feel like we've gone through a lot together after the craziness in town last summer, not to mention the murders. You've really helped me bring the paper back to life, and since you taught so many students who are still around—or their parents are—you're a real part of this town. I'm just a newcomer." He looked out toward the high school where Grace had taught for twenty-five years and mused, "So that's where you were all those years." Then he turned back to her and answered, "No, not married. Close once. And no, no children. I certainly envy you both of those. It's not easy for me to do this, however. Settle down, that is. I've moved all over the country working on newspapers. I'm not getting any younger, and this move to Endurance is my last move. That's my plan. I figure the newspaper is just enough work for a semi-retirement job since it comes out three times a week. This house should be a great hobby, and maybe if I fix it up and bring it back to life, the community will begin to look at me as an insider instead of an outsider. But it's going to take a lot of work."

"More like buckets of money," Grace said, shaking her head as she looked around.

He laughed and pulled her toward him once again. "Grace, I know once you start researching this place, you'll get hooked too. It has to have an incredible history. Just look at it."

Grace looked at the spacious room for a moment and decided it was time to explore the rest of the upstairs. They walked through the other bedrooms and the bath on the second floor. Each room was like a tattered, but proud, old lady: window shades hanging haphazardly, floors that would need lots of sanding and refinishing, dust everywhere, old gas light fixtures from before the age of electricity, windows that undoubtedly needed new ropes or total replacement, a chimney that would take tuck-pointing, and the list went on and on.

Then they climbed the stairs to the room Grace had been eagerly anticipating: the ballroom. At the top of the stairs they walked through an arch, which was repeated several times in the room's architecture. Despite the darkness, a chandelier first caught Grace's eyes, but only a few of the bulbs were still working, and it was covered with grime. Like the stairway, old gas sconces hung up high on the walls. The elegant room's faded green wallpaper was darkened with damp spots where mold had taken over, and Grace also saw places where torn strips of paper hung like cascading tears. Even the ceiling had darkened areas, but she could see the hopeful remains of painted cherubs in spots. They stepped on to the floor, the broad widths of wood revealing a perfect area for dancing. Grace almost held her breath when she considered how beautiful this room would be when it was restored.

"I see where you'll be all winter," Grace said. She walked over to the side of the room overlooking the street and peered out the small, grimy windows.

"Well, not all winter. I'll still have time for you and the newspaper, of course. This is number three on my list of priorities."

She turned to him and said, "By the way, I've found out quite a bit about your house."

"Really?" His voice took on an excited tone. "Okay. Spill it."

"This whole area near the college, north and east of the square, is the historical district. It's not an official, legal, historical district. People just call it that. The college president's house is over there"—she pointed out the window—"along with several Victorians—one said to be haunted. No, not yours. Most were built in the late 1800s—the Gilded Age—with money from land speculation, railroad stock, and supplying Civil War needs. Bankers, retired farmers, and a congressman built these painted ladies. Many were eventually turned into apartments in the 1950s postwar boom. Several have been restored so you'll have some company and probably advice. Judge Charles Lockwood's house"—Grace spread her arms out—"was built starting in 1885. Seriously, I only know the basics—lots more research to do. He married his first wife in 1888, but then he married again in 1893. Wife Number One died in a fall down those long front stairs. Sadly, her unborn baby died too. They are two possibilities for ghosts. And the good judge died in your front bedroom from some kind of stomach ailment. Next, I'm going to look for the obituaries."

"Sounds like a good start."

"I've been over to the Endurance Genealogical Society and the Douglas County courthouse, but I couldn't spend a lot of time. I'll get back to my research again because I can also use some of this information for another historical piece for the newspaper. I think Alfred Peters, the historian who wrote from 1930 till the 1950s, has some articles that may be helpful. I've just barely scratched the surface. However, I can give you the quick version of house ownership."

"I'm listening," Jeff said, leaning back against the wall.

"When the judge built this house, he owned part of a railroad, a dry-goods store, the First National Bank, a pottery, the brickyard, a lumberyard, several properties in town, and some farmland."

"Wow. Wasn't there some conflict of interest going on in some of his cases?"

Grace shook her head. "I don't think it applied back then."

"How long did he live here?"

"Not long at all. The next owner of record was in 1905. A First National Bank president, Jeremiah Baldwin, lived here with his wife and four kids. By then the carriage house on the north side was gone, and a small building, perhaps a garage for a Model-T Ford, was there. Baldwin was killed in World War I, and his widow sold to someone named Malone. The west entrance disappeared, and I suppose the ballroom was more of a storage attic. Malone was a doctor with a wife and three kids. He owned it until 1937, and that was the end of the good times for the house."

"The Depression, I suppose."

"Yes. It took its toll on the whole town. But this house, in particular, stood empty, and eventually went into receivership with the lending bank. It wasn't lived in again until 1942, and the upstairs was divided into apartments. An attorney. He divided the upstairs, lived downstairs, and put in a second bathroom."

"So that's where all the damage was done to the original structure. I suppose it makes sense. It would give him income to keep it up."

Grace walked over to the north end of the ballroom and opened the door to a servant's bedroom. "You can see down there that only some concrete remains of what might have been part of a driveway. When the attorney sold the house in 1950, a real estate agent bought it and rented out rooms to pilots learning to fly for the Korean War. They trained them down the road in Woodbury. A couple of people owned the house after that, but by 2003, it was on the market again."

"Quite a bit of research."

"As far as I've managed to dig. But I'm still working on it." She glanced at her watch. "I need to go."

They went back down to the second floor and stopped at the squeaky board once again.

"Why is that the only squeaky place in this floor?" asked Jeff.

"The boards don't look like they fit exactly as they should." Grace got down on her knees and checked the cracks between the boards. Then she looked at the surrounding floor. "It doesn't look like this board fits square, almost as if the years have either warped the edges, or the original measurements weren't precise enough." She pushed her fingernails into the small crack between the boards and found she could wiggle them. "I don't suppose you brought a crowbar?"

He laughed. "Sure. Right here in my back pocket. I do have a few tools in my truck. Ah, maybe a screwdriver would do it." He disappeared and she could hear him heading down the stairs. Grace glanced around and shook her head. It would take so much work just to get this room into shape, let alone the entire house.

Then Jeff returned and gently began lifting an edge of the board she was guarding. It groaned a bit and then moved considerably. He lifted one end and pulled it up gingerly so as not to break the board, and then he put his hand into the hole. "I think I can feel something that isn't solid," he said.

Grace moved over and got down on the floor beside him. She watched as he pulled out an object wrapped in a faded piece of burlap. Slowly, he unfolded the edges to reveal a book, its cover partly torn but its pages still remarkably intact.

Grace's eyes grew big. "It's a diary. Look, Jeff. The name on it is 'Olivia Havelock Lockwood.' This has to go way back."

"You're right. I know Lockwood's the name of the judge who originally built the house. Do you suppose this was his wife's? Or a daughter's?"

"Hmm. I don't know. Could be one of the two wives. This definitely calls for more research. I can smell a great story for the paper."

He smiled, a huge grin, and handed her the diary. "Here, you take it. Along with the history of the house, it should make a great story."

Grace opened the cover and saw a slight stain. "Water, I wonder? Maybe a tear? Hard to know. Perhaps we'll find out about the ghosts you mentioned, or it might help you figure out how to restore the house. I guess it depends on how much she described of the interior. Oh, Jeff. This could be a priceless historical artifact. I'll bet Sam Oliver, the history department head at Endurance College, would love to get his hands on this! But do you care if I read it first? It would shine some light on the period when the Lockwood family lived in this house. I can't wait to read it."

"Sure. Take it with you. Just don't let it haunt you."

She touched the cover one last time, rewrapped it, and said, "Meanwhile, I have to go put out a fire."

"A fire?"

"Lettie. She has her nose out of joint because of the contractor working on my kitchen. I should probably send you since you can charm her." She slowly shook her head. "I can tell this is a disaster in the making I need to stop."

She turned around, tiptoed her way across the floor, headed downstairs with the editor right behind her, and gave him a kiss. Then she was out the door quickly, but carefully, on the icy steps, holding the burlap-covered diary close to her chest. She stopped, halfway to her car, and looked back toward the house, imagining the twilight falling on the towers, and the shadows deepening within the circle of dense pine trees surrounding the house. She shivered and raced to her car.

★ ★ ★ ★ ★

"I hope you have a good explanation for the interloper in my kitchen when I came over yesterday," Lettie said, before Grace even made it completely through the kitchen door. Lettisha Kimball, Grace's sister-in-law, was sixty-nine, but had the energy of a thirty-year-old. Her garden was the envy of neighbors and friends alike, and everyone said she had a natural green thumb. But she was also an amazing cook, and she continued to cook at Grace's even though the children were grown and gone, and Roger—Lettie's brother and Grace's husband—had been dead for twenty-seven years. He had a heart attack—way too young.

Grace set her laptop down on the counter, pulled off her wet boots, and draped her coat over a chair. Then she turned to her sister-in-law, a woman she loved dearly, but also a woman who could be somewhat irritating. First, she took a deep breath.

"Lettie, the kitchen needs updating."

"Updating? Humph. It's been here as long as you have—even longer—and it's worked just fine."

"Look around, Lettie: green, laminate counters, a 1970s wall oven, no dishwasher."

"Don't really need a dishwasher. These two hands are just fine. And don't send Jeff Maitlin over here to sweet talk me either."

Grace sat down on a chair and pointed at the appliances. "Lettie, the refrigerator is on its last legs, the gasket around the oven door is gone so heat escapes, and the microwave is circa 1985 and probably is making both of us radioactive. The floor was put in when the kids were little. The paint and wallpaper are relics from the 1980s."

"Well, aside from that?"

Grace shook her head. "Lettie, you might as well surrender on this one. I love what you do in my kitchen—the pies, soups, and amazing meals. But I also need a more updated look here. I'll talk to Del Novak and see if he can manage to keep it a working kitchen while he's remodeling, but some of the time he'll have to turn off the water and power."

"How am I going to work in that?"

"We'll have to muddle along as best we can. Oh, and I'm sure you've heard, since you seem to be a main line on the gossip in town, that Jeff bought the Lockwood house."

"I heard something about that, but I didn't believe it. That monstrosity? He's crazy to buy that. He has the sense of a . . . well, I don't know, a nincompoop, which means he has no sense. That place will be a total money pit. I can tell you this right now: when word of this sale gets out, every materials supplier in town will be poised on his broken-down porch with their computer billing programs."

Grace paused, thoughtfully, before she spoke. "We might invite him to come over occasionally for dinner while his kitchen is being updated."

"Updated? Are you kidding? They might as well bring in a demolition team and gut it." Lettie walked to the refrigerator and grabbed some milk, setting it on the counter. Then she turned, her hands on her hips, and looked speculatively at Grace. "Jeff over here for dinner, huh. Does he know you can't cook?"

"I was hoping we could fool him."

Lettie put her hands in the air. "We? All right, all right. I surrender. Just remember the food may not be up to snuff while that terrorist is here pounding away, and plaster dust is flying into the food." She turned to the sink, her back to Grace, and then swung around again. "Is Jeff Maitlin the reason you're updating the kitchen? Don't tell me you're considering moving to his place! You know, we still don't know anything about the man. Where did he come from?"

"New York City," Grace said quickly, a trace of defensiveness in her voice.

Lettie threw her hands up in the air. "I know that. But what else do we know? Absolutely nothing. Why did he move from the enormous city to this little town? He must be hiding or running from something. Mildred at the bakery thinks he may be in the witness protection program. Have you checked on that?"

"I don't think people like you and me can do a web search for 'witness protection' and find out who's in it, Lettie. That's the whole point of 'protection.' "

"So? See? You get my point. What if he was in organized crime? Gladys at the coffee shop thinks he's working undercover for the FBI. All those guys are good-looking like him." She paused a moment and added, "Besides, they have to be in great shape to run alongside the president's car."

"Lettie. Have you been discussing him all over town?"

She looked down at the floor. "No. Well, not really. Oh, all right. Just with a few people—Mildred, Gladys, the Sunday night bingo group, Ginger at the power company, the garden club, and a few others I can't remember."

Grace sat down at the table and put her hand on her forehead. She counted to ten before she opened her mouth. "Lettie, you have to stop this. Jeff is a private kind of person, and he'll get around to talking about himself eventually. He's not used to living in a small town where everyone knows everyone else's business. So no more spreading rumors. Got it?"

"Oh." She paused for a moment. "All right."

"I'm not moving in with Jeff. I hardly know the man." Grace stood up and grabbed her coat. Then she lowered her voice. "We are going to somehow live through this remodeling. Right now I'm going upstairs to change clothes." She turned a moment before heading upstairs. "I think I liked it better when you were reading the tabloids and spreading rumors about dentists being part of a terrorist group putting poison in people's fillings."

CHAPTER SIX

Thursday morning, Grace was sitting on the sofa in the office of her home on Sweetbriar Court, warm pajamas on, her red wool blanket over her legs, and the Olivia Lockwood journal on her lap. She had already checked the weather outside and decided ice and sleet meant she could delay a bit before taking care of some errands. Besides, she couldn't wait to see what was in Olivia Lockwood's journal. A cup of hot spiced tea sat on the end table, its pungent, cinnamon aroma filling the room. She could look over at the bookshelves and see photographs of her husband, Roger, her children, her granddaughter Natalie, and her friends. Then, glancing down on her lap, she unfolded the burlap material and gently laid it on the back of the sofa.

Oh, wait. Maybe I should put on some gloves. She went upstairs, found a pair of old gloves, and returned to the study. Then she gently opened the cover of the diary and moved her hand over the title page. "My Journal, by Olivia Rebecca Havelock," she read. A small space at the end of "Havelock" was followed by the word "Lockwood," written with a lighter color of ink. *She must have started this before she was married,* Grace thought. She slid her fingers behind the thin, fragile paper and examined the first page. The writing was an old-fashioned script, the ink a faded brown on the brittle, delicate paper.

★ ★ ★ ★ ★

My Journal
10 June, 1893

What powerful words—"my journal." Mama gave you to me so I will have a way to express my excitement as my real life begins. Tomorrow I will go to a large town called Endurance to stay with my aunt. I am not sure I will sleep tonight because my heart pounds for both joy and sorrow. To leave all I know behind—our farm, my mama and papa, my three brothers, the lilies outside my window, my dog—Cinnamon—and my horse—Lightning—the little cemetery with the graves of my parents . . . Oh, the list could go on and on. "You are creating a weed patch." I can hear Reverend Ainsley's voice in my ear. "Think, girl. Use your reason to organize your flighty thoughts. Begin again."

I, Olivia Rebecca Havelock, am beginning my new life at age seventeen, in the Year of Our Lord, 1893. I was born eleven years after the Great War to my parents, Jacob and Rebecca Havelock. God sought to call them home when I was a mere three years old. Their carriage suffered an accident, and they were both killed, Mother immediately, and Father three days later. I carry their images in a locket my grandmother gave me. I do not really remember them, alive. Sometimes I think I can call to mind the warm, flowery scent of my mother, but maybe it is just a dream. My grandmother, too, lies beside them in the little cemetery in our town of Anthem. All I can remember of Grandmamma is the smell of lavender. She must have worn a parfum that remains in the deepest recesses of my memory. I was five when she was felled by a stroke.

For the last twelve years my new papa and mama have been Simon and Julia Wheeler. Papa farms, and he and

Mama used to live next door. When Grandmamma died, the Wheelers took me in and adopted me as one of their own. Mama always said she wanted a daughter, having birthed only sons. But they are the rough and tumble loves of my life: Simon Jr., Jeremiah, and William. We call Simon "Sam" to distinguish him from Papa. I shall miss them so terribly while I am gone. We chased away possums, went mushrooming, swam in the creek, sneaked out at night and watched the stars and the moon—well, that was William and me. We could name all of the constellations.

But now Mama says it is time for me to "put childish things away," and learn to be a lady. She has taught me the skills of canning foods from the garden, mending clothing, stitching, reading, and writing. The Reverend Ainsley came several years ago to add piano, religion, sums, and history. My mama says I am very well educated for a woman of my time, and she wishes her own parents had allowed her to be so complete.

But, oh, how I long to be done with my piano practice and out in the wind and the breeze on Lightning. Sometimes I ride so early the sun is just coming up, and the meadows are still filled with dew. I wave at Papa and the boys in the fields, and gallop up to the meadow beyond our range. There Lightning and I sit and ponder all that is to come: being a lady, falling in love with a man, having children and my own house to run, and growing old together. I thought it might happen in Anthem, but we have a paucity of young men in the countryside. Anthem only has a few hundred people, most of them married or old.

So I am to go to a town called Endurance for the summer. I will live with my Aunt Maud, who will teach me more needlework, etiquette, and how to stand and sit properly. My mama says I have so much to learn to walk out in Society. I am excited to start my new life and I can hardly sleep at night. Mama and Papa will come and visit me after the crops are safely in.

Sometimes, when Mama folds the wash or peels vegetables, I can see a tear on her cheek, and she wipes it away, thinking to hide it from my eyes. I often ponder this being a mother. It seems such a terrible waste to love, sacrifice, and rear children, only to watch them go off on their own into another life.

Tears are in my eyes, and I must be careful not to let them fall on my words—another sin, self-pity, according to Reverend Ainsley. I am sure I will make new friends, and Aunt Maud will be as gentle and lovely as my own mama. One life ends, and a new life beckons.

And so I end these first words of my life in my own, private journal.

Olivia Rebecca Havelock

Grace looked up from the diary. *1893. Seventeen years old. I'm trying to remember when I was that young. She seems so mature in some ways, especially when she is talking about her mother. But she's also so sheltered. I wonder what she'll think of Endurance.*

It didn't take long to find out.

14 June, 1893
We have had such an arduous but astonishing trip to Endurance. We traveled by wagon with four of the horses, and it took us four days. We left the farm country while it was still dark and rode through vast prairie lands. The wildflowers bloomed in the fields beside the roads, and they were a joy to see. My anxiety disappeared amidst such beauty. I have already studied the wildflowers and seen their pictures so I can identify many of them. We saw

Indian grass, goldenrod, phlox, rosinweed, and yellow coneflowers. The coneflowers are my favorites. In many of the fields by the road we saw wheat growing, and some of the farms we passed had the John Deere steel plows I have only read about. I saw drawings of them in the newspaper. Mama was right about education being an amazing thing. I have never been more than a mile or so out of Anthem, so my eyes tried to take in everything.

Rev. Ainsley and I looked at a map before Mama, Papa, and I left, and I could see the sixty-five miles we would traverse. Papa said the vast Mississippi River ran parallel to our roads and west of us. Mama gave me a copy of Mr. Twain's book, *Life on the Mississippi,* and I was so amused by his descriptions of the steamboat days, when he was about my age and trying to figure out how to navigate the deep and treacherous river. After he memorized the bends and depths of every inch of the river, he realized the romance and beauty of the river's surface were lost to him. Treachery waited beneath the surface, unseen.

We crossed several railroad tracks too. I have only read about trains, but I hope I may ride on one sometime in my future life. From Endurance, one huge railroad goes south called the Atchison, Topeka and the Santa Fe, and another one goes west and south. It is called the Chicago, Burlington, and Quincy route. I must stop now because we will reach Endurance today. I am so excited my thoughts scatter in fifty directions, and I am unable to think clearly.

We have reached Endurance, and I am writing this part of my journal after Mama and Papa's departure. I miss them already. It is impossible to explain how huge and bewildering this town is. We drove into Endurance from the south, and even though the whole way we had seen trees and prairie and grasslands, all of a sudden we began to see signs of civilization. A small house here, a barn there, appeared on the horizon.

In the distance we could see the spire of a church, and this is good because Mama and Papa will expect me to be there on Sundays. But before we even saw the church, we crossed railroad tracks, and off to our right we saw a gigantic train depot. It was made of black stone, and it rose two stories with a tower and a clock on top. Oh, that I could actually see a train after seeing pictures and drawings of them!

The town is bigger than any place I have ever been. The streets are dirt, but they are dry and dusty since no rain has fallen. So many stores! It is like a wonderland. Everywhere I looked I saw stores laden with any possible requisite or desire. I saw more wagons on the street than I have ever seen in my life. We must have looked like hayseeds since the people all stared at us. We passed a library and reading room. (Rev. Ainsley will be happy to hear about this because I can continue reading.) Next door to the library was a newspaper called the *Endurance Register*. I love to read the newspaper. In Anthem, it was sometimes a week late at the small reading room, but I still liked to read about the rest of the world.

Our wagon rolled around a circle with a fountain in the middle and several benches. This must be the business part of the town. Like Anthem, one street is called "Main." In Anthem, we only have a small dry-goods store and grocery store. Mama laughed at me because my mouth was open and my eyes were taking in sights I had never seen before. We saw gigantic Victorian mansions on the way to Aunt Maud's. I wondered what it would be like to live in such huge places.

Finally, we stopped in front of a two-story house, and Papa said we were here. Aunt Maud's home is about the size of our farmhouse, but with more bedrooms. She has two boarders to help her with expenses. I laughed when I met her because she had a twinkle in her eye and a smile like I imagine my true mother would have had. Her hair is white as snow, and she is a bit plump in the middle. I remained quiet, as my parents told me a lady should do, and I listened. I think I will like her very much. She is actually my great-aunt, the sister of my adopted father's mother.

We had a lovely dinner, and my parents will stay overnight at the Lenox Hotel. From there they will depart early in the morning. We bade each other a tearful farewell this evening, and they promised to write and to come for me in the fall when the crops are in. Then I was shown to my new bedroom—which is furnished spartanly, but will do. I am not used to having frills in my life. While I turned in, my parents visited and discussed details about payment for my board. I could hear their voices murmuring while I changed into my nightgown. Then it was quiet downstairs.

I wonder what Chicago must be like if Endurance is called a small town? I hope I meet other girls my age so I can have friends like Alice back home. I realize how tired I am, and I think I will fall asleep as soon as my head touches my pillow. Good-bye, Mama and Papa, and hello, my new life in such an astonishing town . . . Endurance.

Grace closed the journal, stretched, and glanced at the clock on the wall. "Oh, my," she said out loud. "I need to get cleaned up and take care of some errands. You'll have to wait a little longer, Olivia, for me to get back to you."

She wrapped the burlap around the journal and slipped it

into the drawer of a small end table. *How amazing that she thought Endurance was a huge place. Perspective. And to think that even back then, the good, old* Endurance Register *was announcing the news. This calls for a visit to Sam Oliver in the history department at Endurance College. He should be able to fill me in on more details. I need to find out more about why the first wife fell down the stairs and what happened to this girl, Olivia. Since she married the judge later in 1893, theirs must have been a very fast courtship. Wish I had more time to read her journal since I am curious about the history of the town. Maybe she will describe some of the places we still have today. Well, at least I know she ends up marrying the judge and living in Jeff's house. This seems weird—reading her words when I know a little about what's coming up. Life isn't supposed to happen that way. I wonder if the judge will turn out to be a prince or a toad.*

CHAPTER SEVEN

Emily Folger watched, concealing her impatience, as Conrad left with the children for school. *Friday. Dinner and poker tonight.* She paced around the kitchen, biting her fingernails. *Everything must be perfect. The house, food, drinks, and poker table must be ready.* Glancing at the clock, she recalled Ms. Simmons would be over by noon, and she would help organize and clean the house. *And the caterer. When? When would the caterer be here? Why can't I remember? Oh, yes. I wrote it down. Where?* She shuffled over to the bulletin board on the wall near the door. *Thank God it was there, a blue note tacked on the board. Dinner at 7 p.m. Caterer will be here at 6:15.* She let out her held-in breath.

Conrad had picked up the wine and alcohol last night on his way home from the bank. Catastrophe averted. She sighed with relief, recalling their ritual monthly talk last Wednesday about the bills. Emily had to account for every penny spent on the house and the children. It was always the same. He sat at the kitchen table and examined all the bills she had paid, and then he added the numbers in a ledger and checked and double-checked, as she stood waiting for his verdict. She fidgeted and bit her lip. Behind her back, her fingers curled and uncurled. It must have been minutes, but it seemed like hours.

Finally, when he was finished, he looked up at her and said, "Done. You managed to stay inside the household budget. Just barely. You could do better, but for now we'll leave it at this." He shut the ledger, rose from his chair, and headed upstairs, whistling as he climbed the steps. Emily's withheld breath flew out of her mouth, and her upset stomach still did fluttery turnovers, but she had managed once again.

She remembered the week of Thanksgiving—the last time she had missed the mark. Twenty-five dollars—that was how much she was over with the groceries. Riveted in her memory was the conversation that night.

"Twenty-five dollars. You're over budget by twenty-five dollars," Conrad stated, looking up from his usual position at the kitchen table.

"I—I can't be," she stammered, and walked around the table to look over his shoulder at the dreaded black ledger. Conrad slammed the book shut and glared up at her. It was that "pain look." She knew it and cringed.

"I'm sorry. I made a mistake. I didn't mean to say that. You're right." She crept back around the table to her usual position, head down, curling up her fingers into fists. The room was silent. Conrad leaned back in his chair. The clock ticked, echoing off the walls. Emily could hear her heart beat in her ears, and her stomach ached. She glanced up, under hooded eyes, and saw the "pain look" on his face.

"Well, there's nothing to be done for it."

Emily's muscles relaxed. Slightly. Her breathing slowed. *Maybe this time he would forget it.*

"Nothing to be done. You'll have to call your mother and tell her we can't make it for Thanksgiving. Maybe you will do better with your budget next month."

"But—we can't. They're expecting us. I want to go. I've—"

In seconds, Conrad was on his feet, around the table, and grabbing her shoulders. He slapped her face with a stinging crack, and Emily's breath caught, her eyes lost focus, and immediately her hand went up to her smarting face. He walked back around the table and picked up the ledger.

"You'll call them tonight."

She stared at him. "And tell them?"

His quiet voice was calm and monotonous, the words unhurried. "I don't care what you tell them. Just do it. Maybe in the future you'll be a better wife and keep track of the bills the way I expect you to deal with them. You never get anything right, Emily. You're not smart, and so you're not in charge. You need to do what I say."

Emily shuddered as she remembered that night. *Last November. January*—yes, she remembered. *It's January now. I hate the winter because it's so suffocating, closed in.* Last night she couldn't sleep. *I was probably worried about this dinner,* she thought.

She hated to take a sedative because they made her groggy in the morning, and sometimes she even walked in her sleep. One night she woke up in the back yard and she had no idea how she had gotten there, or why the alarm didn't go off when she left the house. *Maybe she had turned it off in her sleep.* She rubbed her forehead, thinking about that night. Other times, too, she'd awakened somewhere else in the house. One night she woke up on the kitchen floor, two knives beside her, and blood on the floor from a cut on her arm. She had no idea how she got there, or why she had cut her arm.

Sometimes she hated Conrad and wished he were dead. At night she often dreamed of him dead, picturing him in his coffin, his eyes closed, and his ability to hurt her gone. Over forever. She didn't know how she could make it happen. Besides, he would tell her she wasn't smart enough to get away with killing him. And he was usually right, so she would end up in prison and then who would raise her children? *If only I could take the children and leave. But what would I do for money? And what if he found us and forced us to come back?* She glanced at the clock again.

What time did Ms. Simmons say she was coming? She examined the bulletin board. *Oh, yes. Noon. Why do I have so much trouble remembering things? And nervous. I'm always so anxious. The only time I'm not anxious is when Conrad goes on a business trip. Where did he go? Cincinnati? No. Chicago. That was it.* He used to do that regularly, but lately he hadn't traveled for several months.

Emily walked over to the bulletin board and looked at the piece of paper she'd tacked to it. *Ten people for dinner and six for poker afterward. The children will be at a sleepover at the Andovers'. That's good. They won't do anything to upset Conrad.* Then she shuddered. Alcohol and Conrad were never a good combination, and she would be here alone with him for the night. Maybe she could retire early and take a sedative. It might help her forget. Her hands shook and she pushed them together tightly.

She sat down at the kitchen table. Then she got up again and paced around the table, wringing her hands. *So restless today. It must be the party. It makes me nervous to have people in the house. But Will and Darlene will be here. I'll have someone to talk to. The people from the bank make me anxious. Conrad is always watching, and I'm afraid I might say something wrong.*

She peered at the clock again. *When was Ms. Simmons coming? Oh, yes. Noon. What should I wear tonight? Maybe the pearls he gave me for Christmas. That would make him happy. I can't do anything wrong. I have to have everything ready when he gets home.*

Emily tucked her hands behind her elbows, her arms across her chest, and walked out to the living room. *We can set up the table for poker here. I'll need to find the cards and the chips. I think they're in the front closet.* It was so quiet she could hear the grandfather clock tick over in the corner. She looked out the front window at the snow swirling up around the fence. Then she sidled over and checked the thermometer on the outside of the window, attached to the window frame. Twenty-five degrees. The sky was its usual January gray, and she could hear the wind whip between the garage and the house. *I always feel so isolated here in the daytime even though we're only a few miles out of town. But I mustn't go out. I need to have everything ready. It all has to be perfect when Conrad gets home.*

She stared at the long expanse of driveway out to the county highway, the gravel buried in snow. The fence posts were enveloped in gray and white snow, the trees swayed in the wind holding more snow aloft, and hardly a car came down the blacktop road. The world was utterly at a standstill.

Emily turned and walked into the kitchen again. The bottles of alcohol and wine were lined up on the counter under the north windows. She bit the nails on her right hand. Then she stared at the bottles for a moment and shuddered. *All must be perfect for when Conrad comes home.* Looking at the shiny, round bottles filled with amber and colorless liquors, she thought, *but it really might not matter at all—the perfection—as far as the pain that was sure to follow.*

CHAPTER EIGHT

When TJ fell asleep on Friday night, the temperature was bitterly cold at five above zero, sleet was hitting the picture window in her living room, and the streetlight on Sweetbriar Court sported a halo of sparkly moisture around it. She'd left the faucets dripping, worried about frozen pipes. Dreaming about the drip, drip, drip, she was awakened by the vibration of her phone.

She realized, through half-opened eyes, it was Saturday morning. Sometime during the night she must have pulled a navy-blue throw over her legs. Her cat, Eliot Ness, was snoozing on her chest, two empty beer bottles were on the floor with a newspaper on top of them opened to the sports page, and her phone was under the newspaper. Gently removing Eliot, she glanced at the phone and realized it was almost nine o'clock. It was also her day off. "Drats!" she muttered, to no one in particular.

Tapping on her phone, she heard the unemotional words of the police dispatcher.

"Roger that," the detective answered, wearily. She rolled off the edge of her sofa where she'd fallen into an exhausted sleep, and trudged to the bedroom for her clothes, badge, and gun. By then, the dispatcher's message had kicked in, and she said out loud, "Unbelievable! What is going on?" Picking up speed, she took the gun from her dresser and grabbed an extra cartridge. Within eight minutes she was ready.

She glanced at the driveway as the garage door opened, and

saw a thin sheet of ice. "Crap!" she said, shaking her head and pulling the earflaps down on her hat. She drove out through Sweetbriar Court and passed Grace's house where her friend was probably munching a bagel with cream cheese. Last summer, TJ had handled her first big murder cases and figured they would be her last. No such luck. She had relied on Grace to be a sounding board for her theories on those murders. Grace had pushed her hard in high school and earned TJ's reluctant respect. She had never praised TJ for mediocre work, and after the detective graduated from college they had become close friends. She was even welcomed into Grace's group with Deb and Jill. She knew she could trust her former teacher to keep quiet about what she told her. As a good listener for TJ's theories, Grace was a wonderful resource. *Looks like I'll be talking to her again.*

It was eerily silent. Most of the small town's residents were staying off the slick roads, at least until the salt trucks had been dispatched. The ice shimmered on the black, spidery tree branches, and the sun cast a bleak light through the winter-gray sky. TJ's breath was steaming on the windshield, but it was no use to turn on the heater. It would only start working by the time she got there. She glanced in her rearview mirror. *Geez, one less beer, a night of sleep without a cat on my chest, and I might actually look civil.* She turned onto Primrose Street and twisted the steering wheel this way and that for several scary moments as the tail end of her car slid, fishtailing around the corner. Then she drove onto the blacktop leading to the Folgers' place east of town.

The residence was a large brick house without neighbors for an acre on either side of it. A colonial design, it had white-framed windows with white shutters. The garage matched the house, with an eagle plaque, also white, mounted above the three doors. A huge American flag flapped in the breeze from a flagpole in the yard. The Folgers had a man-made lake behind their home with a boathouse and expensive sailboat, useless now while the lake was frozen over. As TJ remembered it, Folger had a long driveway ending at the two-lane county road, and a white picket fence enclosed his front yard. At least they could keep traffic away from the house.

It was 0915 when she pulled in and, seeing a familiar car, she realized her partner, Jake Williams, had arrived ahead of her. Ted Collier, a patrolman, had been the first on the scene, and he was waiting near the back door. That meant Williams was already inside. She knew other officers would follow and set up a perimeter near the end of the driveway so curious residents wouldn't get onto the property. TJ stopped her car halfway to the house and parked on the edge of the drive, partly in snow, partly on tire tracks.

She stared up the driveway at Ted Collier and, grabbing her gear and tightening her hat over her ears, she walked up the edge of the drive, noticing multiple tire tracks and footprints in the hardening snow/sleet mixture on the pavement. *This isn't going to make things easy.* She stared at the sidewalk curving up to the front door, and saw even more footprints in and out of the house. From the looks of them, they were prints from yesterday. They had sunk into the snow, and the sleet was now molding them into permanent impressions.

Approaching young Collier, she noticed his usually ruddy complexion was a pasty white, even in the cold. He was visibly shaken. She asked, "Who's here so far?"

"So far, Jake Williams. Crime techs are on their way."

"What's the story?"

"It's awful, TJ. Just—" And he swallowed deeply, his face contorting to keep from crying. Then he seemed to get his composure back. He pulled some notes out of his pocket. "Hysterical 9-1-1 call from Mrs. Folger around 0825, and an additional call from the housekeeper ten minutes later. Jake's up there now with them. It's—it's—like nothing I've ever seen before." Sniffing several times, he cleared his throat, and TJ heard his voice deepen. "I checked when I first went in, making sure there weren't any suspects in the house with weapons. No one else. Just Ms. Folger and Ms. Simmons. Blood everywhere. Don't worry, TJ. I was careful. Secured the scene and waited for Jake or you. Removed Ms. Folger and the housekeeper to Ms. Folger's bedroom—imagine that—separate bedrooms. I had to, TJ. The larger bedroom where the—the body is"—he took a deep breath—"is—is just like a scene from hell." He swallowed again. "So much blood. I couldn't let those ladies stay there. Jake is checking the crime scene and making necessary calls. Then he's going to take a statement briefly before sending Ms. Folger to the hospital. She's in really bad shape."

"Hurt?"

"Not sure. She has blood all over her, and I could see visible cuts on her foot. But mostly her face is bruised and swollen, and so are her arms. She started to calm down after Jake got here. Housekeeper said when she heard the screams she went upstairs and found Ms. Folger hysterical. I called the dispatcher and asked for an ambulance."

"Okay. Good work, Collier. Stay right here and keep everyone out except the people who should be on the scene. No need to have anyone else tromping over evidence. We may need you to accompany Ms. Folger to the emergency room."

"Yes, TJ. The front door is still locked so no one's getting in there. I heard Jake say Zach Gray would be down at the end of the drive, and Alex Durdle is on the way. First crime scene like this. What an awful start for newbies. It was bad enough for me. And I thought that shooting scene was horrible last summer."

"Hang on a minute," TJ said. She called the office and asked Myers to get whoever was on duty to obtain a warrant for the

Folger house. "Okay, Collier. Keep an eye on Durdle. I think you're right in saying he probably hasn't seen anything like this before. Oh, and remind him it's a crime scene—he needs protective gear."

TJ glanced around before going inside. The sidewalk to the back door and another one out to the garage had footsteps similar to those at the front. Lots of people in and out at some point yesterday. She put on gloves and carefully pried open the corner of the door without touching the knob. She looked around at a kitchen full of dirty dishes, pots and pans, and lots of empty wine, beer, and champagne bottles. *Must have been some party,* she mused. Just inside the door, she pulled out paper protectors for her shoes and put them on.

Walking carefully through the huge kitchen, checking for blood spatter and finding none, she looked out the first door on her left. It led into a living room with a cathedral ceiling and chandelier. In the middle of the room was a poker table with chairs, cards, chips, and more empty bottles. Through the living room window she noticed Alex Durdle pulling up in a squad car. She turned back to the kitchen, walked over and pushed the door open slightly, and told Collier to have Durdle go back and pick up the warrant at the office. Then, figuring the kitchen was safe, she dropped her snow gear on a chair.

While she was getting organized, she considered what she knew about Ms. Folger. Emily was two years older than TJ, and she had graduated from high school in 1986, the same year TJ had Grace for her sophomore English class. Emily married Conrad Folger in '91. TJ could remember that because she was home for the summer from college. It was a huge wedding, but she also recalled people being surprised, and she couldn't remember why.

Glancing across the kitchen, she saw a staircase, and she could hear Jake's voice somewhere above. She started up the stairs, being careful to watch for blood spatter, and seeing none, figured the scene was up on the second floor. She was careful not to touch the railings or walls.

"On the way up, Jake," she called.

"Watch the hallway floor. We're in the first bedroom; turn left, and then right."

The stairs ended at a hallway, which stretched left toward the living room's cathedral ceiling. She could see spindles that were part of a balcony that surrounded and overlooked the living room below. The hallway took a right turn, and that's where she saw it. *Blood spatter from a doorway up ahead and around a corner. Where does it go?* Being careful not to step on the blood, she glanced into the first bedroom, observed the blood trail across the room, and saw Jake with a middle-aged woman and Emily Folger, and Emily was covered in blood. She was sitting on the bed, while Jake quietly talked to her. Jake Williams often worked with TJ on cases, and his calm self-confidence helped her stay centered. She could see him now, leaning toward Emily, speaking quiet and reassuring words. Emily's eyes had a glazed look. *She's in shock.* TJ stuck her head in the door, and Jake nodded his head slightly toward the hallway and blood spatter. *This isn't the crime scene.*

She followed the blood droplets around another corner, which turned out to be a hallway balcony on the south side of the upstairs. Another staircase, evidently the main one, came up from the living room in front of her. *All right,* she thought, *the trail leads into that room at the top of the stairs.* She glanced down the staircase and saw no blood going up or down. Then she turned toward the larger bedroom that must be Conrad Folger's.

Stopping momentarily, she steeled herself for what was inside the room. She could already smell the familiar iron odor of blood, the first sense that death was nearby. TJ had never handled a homicide until last summer, and the scent brought back dark memories. She had learned to make herself objective when she saw the blood and the victim. A little town like Endurance seldom had violent crimes, and she'd never had to worry much about dealing with homicide scenes. Car accidents on the city streets, yes. Crime scenes from robberies, yes. Last summer was an unforgettable education, and she was afraid this might outdo it. In the distance she heard a siren. *The ambulance. No use putting it off.* Her face set in a grimace. *I can do this.*

Rounding the corner, stepping carefully around blood spatter and not touching the door's archway, she immediately went into detective mode, sizing up what she saw as a whole. Emotions in check, detective objectivity on her mind.

Blood spatter on the floor trailed from the far side of the bed, out the door, and into Emily Folger's bedroom, so much blood it had to have fallen on more than one trip. Broken glass was all over the floor on the far side of Conrad's room and at the end of the bed. She lifted her eyes ever so slowly and saw, on the bed, the last remains of Conrad Folger IV, his clothes somewhat on, pants pulled halfway down, his shirt off, a ghastly, dark slit across his throat, blood everywhere, including a pool around his head. On the bed next to him, besides his blood, was a large piece of glass with dark stains all over its edges. Most likely the murder weapon. *We'll see what the coroner says.*

TJ felt the gorge rise up in her throat, even though she hadn't had any breakfast. *Probably a good thing,* she thought grimly. Folger's eyes were open and his head flung back where it had deepened into the pillow when his throat was cut. The entire pillow and part of the bed under his head were soaked in blood. Carefully walking across the room, she studied the blood drip from his bed to the floor and the pieces of glass surrounding the red drops. *Maybe a vase of some kind or a glass ashtray. Not very big, whatever it was.* Despite her concentration, she heard the ambulance people heading up the stairs and knew they would be taking Emily Folger to the emergency room.

While she was studying the blood spatter, Jake Williams came into the room, walking as carefully as she had.

"Rough night, TJ?" He smiled as he sauntered in the door and saw her hastily pulled-together condition.

"All alone, couple of beers, ESPN, and Eliot Ness," she answered with a grin. "So, what's the story on Emily Folger and the housekeeper?"

He looked at a notebook and shuffled back a few pages. "Housekeeper came in at 0830 this morning, expecting to clean up after a night of carousing by Conrad and the boys. You saw the kitchen. Ms. Simmons—that's her name—worked here last night, early, helping get food ready with a caterer, and then she left. They had dinner and a poker game, and I've got the names of the participants. Anyway, the housekeeper left when it got underway and came back to help clean up this morning. Came in the kitchen door. It was locked, by the way, and the alarm was on." He glanced up at TJ, proffering a significant look. "So she shut off the alarm, unlocked the door, came in, and started some coffee for Emily and Conrad. Just as she began picking up dirty dishes, she heard screams from upstairs. She rushed up the back stairs, saw the blood on the carpet, and followed it into Emily's room, thinking she was there. But she wasn't. She saw blood on the floor of Emily's room and the bed.

"So Ms. Simmons followed the blood to Conrad's room, and saw Emily, in full hysteria, rocking back and forth on the floor behind the bed. She rushed in—probably screwing up our crime scene—and grabbed Emily by the shoulders and hugged her, lifting her up off the floor. When she saw Conrad, she was shocked, but had the fortitude to hang on to Emily, keep their backs to Conrad, and grab the bedside phone to call 9-1-1. Amazing woman. She heard sirens very quickly. Evidently, Emily had already called them, but from a different number than the bedside phone.

"By the way, Emily is not even close to coherent. Collier was the first one in. At least he didn't throw up and further screw up our crime scene. Ever the rescuing knight, he moved the two of them out of the room over to Emily's bedroom. Made the necessary calls, and stayed with them until I got here. I was on my way in to work, so I just turned around."

"Who's with Emily now? We'll need to get a warrant for her clothes."

"I sent Collier with her, and a policewoman, Eileen Randall, is meeting them at the ER. I also sent strong admonitions with Collier to have the ER doc be careful about checking for evidence, especially DNA, defensive wounds, and all. The housekeeper went with her too. Ms. Folger's in really bad shape. Shock. I couldn't get much coherent out of her except for one thing."

"What was that?"

"She repeated over and over, 'I killed him.' "

CHAPTER NINE

Before TJ could reply, the crime scene tech arrived to check for fingerprints with his suitcase of powders and brushes. He was followed upstairs by another tech, carrying a camera and other equipment to film the scene. Alex Durdle brought up the rear with the warrant for the house.

"Hey," said TJ, suddenly remembering something. "Don't the Folgers have a couple of kids? Where are they?"

"Housekeeper said they'd been off at some friend's house for a sleepover while the big kids played," said Jake. "Don't worry. I checked their bedrooms and the downstairs just in case."

"Call dispatch and have them talk with Will Folger and his wife. Maybe they know where the kids are, and they need to be notified anyway. Probably will want to go to the hospital to see Emily, so tell the dispatcher to mention, also, the Folgers can't see her until we can question her."

"Where're Sweeney and Williams?" A booming voice could be heard out on the stairway.

"In here, Chief," TJ answered. She glanced at Williams. It was Chief Stephen Lomax, their boss, and Endurance police chief for the past fifteen years. He didn't always come to a crime scene, and Jake and TJ looked at each other and waited for him to round the corner. The chief's usually jovial mouth looked grim, and he hadn't even stopped to put on his uniform. His winter coat was open, revealing a sweatshirt with EPD on it.

"What do we have?" he asked them, and then glanced at the bed. "Jesus!" he sputtered, as he noted the body and the blood that marked the remains of Conrad Folger. "What the hell is going on? Robbery gone wrong? Was anything missing?"

"Not sure yet, Chief. But I can take you through the scene and make some rash conclusions if you'd like," TJ said. "Usually robbers don't cut throats."

"All right, Sweeney. I give up. Tell me what you think happened."

"Housekeeper came at 0830 this morning. The door was locked and the alarm on. That leaves the wife, Emily Folger, as the lone person in the house with the victim. She told Williams she killed him, but she was also hysterical and definitely in shock. I'll see what she says once the doctor has stabilized her. She was pretty beaten up, too. We'll have to find out about that."

"S'pose he hit her?"

"Most likely. At this point that's the theory. We'll see. If you follow me over here—" TJ indicated safe places to walk. "Looks like the perp came into the bedroom. Folger was asleep. From the looks of the downstairs, they had quite a party last night so he was really out. Whoever came in probably used the piece of glass next to him on the bed to slash his throat. The killer must have hated him, and you can see cast-off splatter from the glass, and more blood spatter, which must have been a fine spray from his throat. It's a pretty ugly way to do it, and not something a woman usually does. Curious, Chief. Some grains of dirt are on the bed and no place where they might have originated. No plants knocked over. Broken glass everywhere. For sure, the murderer would be covered in his blood, and Ms. Folger was covered in blood. Not sure I can see her doing that, but who knows what goes on in a house? In fact, I'll get a warrant for the hospital records and see if he's put her in the ER before.

The glass on the floor appears to be from a vase or an ashtray. It was probably over here on this table from the looks of the arrangement of various photos and glass ornaments. So whoever killed him didn't actually bring a weapon. The blood trail leads to Ms. Folger's room and goes in both directions."

"Her cell phone is in there, and it's covered in blood," added Jake. "Probably that's what she used to dial 9-1-1."

"So let me get this straight," Chief Lomax said. "It looks like she came in here, slashed his throat, went back to her room, and called 9-1-1."

"Yes," said TJ. "But the housekeeper found her in here on the floor next to the bed, her back against the wall, incoherent, rocking back and forth, a few minutes later. So I assume Ms. Folger came back here after she killed him, assuming she killed him. She did, in fact, confess to Williams in front of Ms. Simmons."

"Are there any other suspects?" the chief asked.

"Don't know yet. Conrad Folger was not exactly a loved guy. Man like that makes lots of enemies," Jake said. "We've had his brother informed, and Conrad has two kids, so we're hoping Will knows where the kids might be."

"Come out here in the hallway for a moment," Chief Lomax motioned to the detectives. TJ and Jake left the techs working on the scene and followed him into the hallway.

"I don't need to tell you," the chief said quietly, "we'll be getting a crap load of pressure over this murder. Folger is a huge presence in the town. So we need to get this solved, wrapped up with a bow, and put on the shelf as soon as possible. Is this clear to both of you?"

"Perfectly," TJ said, glancing at Jake.

"I was planning to drive to Woodbury for the day. The wife has a hen group coming over to work on something. Guess I'll have to go home, get cleaned up, and head back to the office with this situation. Keep me up to date. I'll have my cell on."

"Sure, Chief," said Williams.

After he left, TJ and Jake went back to the crime scene, thinking grimly about the chief's admonition. The crime techs were working, and Ron Martinez, the part-time coroner, stuck his head in the doorway. Martinez was the local pediatrician, but he also doubled as a coroner when the EPD needed one. The body, however, would be taken to Woodbury for an autopsy.

"Jake, TJ," Martinez said, as he set down his medical bag and looked in the door. "Geez. I think I need to find someone else to do this coroner's job. I'm much happier working with my little people. Mostly they need Band-Aids and vaccinations. So what's the story?" he asked, not taking his eyes off the crime scene.

"Conrad Folger. Throat slit. We'll let you tell us the rest, Doc."

"The banker?" Martinez turned, a shocked look on his face. "You have to be kidding!"

"None other."

Jake was busy making a diagram of the room and noting the closed windows and the temperature on the thermostat. Martinez grabbed his bag, walked purposefully over to the bed, gloves on, and scrutinized the body carefully before he did any hands-on work. TJ and Jake waited until Martinez had studied several areas on the corpse and checked for body temperature. Then he stood up and walked back over to the detectives. "Manner of death is exsanguination, and time is probably between midnight and four a.m. Stomach contents should narrow it down, and the ME will do a tox screen and autopsy. I'll call him now and see when he can schedule it."

"Try to push him a bit, Doc, because the chief is chomping at the bit. Lots of pressure on this." Martinez walked out of the bedroom, pulling his cell phone out of his pocket.

Jake and TJ spent more time examining the room. "Jake!" TJ held up a handgun she had taken from the drawer in the bedside table. "Looks like a Glock." She smelled it. "Not fired. Probably Folger's for protection. They do live in an isolated area. I'll bag it anyway."

Martinez walked back in and said, "Tomorrow morning, TJ. Autopsy will be then. I'll take the body over there today."

"Right. I'll be there," said TJ.

In the hours that followed, the body was removed, and the crime techs finished their photographs and examination of prints. They were working on trace evidence when TJ and Jake went to Emily's room and then downstairs to examine the rest of the house. Passing Collier at the back door, they checked the tire tracks in the driveway.

"This is going to do us no good," Jake said. "Those could have been there last night. Lots of people here. From the looks of the living room, lots of people in and out."

"No blood spatters down the stairs or at the kitchen exit. They'll check the doorknob and the security keypads for prints, but as cold as it is, if someone did get in, he or she was probably wearing gloves."

"Right now it sure doesn't look good for the wife," Jake replied.

"We'll have to get warrants to check his finances, talk to people at the bank, check his bank files, and see who might have had a reason to kill him. You know, sometimes a banker isn't the most loved person in town. He probably says 'no' a lot. We need to get to the hospital, and we'll question the people at the shindig last night too," said TJ. "Plenty to do, ole Jakie. No rest for the wicked. My day off is changing to 'on.' I'm going to stick around and check Emily's bedroom and both the bathrooms, and then I'll meet you down at the station. We'll let the techs see what they come up with. Then we need to check on

Emily Folger at the hospital. She might be lucid enough to talk."

Jake left, and the crime techs were working on photos and fingerprints when TJ went back upstairs. Examining Emily Folger's room, she found the bloody cell phone, which she put in a plastic bag and marked for evidence. Then she poked around the room, finding little else except blood on the sheets and the floor. Walking into Emily's bathroom, she saw a nightgown on the floor and a half-full glass of water with a bottle of sedatives next to it on the counter. Picking up the nightgown carefully, she shook her head as it practically came apart in her gloved hands. It was wet—semen maybe—but also it had been torn open down the front. It didn't take much for TJ to figure out how that happened. She bagged the nightgown and carefully dumped the water from the glass. Wrapping both the glass and sedatives in an evidence bag, she checked the medicine cabinet. Seeing nothing unusual, she signed the evidence bags. Then she went down the hall, pulled a tech out and down to Emily's room, and pointed out the evidence bags to them and the bed sheets.

"Also, don't forget to photograph the blood trail from here into the other bedroom—"

"Will do, TJ."

"Oh, and photograph the contents of both medicine cabinets. I'll walk around and point out what else needs to be bagged."

An hour later, TJ was back in her car driving toward the Endurance police station. A glance at her dashboard told her it was almost two in the afternoon. She felt ravenous. She radioed Jake, telling him she'd pick up some sandwiches and coffee on the way. Then she settled in to drive across the small town of Endurance. As she drove, the evidence from the scene played through her mind. *The alarm was on, the door locked, blood spatter verified the trips back and forth to Conrad's room, manner of death obvious but kind of rash for a female perp, and blood all over Emily Folger. Doesn't look good.*

But then there was the torn nightgown in the bathroom and the sedatives. How did those fit in the timeline and increase her motivation to kill her abusive husband?

CHAPTER TEN

". . . and the high today will be twenty degrees with light periods of snow. Tomorrow's looking better with a high of twenty-five, but then the wind will come in, and it will feel more like ten degrees." Grace snapped the radio off in her car and killed the engine. *More of the same. Gray skies, bone-chilling cold, and "light periods of snow" probably mean two to four inches. How many times can I dig out my driveway?* She grabbed her purse, locked her car, and trudged through the parking lot and into the *Endurance Register* office.

Looking back at the parking lot, she was relieved it had been repaved and was no longer full of holes the way she remembered it last July. A plow had scraped the snow off the surface and salt had done the rest. Last summer she had taken on a part-time job reviewing books and then writing historical articles for Endurance's centennial celebration. The town had thrown quite a party for its one hundred seventy-fifth anniversary. But now she worked almost full time, and besides book reviews, she also wrote *Grace Notes*—articles about the history of the town. She had her own office at the *Register*, but often worked from home. When Jeff came to Endurance last summer, the circulation of the newspaper was only 4,000. It was on its last legs and sinking into oblivion. But with his innovations and changes in content, the circulation was up to 6,000 and rising. He had moved from his newspaper job in New York City to take a part-time job as editor in their small town. To hear him talk about it, he wanted a change from the big city and a less stressful job during his last years before retirement. He was sixty-two—time to slow down a bit. And—bonus—he and Grace had started dating recently.

Grace walked into the main room and saw Jeff's open office door. He sat at his desk, his head bent over some reports. Then he reached for a bottle of water, saw Grace, and motioned her back. She spoke briefly to Rick Enslow, the sales manager, and then walked behind the front counter toward Jeff's door.

"Something's happening out at the Folger house. Lots of police cars, crime tape, an ambulance. They have everyone blocked off at the end of the driveway, and it's a long driveway. Ever been out there?" he asked.

"Not really. I know he built that house out in the country and even put in a lake. But I've never been inside. What could be going on?" Then she remembered. "Oh, how did the poker game go?"

He motioned her to sit down, and she walked in and sat in one of the chairs in front of his desk. "It was quite an evening."

"How so? Did you win?"

"Ha, ha. Not hardly. When I got there, Emily Folger was clearing off the dishes and they were setting up for poker."

"Who was at Conrad's besides the two Folger couples?"

"A bunch of bank people. They set up the poker table in the living room, and most of the ladies left. Emily was still around and so was her sister-in-law, Darlene."

"Darlene stayed?"

"I think she had a feeling ole Will would need a designated driver, and, sure enough, he did. It wouldn't be wise to have the VP at the bank hit with a DUI. Besides, here in small town, USA, it would end up in the newspaper."

Grace laughed. "Oooooh. That would *not* be a proud moment for Conrad or Will."

"No. So Emily disappeared shortly after the game got started. You're right about her, by the way. She seems troubled, has dark circles under her eyes, and generally looks like a little mouse. She hardly said anything all evening. I had a tough time connecting this Emily to the one you talk about."

"Maybe she was worried about the dinner. I know when I have a lot of people over for a meal I worry about how everything will work out." *And whether my food will be edible,* Grace thought, *or whether I might poison someone accidently.*

"Perhaps. I assume they've had these parties before, and that's why the ladies leave. They go into the wee hours of the night. I stayed till the bitter end, however. You were right. No love lost between the Folger boys. Highly competitive. Several times Conrad made some nasty, ugly comments, and Will just shook them off. I was a little embarrassed, but the other players acted like it was normal."

"Doesn't surprise me. Conrad was all smiles and charm when we saw him at the bank. I always liked Will better. I can't remember exactly what happened, but Will was gone from Endurance for a long time, and when he showed up again— around 2000—he had a wife, Darlene, in tow. Next thing anyone knew, he was working at the bank. Of course, I knew much of this via Lettie, but I've also had dealings at the bank."

"They are an interesting pair of siblings. I remember a sister, too, in those photographs. Wonder what she's like."

"Jessalynn? She was always a little kinder, a bit more patient than either of the boys—at least from what I knew of them. She was a good student—not spectacular, but good—and I thought her personality lacked their aggression and competition. She was the only Folger child I had in school. The others were already out when I began teaching. I haven't seen her in years either. I have no idea where she is now." She paused a moment. "What time did it all break up?"

Jeff scratched his head. "I think it must have been one o'clock. I got home around one-fifteen, so it sounds about right. We all headed out at once. No one had drunk much except Conrad and Will, and Conrad wasn't driving anywhere. Will's wife stuck around and knitted or crocheted or something in the den or family room, and watched some late-night show on television. As I mentioned, she drove Will home."

"Is someone from the paper out at the Folger house?"

"Yes. Jack Gillenhall, the college intern. He's supposed to call." Jeff glanced at his silent cell phone.

Grace started to get up and then remembered she was going to ask Jeff about his house.

"Well," he answered, "the property transfer of my house in the newspaper listings has certainly made me popular. Everyone is curious and everyone has advice. They're dying to get inside."

Grace laughed. "In Endurance, people watch workers paint houses in the summer. It passes for entertainment. Oh, and I brought the latest notes from Lettie, speaking of entertainment." She reached in her purse and pulled them out. Then, arranging them in order, she read them out loud. " 'Gracie, that man'—she never calls him Del—'told me everything has to be boxed and moved to the dining room so he can remove the counters. I can't cook in the dining room. It's time to fire him. Besides, we still don't know if he's hiding something. Lettie.' Second one: 'Gracie, Doesn't he ever clean up after himself? There's sawdust all over the floor whenever I come into the house. It could catch on fire with autonominous combustion. This has to stop. He could be a convicted felon, you know. Have you done a background check? Lettie.' "

"I can hear World War III in progress."

"That's not the end of it. Besides the notes, she's proven herself impervious to Del's charms. She told me she was in the kitchen and the front doorbell rang. So she checked the door and no one was there, but a bag was hanging on the doorknob. She carefully opened the bag and saw a box with white powder on it. Panicking, because she figured it was anthrax or ricin or who knows what she's read about in the tabloids, she dropped it in the garbage bin in back of the house. While she frantically looked for the number of Homeland Security, Del called and asked her if she'd gotten his present. So she had to play along with him and not tell him she'd thrown it in the garbage. Then she went back out and trolled through the bin. It was powdered donuts from Abbey's bakery shop at The Depot." Grace shook her head. "I keep thinking I'll come home someday and find Del on the floor, unconscious, blood everywhere, and an iron skillet nearby. However, knowing Lettie, she loves that skillet. It's more likely she'd grab something heavy, but expendable, like ceramic."

Jeff laughed, and Grace noticed he forgot to look at his silent phone.

"How is the work on your house going?"

"Slowly, but progressing. When you have to peel back layers to get to the original walls and window frames it takes a long time. But it will be worth it to see so much history come alive. The last time I stopped in, Todd Janicke had discovered '1892' etched into part of the frame on a window. Pretty exciting!"

"You really love history, don't you?"

"I've always loved history," Jeff said. "That's what got me into journalism in the first place."

Grace, seizing an opportunity to pry his hidden past open, said, with a brief hesitation, "And how did you happen to get into journalism? I know you worked at a small paper because you told me about your interview with that young fire starter."

Jeff studied the wall over her shoulder a moment, and Grace watched an internal struggle on his face. Then he looked into her eyes. "I know I don't say much about myself. It's a habit, I guess." He took a deep breath and Grace thought his face slowly resolved itself into a decision. "When I finished college, I got a job as an assistant for an author who lived in the Smoky Mountains. It was a gofer kind of job, but I kept at it for a couple years. The hours were long, the pay low, and I didn't learn much about writing. Research, yes. So I sent my resume out to several newspapers in a three-state area, and ended up with an interview at the *Smoky Mountain Gazette,* circulation 18,000. Again—long hours, low pay—but I was a news reporter, and it was romantic with the 1970s such a volatile time. Quite an education compared to college."

He paused and glanced at his cell phone, willing it to ring. Then he looked up at Grace again. "A few years after that, I left for a newspaper with a little larger circulation. And I kept doing the same thing—moving to larger papers. I worked at the *Richmond Times-Dispatch* and the *St. Paul Pioneer Press.* A story I wrote for the *Press* got quite a bit of recognition, and the next thing I knew, I was at *The Philadelphia Inquirer.* I was in the big time! I loved the city, I was still relatively young, and life was exciting. I was a managing editor, but I still was able to write a story occasionally."

He paused a moment. "We had a series of murders in Philadelphia, and I covered the serial killer, staying close to two of the detectives on the case. Eventually, I broke the story when they caught him. I won an award or two, enough to catch the attention of others in journalism circles. The next day the *Chicago Sun-Times* called me, and I moved to the Midwest and learned about a whole new region. Those times were some of the best in my life. From there I moved on to New York." He smiled and added, "We have a love of history in common, don't we?"

"Yes. In fact, I just stopped in to get my recorder and laptop because I'm going over to Endurance College to see an old friend, Sam Oliver, who's the head of the history department. I found the obituaries for two of the Lockwoods. Still haven't found one for Olivia, the writer of the diary."

"Oh, yes, the diary. How is that going? Intriguing?"

"Amazing. She was so young and totally innocent about the 'big city' of Endurance," Grace said, laughing. "I'm hoping Sam can fill me in on some facts."

"Like what?"

"Well, the judge died May 20, 1894, the year after he had married wife number two, Olivia. But before she came into the picture, he'd had the usual childhood with a common school education. That's where 'usual' ended. He went to Harvard and studied law with some impressive guy in Philadelphia, and then he came home and got involved in local politics. Circuit judge, and then he built your house. Dabbled, as you know, in a great many businesses. His first wife was a Jane Maud Spencer. Her death was really soon after they married, and she was only twenty-three when she died. Fell down the front stairway, losing an unborn child. They'd had a big society wedding and a honeymoon. She was quite the beauty. Joined the correct clubs and did volunteer work. Her death is kind of mysterious. The newspaper made the suggestion she might have tripped on the train of her dress."

"But nothing more than that as far as whether it was an accident?"

"No. The same year he was made a federal judge and married Olivia Havelock. She was only seventeen and from a small town south of Endurance. He must have been forty-four and thinking about a run for the governor's office. But he died suddenly of what they called gastritis. Here, I wrote down the description." She pulled some papers out of her purse and unfolded them, checking for the right page. "Here it is. 'Despite the care of his physician, who used moderate doses of subnitrate of bismuth, he died suddenly of gastritis. At his bedside were his wife, Mrs. Lockwood, and his attending physician. He was unconscious at the end.' "

"That seems strange. Why would a seemingly healthy man in his forties suddenly die of a stomach ailment? Some undiscovered illness? Something he ate? A fight? Surely not. No autopsy, I suppose."

"You suppose right. So far I haven't found any more mention of Olivia, the second wife. But maybe Sam will have a clue."

"Sounds like quite the mystery to me."

"Mysteries, plural. I'm becoming obsessed with this story. It's crazy. All I did was look for information on your house. The deeper I dig, the more mysteries I seem to find."

Suddenly, Jeff's phone buzzed, and he checked the caller. "Oh, this is Jack Gillenhall. I'd better take it." He pushed the accept button and said, "Yes, Jack. What did you find out? What?" Then he listened for at least a minute and a half by Grace's estimation. "Right. I'll be out there in a few minutes. Thanks."

"What's up?" Grace asked.

"Someone's killed Conrad Folger, and it's definitely a murder."

"What?" Grace jumped up and leaned across his desk. "What about Emily? Is she all right? The children?"

"I don't know. I only know," he said, pausing and looking at Grace, "Jack said someone slit his throat. I'm on my way. Got to go." He grabbed several items off his desk, pulled his coat off a hanger, and kissed Grace as he ran out the door. She just had enough time to shout, "Call me when you find out about Emily and the kids."

It seemed so quiet after he left. Grace walked over to her office to pick up her recorder and her notes for Sam Oliver. She also needed to take her laptop so she could use it at home. She was just about to lock her office door when her own phone began playing Bon Jovi's "Wanted: Dead or Alive."

"TJ. What's going on?"

"I'm out at Conrad and Emily Folger's and just took a break for a moment. Folger is dead, murdered."

"Oh, TJ. Jeff just got the message too. Emily? Is she all right? And the kids?"

"Kids are fine and at a friend's house. They weren't here last night. Emily is off to the ER because she's in shock. She isn't hurt, but we'll have to wait to talk to her. Still trying to put the pieces together. I know you had her in school—she was at the high school when I was."

"TJ, this is awful." Grace paused a moment, thinking about what else to say. "What can I do?"

TJ paused. "Nothing for now. But I think you should get a grip on the fact that she's the prime suspect in her husband's death."

"What? You can't mean it. Emily Folger?"

"Yes. Only one here. Doors locked. Lots of blood on her. Looks bad for her."

Grace could feel tears rolling down her face. *Emily Folger.* "You have to find the real killer, TJ."

Again, there was a long pause at the other end of the phone. Then, a deep sigh. "Why did I know those would be the next words out of your mouth? The Grace Kimball 'My Student Could Never Have Done That!' reaction. Grace, you knew her a long time ago. Lots has happened in between."

"You do what you have to do, TJ. Remember, you are the person who looks for *all* suspects. And—"

"Don't even start on the rest of that sentence, Grace. Remember what happened the last time you went off half-cocked and tried to find a killer. That's not happening again."

Grace sat down in her office chair. "Then promise me, TJ,

you'll find the real killer." She ended the call and sat back in her chair, thinking about Emily Folger. Every fiber of her being knew *her* Emily could never have killed another human being. *Should she go to the hospital? No, the police probably wouldn't let her in to see Emily at this point. So, Plan B.* Pressing her lips together, she stood up, gathered her purse, laptop, and recorder, and headed out the door, determined to deal with the Lockwoods and then start on the Folgers. She left the office, headed for her car, and hummed "I Am Woman, Hear Me Roar."

Chapter Eleven

Fortified with two cups of strong coffee, Grace traipsed down the wide sidewalk to the main doors of Spencer Hall at Endurance College. It was ten twenty-five, and the campus seemed devoid of students on the various paths leading to the student union or the dorms, but she figured, on a Saturday morning, they were probably huddled under thick blankets, still in bed. The sidewalks had been plowed and salted, and she didn't have any problem walking, but it was sure cold, and she watched her breath disappear into the wintry, dry air.

Climbing the stone steps carefully, she walked into Spencer Hall, looked around at the portraits of the college presidents on the walls, and then turned down the hallway, her footsteps echoing on the marble floors. Bulletin boards, filled with event flyers, covered every inch of space in the corner near the stairs, and she turned and walked up to the second floor. The ancient marble steps had half-moons worn into the middle of each step, and she walked carefully. She watched for Sam Oliver's name on an office door and found it, the second one on the left. Opening the door, she walked past a teakettle on a hot plate, plants hanging from wall hooks, and a table with graded papers left for students to retrieve. She meandered into the next room and saw her old friend, Sam, working away on a thick pile of papers. He hadn't seen her yet, and she took a moment to study him. He was wearing a heavy, navy sweater over a black turtleneck shirt, and a small, gold earring dangled from one ear.

He was a fixture at Endurance College, having come to town a few years before Grace, so he could be approaching sixty. He and his wife, Glenna, were friends of Grace's and Roger's back in the long ago.

She cleared her throat. Sam looked up, and a pleasant smile came over his face.

"Grace! I lost track of the time." He checked the clock behind him. "I knew you said you'd be here about now, but I needed to grade Western Civ papers. You're a welcome distraction."

He stood up and enveloped her in a huge bear hug. "Glad you're here. Can I take your coat?"

Grace shook her head. "I think I'll keep it on. Don't they pay the heating bills at the college?"

He laughed. "Oh, yes. However, the powers-that-be believe the ivory tower ambience is one of austerity. It keeps us academics humble and grateful for our little pleasures in life." He glanced around his office, indicated she should move back a few steps, and cleared off the clutter and books on a chair near his desk. "There. Now you have a place to sit. May I bring you some coffee, such as it is?"

"Sure," said Grace, and she opened her notebook and fished for a pen and her recorder in her purse.

He called to her from the outer office. "It's kind of like police stations."

"What is?"

"Coffee's pretty bad. No one really worries too much about it because everyone has too much to do," Sam said. He handed her a steaming cup, and then he patted his silver hair, which was pulled back into a small ponytail at the nape of his neck and tied with a thin, leather strip. Sitting down, he looked around the room and said, "You know, this hall was named for Judge Lockwood's first wife, Jane Spencer. The judge gave a large endowment to the college, and they named the building for her way back in the late 1800s."

"Guess I hadn't connected the name." Grace gingerly sipped her coffee and winced. It was bitter and nasty.

"When you said on the phone you were interested in the Lockwood family, I was delighted. I've researched them extensively as part of the history of the town. But I always come to a dead end on the mysterious deaths in their story."

"Mysterious deaths?"

"Yes. It's hard to tell, for instance, what killed the judge so young. He was only forty-four."

"I noticed that when I read his obituary. You know Jeff Maitlin bought the Lockwood house, and he wants me to research the family and the house for the newspaper."

"So that's who bought it. I was so glad to hear someone did buy it. Those old buildings deteriorate so quickly, and they cost prodigious amounts of cash to keep up. It's like driving a Brinks truck off a cliff into a dark hole."

Grace watched Sam rise and walk over to a wall filled with books of various sizes and shapes. The bookcases went from the floor to the high, vaulted ceiling, and books were crammed into every square inch. She wondered how he knew where anything was. "I can sure help you with the Lockwoods. Just a minute." He moved a small ladder over to the far end of the bookshelves and maneuvered it around piles of books sitting on the floor. Climbing up slowly and carefully, the academic peered at several book spines and then, with some effort, pulled a dark-covered book from the shelf. He looked down at Grace and the book-strewn floor. "Don't know how I will clear out this office when I retire. Too many books. But maybe I won't retire," he said, and chuckled. He climbed down and handed the book to Grace. "Here you go. This is a book I wrote in 1985 about the history of the town and the Lockwoods. That family is an intrinsic part of the town's story."

"Do you mind, Sam, if I record our conversation?"

"Not at all."

Grace looked at the book cover. "This is wonderful, Sam. It should help me immensely."

"Thought the book might help. You can keep it till you're done with your research."

She thumbed through the pages. "Oh. Photos of the family. Here's one of Olivia, his second wife. My, she was very beautiful, wasn't she?" Grace stared at the gray-toned photo of a young woman in a high-collared, white dress, a necklace with a heart suspended from her neck. Her dark hair was long and pulled back with a ribbon, and her eyes stared at the camera with a curious expression. "And terribly young."

"That she was. It's another story with many question marks. After the judge's death, her trail grows cold. Not sure what happened to her. Like I said, lots of questions about the endings of both those people. And, for that matter, even more questions about the death of his first wife."

"Tell me about your research; the Lockwoods must be fascinating for you to spend so much time on them."

"If you get me started, I won't stop, you know," the professor said.

"It's fine. I can see the clock behind you, and I have to do another errand around twelve o'clock. I'm not intimidated by your vast store of knowledge. I'll tell you when to stop." She grinned and took another sip of the dreadful coffee.

"Well, then. Give a man an audience and he'll talk. Where should I start?" He took a deep breath and considered his first words carefully. "The judge's father, Benjamin Nathaniel Lockwood—good old New England name—came here from Delaware in 1840. Started a dry-goods store, and was quite the master of marketing and merchandizing. The store flourished, and he enlarged it several times—down on the public square on the southeast corner. Eventually it took up the whole block. Then he married Sophia Endicott in 1846. She was quite the lovely girl—only sixteen when they married. But, as luck would have it, they had two stillborn daughters."

"Was Sophia from the area?"

"Actually, her family had been friends with his family back in Delaware, and they came out to visit. Guess she stayed," he said, "much to her misfortune. The Lockwood family was a major pillar of the Methodist Church, and I suppose her inability to carry a child disturbed him and disappointed him. He must have thought God was punishing him—or her. I don't think Sophia had an easy time of it."

Grace paused in her note-taking and looked up. "You mean he was unfaithful?"

"Well, I found examples of speculation that he was both unfaithful and also a little bad-tempered. Some of the medical records of the family doctor were saved, and I found them years ago in the college archives. Evidently, Sophia went to him for some bruises, sprains—and once, a broken wrist. But in 1848, as they said back then, 'she was delivered of a son,' Charles Benjamin, and he was the fair-haired boy. The father had purchased railroad stock by that time, and he also had his hand in a brickyard. The son, Charles, grew up, went to college, became a lawyer by 1871, and returned to town, where he proceeded to sow his wild oats with alcohol and whorehouses. His father often intervened, especially when the boy didn't treat the women kindly."

"You mean he hurt them?"

"So the story goes. Not sure what the old man finally did to bring him in line—maybe threatened to disinherit him. Back then, you know, abuse was considered a family issue, but if people found out about abuse, it was still frowned upon. Women didn't have much protection and were at the mercy of their spouses. Law enforcement—such as it was—figured a man's home was his castle. If he wanted to get drunk and beat his wife, well, so be it. Some people believe that's why the women eventually took hatchets to saloons and barrels of alcohol. Anyway, Charles got involved in local politics, and, by 1884, his father had died and left a huge estate with orders for Charles to take care of his mother."

Grace scribbled on her notepad. "So that means the father died at age sixty-six, and Charles Lockwood was thirty-six when he came into his inheritance."

"Correct. Your math is excellent, Grace."

"This must have been around the time he also began to build Lockwood House. I know attorneys didn't make all that much income back then, so I assume the inheritance was substantial."

"It was enormous for the time. I imagine Charles hired someone to manage the dry-goods store. But he lived in a period where corruption was rampant, and he was in a position to take advantage of that. He was appointed a circuit judge in 1885, and that's when he commissioned the house at 402 East Grove Street. Once the amazing edifice was built, he needed a wife, so he courted Jane Spencer in 1888, and they moved into the new house after their honeymoon. She was, I believe, twenty. When you look at your social pages in the *Register,* Grace, you'll note all the pictures of the couple at the opera house, the Lenox Hotel Dining Room, and other society weddings. Lots of pictures of the young, influential couple. Study their faces in those photos, and you will think they are having the time of their lives."

"But it wasn't the case?"

"Rumors abounded. Many sources from the town—diaries and journals—attest to the idea that Lockwood had a fondness for the madam of a local whorehouse on South Mercy Street, and he was whispered about when it came to corruption. He had a lot of rich friends, so he ran in fast circles and bought a great deal of property in the town."

"That would include, besides the inherited brickyard and railroad stocks, the pottery and lumberyard, right?"

"Correct. And, of course, when it came time to pave the streets, which brickyard won the bid but that of Judge Charles Lockwood?"

"What about the conflict of interest thing?"

"Didn't exist back then. And, I imagine, with Lockwood's inclinations, his young wife spent many nights at home by herself . . . until, of course, she did finally get pregnant."

"But that didn't last either."

"No. You would think she would have a happy ending, but she didn't. She died in an accident—fell down the huge stairs at the front of the house while she was pregnant. Both of them— she and the baby—died of her injuries."

"But it was an accident, right?"

"Maybe. The local coroner was also the family physician— Dr. Milton Brown. He called a rapid, efficient, coroner's jury, and the unanimous verdict was that her death was an accident. But people still talked and speculated."

"Didn't this bother the judge?"

Sam shook his head. "No. Life went on and he moved up the ladder. In 1891, he was appointed a federal judge. His mother had died the year before, so he no longer had that responsibility. Time for the bored Charles to consider politics on a higher level, but he needed a wife by his side. Word was he might want the governorship."

"That was when he met Olivia Havelock?"

"Yes. She was a young thing, just seventeen, and fresh off the family farm from a small town south of here." He sighed, and a troubled look came over his face.

Grace chimed in. "Then he wined her, dined her, and married her."

Sam's voice broke into her thoughts. "Yes, you can read about it in my book or in the social pages of the *Register.* Tuesday, September 26, 1893, at Lockwood House—the wedding and a levee—that's a dance—afterward."

"In the ballroom?"

"Of course. You'll see photos in my book." He got up and came over to Grace, turning corners of pages with practiced assurance. "See—there on page 214. You can read the description of her dress."

Grace read, " 'The bride wore a white silk dress with three lace flounces, a veil of lace and tulle, and a bouquet and hair wreath of white roses and orange blossoms.' Sounds quite traditional." She turned a page. " 'Lockwood House was splendidly decorated with ferns, flowers, and tall vases of roses at the front entrance and at the ballroom door.' " She looked up at Sam. "Quite an exquisite wedding, Sam."

"Oh, yes. The best. And—to top that—a honeymoon to the Columbian Exposition of the World's Fair in Chicago—all the way by private railcar."

Oh my, thought Grace. *She did get her wish to ride on a train.*

"If you turn a few more pages," Sam said, "you'll see a photograph of the couple taken after their honeymoon. They had celebratory teas and the expected dinner with Olivia Lockwood's parents."

Grace stared at the photo of the couple. Judge Lockwood was in a dark suit with a pocket watch and gold chain. Olivia was in her wedding dress. There was also an exquisite ring—an heirloom ruby with pearls on either side. *How beautiful she looks,* thought Grace. *Her hair is up in a fashionable set of curls as befits a married woman. She stands so stiffly in her corset. The delicate lace of her bodice goes up to a high collar. She looks happy . . . Her goal as a woman has finally been reached. She doesn't realize her husband will be dead in months. How strange to look at this photo and know what lies ahead.*

Sam's voice brought her out of her reverie. "And again, rumors, strange absences of the young wife from social events, whispers of abuse, and his frequency at the saloons on South Mercy Street. I kept seeing rumors of those thoughts braided through several diaries of the time."

"I've seen pictures of her in the social pages. As you say, she was both hauntingly beautiful and also innocent looking."

"Yes. And it's probably a story for another day," he said, glancing at the clock. "See. I did say I could go on forever. You'll find more about the second marriage in my book. Another un-pretty story."

"But you did say something about a mystery," Grace said.

"Ah, yes. That's in the book too. Maybe you can solve their secrets. The deaths have been real subjects of speculation. What happened to his second wife—period? The judge's money did not end up with local charities, which makes me suspect she lived on elsewhere. How did the judge die? Someone he had sentenced looked for revenge? Poison? Still more questions."

"I'm going to try, Sam. I'll bring your book back, and we'll see if I've managed to figure it all out."

"After your 'figuring' about those murders last summer, you just might be able to do it," Sam said and chuckled. "Don't believe everything you read on the social pages of the *Endurance Register,* Grace," he warned.

"What do you mean?"

"Those were dark times, especially for women."

"Thank you, Sam. I appreciate your help with this." She took a deep breath. "And, since you've been such a great help, I have a secret to tell you."

He looked up, a huge smile on his face and his eyes twinkling. "Great. I love secrets."

"Olivia Lockwood left a diary." The shock on his face made Grace laugh with glee.

"Wh—at?" he stammered.

Grace stood up and walked over to him, putting her hand on his arm. "Don't have a heart attack on me, Sam. You heard me right."

"How—how do you know this?"

"Jeff and I found it in the house, secreted away under a floorboard."

"Grace! I—I don't know what to say!" He paused. "You must announce this to the world."

"Not just yet. I'm reading it—carefully, with gloves on. I suppose it is Jeff's property, but I'll ask his permission to let you read it when I'm done. I'm sure he'll be fine with it."

"I take back what I said about you figuring this all out the hard way."

"Oh, come on. Don't be a poor loser."

"Grace, that's fantastic. I can't wait to see it. I've spent years wondering about the missing details."

"You won't have to wait much longer. Now, I have to go, and you have to get back to work. I've taken up enough of your time."

"Gets me away from grading exams, Grace. But you know all about that, too, I suppose."

She smiled and gave him a quick hug. "Uh, yes."

"Call me if you have questions. Be glad to help. And Grace—"

"Yes, Sam?"

"Read fast!"

"I will, Sam. Thanks for your help."

Grace walked down the hallway, deep in thought about Sam's ideas concerning the Lockwoods. About the time she passed the college president's office, a few groups of bundled up students in winter gear—but also some of them barefooted in flip-flops—

came down the hallway. Grace looked at their young faces, as they talked energetically to their friends and laughed.

They're about the same age as the Lockwood wives, Number One and Number Two, thought Grace.

CHAPTER TWELVE

Grace checked with TJ, and the detective told her she could see Emily Folger at the hospital. So the following Monday morning she was walking down the third-floor corridor of Endurance Hospital when she saw a familiar face. He was a well-muscled aide pushing a patient in a wheelchair. *Andrew Weathersby. His locker was right outside my classroom his sophomore year. One day I heard a commotion and walked out to the hallway. It was a girl fight—the worst kind of fight. Andrew nonchalantly leaned against the wall and pointed out his twin sister, Ally. "She's the one on the top, beating the crap out of Lisa Watkins." Then he leaned forward and shouted, "Hit her again, Ally!" Alphabetical propinquity. That year my hallway was a war zone. It was quite the entertaining year, but the following year their lockers were moved to the lower junior hallway, and all was quiet once again. At least he was using his muscles in a good cause now.*

Grace shifted her bundle of pink roses and checked the room numbers to make sure she was in the right place at Endurance Hospital. 332. She thought about what she might say to Emily Folger, took a deep breath, and stuck her head in the door. It was a double room, but the first bed was empty. Walking in, she passed the unused bed and peeked around the privacy curtain at Emily Folger. She was sitting up in bed, staring out the window, but her eyes were empty. Her face was still a little swollen, her left eye had black and blue bruises around it, and her neck had still more bruises. Her left arm peeked out from a

111

hospital gown, and Grace could see dark-purple bruises on her upper arm.

"Emily?" Grace said, quietly.

Her head turned, and Emily stared at her old teacher. Then, briefly, recognition showed in her eyes. She looked back toward the windows.

"Hi, Emily. It's Grace Kimball. You do remember me, right?"

Emily turned toward Grace, blinked twice, and said, "Yes," in a flat, disinterested voice.

I wonder if she's still medicated, Grace thought. "I brought you some flowers from All That Blooms. I remembered pink was your favorite color, and they had pink roses. Shall I put them over here on the ledge where you can see them?"

After a long pause, Emily mumbled, "Sure."

Grace set the flowers down, pulled a chair over, and kept a distance between them. Instinctively, she figured her long-ago former student would not want her too close. She needed to take Emily's hand, but didn't think it was the right thing to do in her present state. Grace watched Emily look at the roses, and eventually her gaze came back to Grace. But she didn't say a word. Emily pulled up her blanket, and Grace looked down at her hands—her fingernails were ragged, and she had bitten them down to the quick.

"I know you've been through a terrible experience, Emily. I can't remember the last time I saw or talked to you. I feel guilty. Can I do anything to help?" She waited. "Who has your children? I saw their pictures in Con—"—she stopped and corrected herself—"at the bank. Can I help you with them?"

For at least half a minute Emily said nothing. Then she seemed to gather her thoughts and said, "What will I do, Ms. Kimball, with Conrad gone? Where will I go? How can I ever manage without him?" Her voice trailed off into silence.

Grace leaned forward a little. She thought about what her

best words might be. Before she could even speak, Emily said, "I tried to do things right."

"I'm sure you did," said Grace. "This was a terrifying experience. Have you been able to talk with anyone about it?"

Emily looked up and answered unemotionally. "The police. That woman detective, TJ Sweeney. She's . . . been helpful. The problem is I can't sleep. I'm so tired. When I close my eyes I remember how horrifying it was . . . seeing him there. All the blood. I can't remember much when I'm awake, but when I close my eyes it's so frightening."

Grace could tell from Emily's lack of vocal inflection and her slumped shoulders that she was still in a cloud of confusion. Then, for a moment, Emily sat up, leaned forward toward Grace, and said, "People think I did that. How could I? He was everything. I can't remember what happened. I'm so confused. I don't even remember how I got here to this hospital."

Grace leaned over and patted her hand. "You will, Emily. It will eventually come back. I imagine the confusion is from drugs. They've probably had to keep you sedated. The mur— experience was a terrible shock to your system. You need to get some rest and give yourself time. Do you have any friends who can help?"

Emily thought a moment. "No."

"What about your parents? They don't live too far away."

"They're coming." Another long pause. "They're going to take Caitlin and Conrad back to their home."

"That's good—to get them away from here for a while. The children know their grandparents, and they will feel safe there."

Suddenly, Emily repeated, "I tried to do things right."

"Oh, Emily, I know you did," Grace answered, somewhat confused.

"I don't know what I'm going to do . . . where I'm going to go."

"I don't think you need to worry about it yet. You're safe here in the hospital."

Just as Grace reassured her, Will Folger came in the door quietly.

"I'm back, Emily." He smiled. "Oh, hello, Ms. Kimball."

"I think you can call me Grace, Will." She noticed the curly hair from the bank was now disheveled, and his anxiety was more evident in his quick handshake.

"Grace." He smiled and turned toward Emily. "How are we doing today, Emily?"

"Will, I don't know what I'm going to do. What am I going to do without Conrad?"

Will walked over toward the side of the bed opposite Grace. He took Emily's other hand and said, "Don't worry, Emily. We have everything well in hand. Darlene and I will help you however we can, and she's at home with Caitlin and Conrad right now. We're waiting for your parents to come, since you'd like them to keep the children. I think that's a good idea. I went to your house and picked up some things for the children to take with them. No need for them to go to the house." Will spoke with concern, but his voice was confident, as if he had a new purpose.

A single tear slid down Emily's cheek. "What happened, Will? How can Conrad be dead? Who did this? Did I do this?" She shook her head and put her hands over her eyes. "I can't remember."

Grace glanced at Will's eyes, which darted toward her and then back to his sister-in-law. Emily became agitated, her hands shaking, so Grace said, "We don't know yet who could have done such a horrible thing, Emily."

Slowly, Emily said, "I think I did it. It might have been me. I can't remember. I remember all the blood, everywhere, all over me and the floor. I was there." She shook her head slowly. "Oh, why can't I remember?"

Will, his voice reassuring, said, "Try not to think about it right now, Emily. Let's talk about some other practical items. I checked at the bank, and everything is in Conrad's name. This means your money will be frozen until all of this—situation—is straightened out. Darlene and I will set up an account and put money in it for you so you'll be able to pay for food and other things when you go home."

"Home? How can I go home? All that blood . . ."

"Will," said Grace, "I'll be glad to help clean the house up or make arrangements for carpet cleaning, if it's all right with you. I imagine you're really busy at the bank. I have the time, and I can do it. I'll wait, of course, until the police say it's all right."

"Grace, you're wonderful. I appreciate your help. As you say, the bank is a mess. With the president gone so unexpectedly, the board will need to name someone, even as an interim, to get bank business straightened out. Reputation is so important for a bank, and we need to clean up any vestige of concern. I've hardly had any sleep myself because I've been at the bank going through all the papers. I know Emily thinks the world of you, and I'm sure Conrad did too. I'll be in touch with you about keys and all. Yes, we'd appreciate your help."

Then he turned to Emily. "Now, Emily," he said, his voice taking on a new urgency. "I've hired a lawyer who will be in to see you later today. His name is Aiden O'Malley. He's the best that money can buy. You need to trust him, and tell him what you can. He is your lawyer, and he can't reveal what you tell him to anyone. Obviously, when you feel better you'll be able to deal with this and him more clearly. But do not—I repeat—do not talk to the police without Mr. O'Malley with you. Understand?"

Emily sagged back into her pillow. "The police again? A lawyer? Why?"

Will glanced at Grace. He reached over and touched Emily's hand. "Let's just say it will be better to have some representation with you. No one knows what the police will do or ask. It's better to have a lawyer with you if the police should want to talk to you."

"I think the lady detective, TJ Sweeney, has already talked to me. But it's all so hazy."

"She may be back again. If she does return, Emily, Mr. O'Malley will make sure you have a way to contact him. You should have him with you if you talk to the police. I can't emphasize how important that is. Promise me you will not talk to the police without him."

"Promise," Emily mumbled, and Grace could tell she was worn out.

"You're tired, and I think I'd better go, Emily, but I'll be back. Don't worry about anything. Get some rest," Grace said.

Emily's eyes were already closed, and Grace began to button her coat and find her scarf as she and Will walked quietly out into the corridor.

"Thank you, Grace, for coming over today. Darlene and I have been so worried about her. I know she's still in shock and the doctor will keep her quiet, but we have no way to tell what she will remember once the drugs begin to wear off. We'll try to keep an eye on her. And I'll take you up on your housecleaning offer. Thank you. You're a kind woman."

"Emily was always one of my favorites, Will."

His face took on a darker look, and he added, "I think she's in serious trouble. I know my brother wasn't a saint, and he learned how to be a bully from the best—our dad—but I didn't realize it had gone this far. I truly had no idea. I think the police have Emily on their radar as the killer. I can't imagine she could have killed Conrad. It—it just doesn't make any sense. Conrad was my brother, and I'm horrified he's dead, especially in this way. God knows we had our differences. But I will try to protect Emily, and I've hired her good legal counsel in case the worst happens."

Grace was too startled at his personal comments to even think about what to say.

With that, he turned, and they both walked down the hallway a few paces apart, thinking their own separate thoughts.

By Monday night Grace had spent much of the weekend going over her notes about the Lockwoods and reading parts of Sam Oliver's book about them. She was still thinking about her visit with Emily Folger and her shock at the change in her former student. She carried a warm cup of tea upstairs, and settled in her bed with the electric blanket dial set to a toasty number. "All right, Olivia Havelock. Let's see what you have found out about the huge town of Endurance." She put on her gloves and pulled the diary out, opening it to the next entry. Soon she was engrossed in the young girl's thoughts.

June & July, 1893
Aunt Maud must think me a country bumpkin since she has ordered my dresses and begun teaching me about rules ladies must know. She showed me *Godey's Lady's Book,* which had fashion plates so I could see the look of my new dresses. Aunt Maud says "The Gibson Girl," created by a Mr. Charles Gibson, is how everyone wants to dress. The shirtwaist dresses have "leg-of-mutton" sleeves. What a funny name. If only the sheep on our farm knew.

Everything I must wear fits so tightly I can hardly breathe. Even the long sleeves fit closely at my wrists. I also have a corset and a bustle. None of these is comfortable, and I am not sure how I will breathe in the corset, let alone get it off and on. It feels like I am in a whalebone prison, one necessitated by my parents' wishes I become a lady. Wait, that is not fair. If I were honest, I would admit I, too, want to be a lady. But this seems a severe price to pay.

I met a boy. I met a boy. I met a boy.

My head is spinning, and I dance around my room. He is a law student named Tyler Quinn, and he is twenty-three years old. His looks are handsome and robust, and he has blond hair and a tiny moustache. I noticed his divine smile first, and his eyes are the deepest blue. My face is flushed just writing this. "Mrs. Tyler Quinn. Mrs. Olivia Quinn."

Mr. Quinn was at the church social, where we were introduced by two of my new girlfriends, who know him because they have all lived here their whole lives. At first, our conversation was filled with long pauses. But once we walked over to the band concert, he talked about himself, the town, and his mentor, Simon Barclay, an attorney. He asked me about my life before Endurance, and it was so easy to talk to him. Our hands barely grazed each other once, and I felt a shock of warmth. I had to take my fan out of my reticule, and help the redness go out of my face and my breathing slow down.

I saw Mr. Quinn again at the Fourth of July picnic and band concert. Aunt Maud packed a picnic basket early, and we walked to the park. The entire town attended, and we enjoyed games, bicycle rides, and a band concert filled with patriotic music. My favorites were "The Battle Hymn of the Republic," "When Johnny Comes Marching Home," and "Yankee Doodle." I both smiled and was sad because Father used to whistle "Yankee Doodle" when he worked. Mayor Paul Andersen gave a speech about the town, and the hardy Scotch Presbyterians who settled here on the edge of the wilderness and began Endurance College.

Mr. Quinn was also at the picnic, having been released from his work for the holiday. We walked over by a small pond—still within sight of everyone as Aunt Maud prescribes—and sat on a bench, well away from each other. We have agreed we will call each other "Tyler" and "Olivia" when we are not in company. I feel so relieved—this is more like Anthem.

The balloon ascension was the highlight of the day. I want to do that someday, float through the sky, up near the clouds and heaven. Once the balloon had taken off, I turned to see a man talking with Aunt Maud. She signaled for Mr. Quinn and me to come over and introduced me to him. His name is Judge Charles Lockwood, and I realized I had seen him at a distance during the day. He is old—I believe he must be at least forty. I later found out he owns a huge mansion on Grove Street, and he told Aunt Maud he would send his card around. He glanced at me, smiled and bowed, and then left. He has very polite manners.

On our way home, my friends and I walked past the reading room and library, and I resolved to make a trip there to find books to read. We also passed the *Endurance Register* office, the local newspaper's place of business. It has a plaque on the door, which says it was founded in 1852. I touched the numbers for luck.

Oh, thought Grace. *I must remember to touch those numbers at the* Register *office. It will be just like connecting with Olivia.* Then she went back to the journal.

Tyler stayed briefly at Aunt Maud's house, sitting on the porch swing with me. Decorum dictated fifteen minutes for a visit, and Aunt Maud watched the time closely. I like him more and more. He is not like one of my brothers, but then he is. It is easy for me to talk to him about my thoughts, like my brother William. He asks me opinions about topics, and that reminds me I must go to the library. He seems interested in what I think. This is counter to Aunt Maud's prohibitions that I must listen and not sound too smart or educated. Mr. Quinn works very hard so he may someday have his own law practice. Only once did a dark look pass over his face: when I mentioned Judge Lockwood said he would leave a calling card. I could tell this news was unsettling to Tyler, but he did not say so.

Grace closed the diary and smiled. Here was a young girl falling for a man whose touch electrifies her. Over a century ago. The old ritual of love and courtship are the same, no matter what the time or place. Deep inside she felt a stirring as she remembered her first date with her husband, Roger. He had come to her campus in Indiana as a guest lecturer, and she was assigned to escort him around the campus. She could think about him now and smile at the good memories. She felt the same warmth as Olivia did when she described Tyler Quinn.

But, of course, Olivia won't end up with him, Grace thought. *I wonder how this will play out—Tyler Quinn and Judge Lockwood. I know which one she marries, but I wonder why.* Grace's eyes were getting drowsy and she thought about Jeff and his blue eyes. Turning out the lights, her last thoughts were, *And which one will I dream about—Roger or Jeff?* She fell asleep still smiling.

CHAPTER THIRTEEN

Grace lifted her head from the collection of newspaper articles she had been reading and rubbed her eyes. She heard a familiar voice.

"Hey, Grace, I'm just coming on shift. What's the latest on the Folger murder?" It was Grace's friend, Deb O'Hara. Deb flung off her coat and hung it up on a hanger. This was followed by two scarves, a knitted hat, mittens, and boots. Sitting down, she pulled a pair of dry shoes from her bag.

"Hi." Grace stood up and stretched her legs. "I stopped to see Emily at the hospital yesterday. I feel so sorry for her and those two little kids. This is crazy. I saw Conrad just last week. We hardly have a murder in thirty years, and then between last summer and now, we are stacking up bodies. This can't be happening again. And Conrad Folger? Why would someone kill him?"

"Well . . ." Deb said, "I don't think this has anything to do with last summer. But the gossip is already flying around town. People have him shot, hanged, and knifed to death. Oh, and their money seems to be on Emily Folger, the wife you just visited."

Grace's eyes narrowed, and her voice trembled. "What? I can't believe it. Emily would never do something like that. She couldn't kill anyone."

"Word has it he's been abusing her—physically—and she just had enough of it. Hard to believe."

Grace paused for a moment, thinking about Emily. "I think the abuse idea may be true after seeing Emily. But someone in Conrad Folger's position? People like that—powerful people with lots of money—they don't do those kinds of things. If they're unhappy, they just divorce."

"Not Conrad Folger. He'd never divorce anyone and have people in town talk about him. And Emily. She seems like such a little mouse; I can't believe she'd divorce him, let alone kill him. You never know, Grace, what goes on behind closed doors. Ask TJ. I'll bet she's seen stuff she never tells us."

Grace sat down and motioned Deb to take a closer chair. "I imagine this means long hours for TJ. She got more than she bargained for when she came back here and became a police-woman. Moving up to detective has kept her busy, especially with these homicides."

"Don't worry, Grace. She'll manage. She's tough—has to be. She'll figure this one out too."

"I know you're right," Grace said quietly. Then she remembered her research. "I've found out a great deal about Jeff's house, but now I'm starting on the social life of the Lockwoods. Between the *Register* and Sam Oliver's book, I'm learning how stifling life was for women back then."

Deb smiled and rubbed her hands. "That should be exciting. First wife or second?"

"The second for now. I just talked to Sam and he hinted—well, more than hinted—that Judge Lockwood was an abuser, like Conrad Folger."

Deb looked up from her desk and said, "Really?" She paused and turned back around toward Grace. "How strange that both of those men were powerful and connected with the town in so many philanthropic ways, yet violence is also in their stories."

Deb turned around to start working again and then had second thoughts. "I think that woman is in deep trouble. She's undoubtedly their number one suspect."

"TJ will get it straightened out. I'm sure. I'm pulling for Emily."

"So," Deb said, "what have you found out about Lockwood's second wife? I forget her name."

"Olivia Havelock. From this 1893 article, it appears she was inducted into the Endurance Garden Club. Back then you had to have a sponsor to be invited. Looks like they made bandages for the hospital and supported the missionary work of the children of the Reverend and Mrs. Josiah Andrews."

"That would be kind of like the 1950s in middle-class America. Even then people had clubs with secret handshakes and all the silliness. I remember my mom talking about it. Only in the 1890s, it was more the upper crust evidently."

Grace smiled. "Different times—same silliness and exclusivity."

"So what else did the bigwigs do socially?"

"Well, the esteemed judge and his wife invited couples in for their Christmas Open House. Here's a quote for you: 'Built for the judge by the renowned architect Ainsley Lorenzo Stierwalt, Lockwood House is a premier home on East Grove Street in one of the most desirable residential sections of Endurance.' How's that? Now we know Jeff will be in the upper-class, desirable neighborhood."

"Well, la-de-dah. I hope he still speaks to little me." Deb paused a minute, remembering the coffee she just had time to grab on her way out the door. Her stomach was rumbling. "Does it say what they had to eat at this open house?"

"Of course, Deb. It's the society page. Let's see. 'A repast of roast beef and ham with various sauces; turnips, parsnips, and potatoes; and hot breads soaked in butter.' They obviously didn't know about cholesterol."

"Dessert. It's the most important part. Surely they had dessert."

"Oh, yes. 'Dessert pastries, including taffy, fudge, peanut brittle and pralines, cherry pies, and plum pudding.' "

Deb sighed. "How did they weigh less than three hundred pounds? That does sound yummy." She felt her stomach rumble again.

"Sorry, Deb. You'd have a corset on and you could just nibble at the edges."

Deb threw her hands up in the air. "Thank God for the twenty-first century."

Grace laughed. "So true." She looked at her watch. "Got to get back to work."

"Me too."

Grace pulled out her notebook and checked on the box of microfilm for the latter part of 1893. Then she settled in to adding rolls of film to the monitor and trying not to get motion sickness. She began scanning the social pages and the photos of Olivia Lockwood.

As time flew by, she realized some very hard truths. She looked at the photographs on the social pages and remembered Sam's words about domestic abuse. As she studied them she thought, *These are amazing articles chronicling the decline of Olivia Lockwood. Each story has a photograph taken at the time of the social event. While the photos are gray and grainy, it's easy to see in November Olivia has lost quite a bit of weight since her honeymoon at the end of September. That's only about eight weeks. And, if I enlarge the photos, her weight loss is even more pronounced. Sam Oliver may be on the right track when he says the judge was another Conrad Folger. Hard to know without documentation. And at Christmas time, Olivia is decidedly thinner, and she has dark circles under her eyes. Her face appears more pale and sallow, as far as I can tell from the grainy photos. Her mother must have been very worried about her. They leave a beautiful, innocent girl on her wedding day, and when they return she looks like this. That poor wife. That poor mother.*

After two hours of extensive scanning and writing, Grace pushed her chair back, rubbed her eyes, and looked at her watch. "I don't know how people look at these machines for so long," she said to a quiet, working Deb.

"Me either. Can you still see?"

"Just barely. My eyes always get so tired, but I'll be fine. Found some good stuff."

"Oh?" Deb said. She wheeled around in her chair and asked, "What was the most interesting tidbit of information?"

"Short engagements."

"What do you mean?"

"Back then the wedding was sealed up and delivered very quickly. The idea was if couples had a long engagement, they might get to know each other and decide a wedding wasn't in their futures."

"That is hilarious. And nowadays we tell our children to date for a long time so they'll find out if they want to stick it out. You know the old saying from Ben Franklin—'Marry in haste, Repent at leisure'? So, did you find anything?"

"Yes. Found the engagement, wedding, and honeymoon information on Olivia Havelock Lockwood. She looks so young and so joyous, as if she has her whole life ahead of her. Of course, she did at that point, I guess. But I can see a steady downhill progression after the marriage. Her whole physical being is shrinking and fading into oblivion. What did he do to her? It's only after his—the judge's—death that Sam Oliver lost any trace of her. Obviously, the judge didn't kill her because she outlived him. I am going to figure out this one if it kills me."

"Don't say that. The last time you tried to become a sleuth, you almost did get killed."

"That was different."

Deb gave her a skeptical look.

Just then, Laura Downey came in to borrow a yearbook because she was on a committee to organize a class reunion the next summer. Grace spoke to her, asking where her younger sister was. *Another one I remember. Laura had brought her baby sister, Lucy, into my class to do a demonstration on how to feed a baby. After three bites, Lucy threw up all over the carpet. That was the year I put in a new rule that students couldn't bring in anything live to demonstrate. It was a perfect rule that eliminated dogs, cats, alligators, snakes, and baby sisters.*

After Laura left, Grace began packing up her research.

"I'll be careful, Deb. Right now, though, I need to go back home and check that Lettie hasn't bashed anyone over the head."

"Oh. You mean Del Novak."

"I do. I'm not sure my homeowner's insurance would cover death by frying pan."

Grace began putting on her layers of winter clothes and gathering up all her research. "Hope all goes well, and I'll be back—well, tomorrow's Wednesday—see you, maybe."

CHAPTER FOURTEEN

When Grace reached Sweetbriar Court, she could see that TJ's garage door was closed, and the lights were out in the house. The lights were on at Grace's, so Lettie was there. No Del Novak truck, however. She breathed a sigh of relief she wouldn't have to deal with Lettie and Del together this afternoon. Hurrying into the house from the garage, she set her bag full of research and her laptop down on the table in the front hallway. "Lettie, I'm home. Whatever you're cooking, it smells great."

"Applesauce."

Yum, thought Grace. After taking off her winter gear, she went to the kitchen and saw Lettie at a makeshift table reading the *Endurance Register*. The sweet, fragrant smell of applesauce drifted from a simmering pot on the stove.

Lettie looked up. "Lots of rumors around town about Conrad Folger."

Grace nodded.

Lettie, of course, continued. "Must be a line a mile long of applicants to do him in."

"Oh, Lettie. Be nice," Grace said, and she checked out the applesauce. "The man's hardly cold, and you're already saying unkind things."

"Grace, you don't know. Mildred at the bakery says he's had all kinds of affairs. Probably had to pay those hussies off. And Emily, his poor wife, has had to put up with that. He runs around with every unmarried—and married—woman in town.

127

You don't see his wife out in the community cavorting with other men. No, she stays home and takes care of their two children while he goes drinking and fornicating with whoever he pleases." She looked at Grace. "All right—make that 'whomever.' I must have learned something from your grammar corrections all these years."

"Lettie, you don't know it's true."

"What? That 'whomever' is right? Of course I do." Grace glared at her, and Lettie said, "Well, isn't it?" Lettie folded up the paper and sniffed. "Gladys at the coffee shop said he even came in there and winked at her, and—what is it they say?—'smacked on' her."

"I think the phrase is 'hit on her,' Lettie, and somehow I can't imagine that. Gladys is close to seventy if she's a day, and not exactly Conrad Folger's type."

"To hear people tell it, I think his type was anything in skirts."

"Do you ever hear any gossip about Emily?"

"I thought about that today. She's been pretty quiet. Of course, I don't ever see her anywhere either. I remember sometime in the past she ended up with a broken arm. The rumor mill in town says he did it to her."

"How do you know these things, Lettie?"

"I ask questions."

"But sometimes doesn't it seem nosey to ask people questions about their personal lives?"

"Nosey? Small towns don't know the meaning of the word. Take this murder. People in town are already saying Emily Folger killed him. Most of them aren't too sympathetic toward Emily. The housekeeper's been talking. She told people about the blood everywhere, and only Emily was home when they found the body, and she was covered in blood too. House locked up tighter than a drum."

"I can't understand that. If he was abusive to Emily, why

didn't she just leave and take the kids? I have never understood why abused wives stay with their husbands."

Lettie took off her apron and hung it up. Then she pulled the applesauce away from the burner to cool off. Turning to Grace, she said, "Some women maybe don't feel they have any other choice. And sometimes it's simply easier to stay."

"It makes no sense. She has a college education, and she worked before she met Conrad. Her parents live only a few hours away. She could move closer to them."

"Conrad would still be around with lots of money and a legion of lawyers. He'd make sure she wouldn't get her kids. I think it's a power thing. Bullies like Conrad Folger like to be in charge. They make sure their wives are afraid to leave."

Shaking her head, Grace said, "I used to know Emily when she was in high school, and she was amazing." She walked to the window and caught a glimpse of a black SUV driving slowly toward town. It looked like Will Folger in the front seat. Turning toward Lettie, she asked, "What do you know about Will Folger? I heard in high school he was a wild child."

Lettie poured a cup of coffee and sat down at the table. "Let me think. He came back here a few years ago with his tail between his legs. I remember he was the black sheep of the family. I think I heard way back then that in college, and even after, he'd had quite a problem with alcohol and drugs. Met his wife somewhere. Conrad gave him a VP position at the bank, maybe because he was family and he believed he had to. But Will Folger still drinks too much. Closes one of the bars uptown too many nights."

Grace turned away from the window and sat down, pushing the newspaper to the side of the table. "Roger said Will was a smart kid, smarter—he thought—than Conrad ever was."

"Well, you have to consider their home life too. Conrad III dominated and bullied his wife and kids. Wouldn't be surprised if he didn't abuse them also. He hated weakness. Our Roger had some dealings with him back in the day.

"I remember one time I saw the whole family at the bank. The missus and the three kids came out of Conrad's office. They stopped over by one of the teller's windows, and the kids were little and all dressed up. Mrs. Folger did her best to keep them rounded up." Lettie drained the last of her coffee. "Evidently, they'd been to the doctor's office for their vaccinations, and the father, Conrad, reached around the teller's window and pulled out two suckers. He gave Conrad a sucker because he hadn't cried, and gave Jessalynn a sucker because she had cried, but it was all right because she was a girl. Girls were supposed to cry. But Will, he got no sucker because he had cried. His younger brother, Conrad, was lording it over him even then. And I thought to myself at the time, 'My, my. I can see trouble down that road.' "

"So Will is actually the older brother, isn't he? I should have remembered," Grace said.

Lettie rose and stirred the cooling applesauce on the stove. Then she said, "Yes, and usually the oldest son got the bank job in the earlier generations. But the old man skipped over Will. Too weak and not biddable. He and his father fought terribly, and Will left after college and stayed away. By the time he came back, the old man was dead, and he didn't have to face him. Only Conrad."

"What about Jessalynn? I rarely hear a word about her."

"She got away forever. And I say, 'good for her.' Women aren't given much rope in that family. Nothing's expected of them except obedience, and no one thinks much of them. Jessalynn did manage to get to college, although that was a huge argument. Her father didn't think a woman needed an education. He was of the old school where the man was in charge. Once she graduated from college, she got a job somewhere. From what I've heard—and it's little—she did quite well and put herself through graduate school. I wonder if she'll even come home for her brother's funeral."

"Families are sure tricky, aren't they?" said Grace.

"True." Lettie took a deep breath. "Think about how all of those kids were shaped by their parents and even the generations that came ahead of them."

Suddenly, Grace's phone started playing "Nine to Five," and she fished around in her purse to find it. "Hi, Jill . . . Yes, she's still in the hospital. I only saw her once and she was pretty banged up. Kids are with the grandparents . . . Sounds good. See you."

Grace punched the phone call off, and then she stood up, took the folded newspaper, and said, "Well, I think I'll go upstairs and change clothes." She looked around. "The kitchen is coming along nicely, isn't it?"

Lettie's face turned sullen, and she retorted, "The man is driving me crazy, over here pounding and measuring and drilling all the time." But her words lacked a bit of passion, Grace decided. Then Lettie asked, "How are you coming on Jeff's house research?"

"I'm still researching, and I think the newspaper articles add a lot to the picture." Grace climbed back down the two steps she had already taken toward her bedroom. She walked up behind Lettie, grabbed a spoon, and scooped up a little applesauce. "Mmmm. This applesauce is wonderful. Maybe you should save some for Del." She smiled, and before Lettie could give her a disagreeable retort, Grace started back upstairs again. "That house—Jeff's house—has an air of sadness about it. Maybe the Folgers aren't the only family influenced by the past."

CHAPTER FIFTEEN

Grace took a deep breath and shook her head. "I only spoke to her yesterday—Monday—at the hospital. She's in terrible shape, TJ. Why would you arrest her when she can hardly even think? The poor woman has not a clue about the whole situation."

"Grace, I know you had this special bond with Emily when she was much younger, but she isn't the same person now. We had to arrest her this morning. The evidence is overwhelming. She has a great attorney, and my guess is they'll plead self-defense." TJ had been pacing around Grace's disheveled kitchen. Now she sat down.

Grace poured some more coffee for each of them. They didn't hear hammering because Del had called earlier and explained he wouldn't be over until late afternoon. TJ had discovered long ago that Grace was a great sounding board when the detective had complicated cases. And, loyal friend that she was, Grace had never revealed a confidence. It was especially true since she'd started working for Jeff Maitlin at the *Endurance Register*. These days, she walked a tightrope.

"I know she's not the same person, TJ. I remember a vibrant, self-confident Emily who had lots of friends in high school. How could she have turned into the barely functioning Emily I saw at the hospital? I hardly recognized her. Of course, it's been years since I've seen her—but still. And if Conrad Folger hurt her, why didn't she leave? I will never understand why women don't leave someone who abuses them."

TJ poured a few drips of cream into her coffee and settled in. "It doesn't happen overnight, Grace. Women like Emily suffer from what's called battered woman syndrome, and it's similar to the post-traumatic stress disorder soldiers go through when they've been in battle, say, over in the Middle East."

"But she's not in the middle of a battlefield away from her friends and family. She's right here."

"True, but abusers make sure they take steps to isolate their victims. Her parents live several hours away. She said, remember, that she didn't have any friends. Stop and think. How many times have you seen her since she married, and this is a small town? He would have made sure of it. Then he would check on her at different times of the day to keep her in fear that he might show up when she didn't expect him. She's totally economically dependent on him, and he's stripped away all of her self-esteem. The Emily you see now can't even trust herself to make good choices. Her only focus for a long time has been on how to survive from one day to the next and protect her kids."

Grace sat back in her chair and pressed her lips in a thin line. Finally, she said, "It's true. Will Folger said all the bank accounts were in Conrad's name. But Emily was, or is, an intelligent woman. How could she let this happen? She could easily hold down a job when the kids are at school, and she could open her own account. She has all of these wonderful qualities, and I know she's a good mother. Conrad made plenty of money at the bank, but why couldn't she work so she'd have something to make her feel good about herself?"

"Ah, Grace, my naïve Grace . . ."

Grace shook her head. "I know, I know. You tell me I'm too trusting."

"Conrad would never have let her have a job. It would give her independence, possibly allow her to leave him, and, yes, she would feel better about herself. All of that goes against his plan."

"His plan?"

"Sure. He's like all those other bullies. He undoubtedly humiliated her, hurt her, and—I hesitate to say this to you—brutally raped her."

"Oh, my God! You can't mean that, TJ."

"We have evidence he raped her the very night of the murder. Since you went to the hospital you know how her face and arms look. We believe Conrad did that to her."

"But why? What would he get out of hurting her instead of loving her and being kind to her?"

"Good question. It's a matter of control and power. Most abusers feel a lack of self-confidence despite their appearance to the rest of the world. Controlling her made him feel powerful. He was probably highly manipulative. After he beat her or raped her, he'd buy her flowers or take her out to dinner. He'd convince her she deserved what she got. She never knew which Conrad would come in the door from one day to the next. He'd chip away at her confidence by constantly telling her she didn't do things right."

"Oh," Grace put her hand to her mouth for a moment. "That's exactly what she said at the hospital."

"Typical. If you get a chance, I'd encourage her to talk. She will go to a therapist—her attorney will insist on it. This is the way you can help her best and leave the investigation to us. We can check on the abuse. We may be able to verify it through other people, and also through hospital records. I'm sure her attorney will look for a pattern. Domestic violence is one of the ugliest and most dangerous calls we deal with at the police station. Often, alcohol and weapons are involved." TJ got up, looked out the kitchen window, and turned back to Grace. "We found a gun in the drawer by Conrad's side of the bed. It's legally his, but I'd bet he used it to threaten her. My guess is her lawyer will use a self-defense plea, but it might be difficult to prove since he was asleep at the time he was murdered." She paused, and sat down again. "His throat was cut."

Grace's hand flew to her throat, and she suddenly felt chilled. "Jeff already told me that." She reached across the table and grabbed TJ's arm. "Dear God. Emily could never have done that. How could anyone?"

TJ patted her hand and fumbled for words. "I'll admit—I mean, I know—it's an unusual way for a woman to murder someone. More a man's style. But whoever did it obviously hated him a great deal. Years of being battered could make a woman do that. Check the prison population. The cells are filled with battered women who killed their husbands."

"TJ. Do you really think she'll end up in prison?"

"Most likely. All the evidence points to her at the moment. It's highly compelling. We had a major crime task force meeting with our personnel, plus investigators from the Illinois State Police and from Douglas County. Add the crime techs and a crime scene analyst to the group. It was an articulation discussion to go over what we already know."

"Why is the evidence so devastating for Emily?" Grace asked.

"Because there's so much of it. She made sure her children were gone that night, and God knows what they've already heard and seen. He raped her after the poker party, and he was quite intoxicated and brutal. Witnesses will agree to the alcohol, although the tox screen isn't back yet. It will substantiate his state of mind. After he raped her and beat her—thus the bruises—he fell asleep, with most of his clothes still on. It appears she left, went to the bathroom in her own bedroom, cleaned up briefly, and threw the nightgown he'd ripped on the floor. She changed into another nightgown, and then she killed him as he slept. The second nightgown is the one she wore that morning, and it was covered with blood.

"She says she took a sedative because she has trouble sleeping, and we did find the sedatives in her bathroom with a glass of water. But she might have taken those after she murdered him. It was a crime of opportunity because the glass vase or ashtray she used was on one of the tables in the bedroom. To top that off, her fingerprints were on the piece of glass that killed him. The blood spatter goes from his room to hers and back again, and her foot had a cut from the broken glass on the floor of his room."

"Can't some of those things be explained? For instance, if she did go into the bedroom, she might have gotten the blood on her because someone else had already killed him?"

"She did go back to her bedroom after she killed him because she called 9-1-1. But the blood pattern indicates she traveled in both directions. It doesn't show how many times. Just the fact that she called 9-1-1 after she killed him shows her confused state of mind."

"And her motive was that he battered her, and she'd had enough?"

"A perfect motive. Why she hadn't done it sooner we'll never know. But something must have happened that night. Whatever it was, it clicked, and she couldn't take it anymore. She had the kids safely parked elsewhere, and no one was around. He was drunk and was sleeping heavily—the perfect situation, except for an alibi for her."

"You will think about more possibilities, right? You won't just look at Emily."

"Correct. I am the number one alternative theory person at the EPD. Ask the chief. Everyone down there, especially the chief, gets frustrated with me. But we haven't touched on a couple of items here. First, the doors to the house were locked and an alarm set. It never went off. She was alone in the house with him. He didn't slit his own throat. Second, I'd imagine he is worth a huge chunk of money, and she's the only possible beneficiary, unless he left some to his brother and sister-in-law. He also has a sister, Jessalynn. But I don't think there's a lot of love among those sibs, so I guess we'll see what the will says. That's next. Of course, if he left everything to Emily, including life insurance, she won't get it if she's found guilty. Illinois has a slayer statute."

Grace shook her head, slowly, from side to side. "This is so far beyond my understanding of what marriages are like, TJ. Roger and I were lucky, but we only had a few years of happiness. I guess I don't get how an intelligent woman like Emily could marry into such a horrible situation."

"I understand, Grace. I'm not sure I know a lot of happy marriages, but, on the other hand, abusive marriages are few on my personal radar too. I think most lie between those extremes. It's been my experience abusive partners can be charming and tender-hearted at times, and perhaps that's how the Folger marriage began. But I think even charm reveals some cracks on the surface. Emily simply didn't see them."

"Keep looking, TJ. I'll clean up the Folger house if it's all right to do that now. I realize it may be a while before anyone is in the house, but I'd feel better if I took care of it."

"Sure. We're all done, and it will be a mess from the fingerprint powder and the blood. I've got the name of a carpet cleaning firm that's good with bloodstains. If anyone can get those stains out, they can." She handed Grace a business card. "You might have to talk with her about how to buy a new mattress for the bed. Actually, both beds."

"I'll talk with Will. He has the purse strings at the moment."

"So far, Jeff has asked the right questions and will publish the facts as clearly as possible. Unfortunately, the *Woodbury Sentinel* editor seems not to have the same journalistic code. His name is Adam Shumacher, he's new, and I think he's a yellow journalist at best. He'll stir up plenty of trouble as far as the gossip circuit. I don't know how they'll have a fair trial in this venue."

"Maybe it won't come to that. I trust you to figure out the real killer, TJ."

"Working on it. As we investigate, we'll look for other possible suspects. But, as I said, the clues are mostly headed in Emily Folger's direction." She shook her head. "It'll be an uphill battle for her, I'd say."

"No one should have to live in fear, TJ, and especially from someone who is supposed to love her. She doesn't deserve this. I know she could never have killed Conrad, abused or not. And, by the way, why is it everyone believes she did it when they don't have a clue about her situation? Why don't people ask why her husband was allowed to abuse her—evidently for years? How come he gets away with that and isn't thrown in jail? I'm going to work on clearing her, TJ, if it's the last thing I do."

"That's the Grace I know, always out there helping the underdog. But I seem to recall your own curiosity put you in jeopardy once before. Don't poke your head, hands, or even your little toe into a viper's nest this time. Got that?"

"I won't, TJ," said Grace, but she had already concocted a plan in her head and crossed her fingers behind her back.

CHAPTER SIXTEEN

After TJ left, Grace continued to think about Emily Folger. From what she had researched about Olivia Havelock, she could see such parallels in the lives of both women. And so much was about appearance versus reality, both then and now. *How many people live their lives worried about what others might think of them, and so their public lives don't necessarily reflect what is happening at home? I'll bet TJ sees that all the time.*

She considered how radically the times had changed when it came to the law and domestic violence. But still, Emily Folger had lived in such terror during her married life. Grace shook her head. *How sad so many women find themselves in that position and, even in this day and age, believe there is no way out, especially when it comes to supporting their children. All right, Grace. Banish those thoughts. It's time to go back and see Olivia at her finest, when she is still happy and not yet married.*

July, 1893
What a modern place Endurance is. The town council has begun to put bricks on the streets instead of dirt, but alas, the bricks are only near the square so far. As I walked to the library today, I noticed all the milliner and notions stores, and the gunsmiths, livery stables, and law offices. It is hard for me to imagine what stores will be in these buildings a hundred years from now. How amazing to consider that people then will walk here where I am walking and

imagine what the stores might have looked like in my time. I noticed several attorneys' offices, and I am sure people will always need lawyers. I told Mr. Quinn that.

On the way to the library and reading room I must pass several banks. The Second National Bank, which belongs to a family named Folger, is on the square. Sometimes I see a gentleman—perhaps Mr. Folger himself—come out the front door, glance at his pocket watch, and make a terrible face. I do not believe he is a happy man.

I examined the novels at the library and checked out one by Louisa May Alcott, called *Little Women,* and another called *Jane Eyre* by Charlotte Bronte. I also borrowed a biography of President Washington to make Aunt Maud happy. She considers biographies of heroes the proper reading for ladies. I may have to sneak the novels into the house. I was also able to read newspapers from New York City and Boston. Of course, they were a week old, but still I find this exciting, since I could not read such newspapers in Anthem.

I found an article about a woman named Lizzie Borden who was found not guilty of the murders of her stepmother and father in New Bedford, Massachusetts. Their murders were gruesome. Imagine: Her trial took a full fifteen days—over two weeks to discuss the details of such a horrendous act. Since I was curious, I looked at the map of Massachusetts and found New Bedford, clear at the end of our vast country, nestled near a cove of water called Buzzards Bay. What a picturesque name. Perhaps sailors died there, and buzzards picked at their bones. Aunt Maud would say, "This is not suitable material for a young lady to peruse."

I spoke with Mr. Quinn about Lizzie Borden. Walking home from the library, I saw him on the other side of the street, leaving the courthouse. He waved and crossed the street to walk me home. He knew all about Lizzie Borden and was able to supply me with more details of the story. He was neither surprised nor censorious about my choice of newspaper reading or my novels. He seemed pleased to talk with me about events of the day. It was so easy to talk to him, and we fell into mutual silences without dismay.

Still, Aunt Maud has been in communication with Judge Lockwood, and she is planning our luncheon at the Lenox Hotel. She sings his praises—his stables and horses, his huge mansion, his notable standing in the community, and his correct bereavement behavior after the death of his first wife. Compared to Mr. Quinn, she says, the judge has an impeccable list of future stability and finances.

Luncheon with Judge Lockwood: We walked to the Lenox Hotel, and since Aunt Maud was nervous to make a good impression, she stopped to check her shawl and finger the necklace at her throat. She had brushed my hair until it shone, and I wore one of my new dresses—a lavender confection with lots of lace around the collar and sleeve cuffs.

When we entered the hotel he was waiting for us and shook hands with Aunt Maud. To me, he bowed slightly and acknowledged my name, "Miss Havelock." The dining room was all linen tablecloths and shiny silverware, and the tables had vases of flowers. The judge had already "taken the liberty" of ordering our luncheon. As we began on the various courses of soups and meat, Aunt Maud looked at me as if I were being naughty. The judge must have thought my mind wandered, and I was not following the conversation. But my blasted corset oppressed my breathing, and filling myself with food would simply make it worse. So I nibbled at the edge of each course. We had relishes, fresh fish and a filet of beef, followed by bread and churned butter. By the time the waiter brought ice cream—a delicacy I have only read about—I could scarcely breathe. No wonder Aunt Maud says gentlemen like ladies who are restrained in their appetites.

Judge Lockwood did not look so old and scary when I sat across the table from him. His eyebrows were bushy and dark, but without a sign of gray. His hair was thick and black, and he had long sideburns on either side of his face. His dark eyes gazed around the room, taking in everything, and occasionally they settled on me. His stare disarmed me, but I followed Aunt Maud's admonition to say little and keep my eyes on my food.

He and Aunt Maud talked about the weather, how the crops progressed at the summer midpoint, the dusty streets from lack of rain, and the recent shipment of goods from France for his dry-goods store. Then he inquired about my horse, Lightning, and asked about my parents and their agricultural holdings. As I described my brothers, I fought hard not to shed a tear because I suddenly realized how much I missed them. He handed me a handkerchief with his monogrammed initials. Then he explained he has stables on the edge of town, and I am welcome to use one of his horses if it would help my homesickness. I thanked him, and Aunt Maud's face resumed its only slightly anxious look.

The luncheon went well, and Aunt Maud has sung the judge's praises ever since. But deep down inside of me—in a place Mama always told me to heed—a feeling grows that, despite his lovely manners and his many possessions, the judge makes me uncomfortable. I cannot decide what makes my insides feel this way. Perhaps I only imagine it because I am tired and unsure of this new world in which I've been placed. When I consider how these rituals—

courtship and marriage—are worked out between families and eligible men, I feel like one of my father's lambs that marches to the slaughterhouse with no knowledge of what lies ahead.

Grace's eyes were heavy, and she decided it was time to go to bed, but her mind couldn't shut down her thoughts about Olivia Havelock. *What a little rebel she was at first. It was weird to read her diary and know the future. Life isn't supposed to happen that way. Obviously, Olivia will end up marrying the judge, but what happened to the young man she met so soon after she arrived—Tyler Quinn? He wasn't part of Sam Oliver's history book at all.*

How like the old Emily Folger is Olivia Havelock. She is filled with intellectual curiosity, and is funny and smart. She listens to her intuition and realizes when things are not as they should be. How strange Olivia should meet a relative of Conrad Folger. But all of her strength and intelligence will not keep her away from marriage to the judge, any more than the same attributes kept Emily from marrying Conrad Folger. Grace thought about Deb's words as she turned out the light and took the diary back upstairs: "Marry in haste, repent at leisure." *Ben Franklin was one smart man.*

CHAPTER SEVENTEEN

Grace finished unloading the dishwasher in Emily Folger's kitchen. It hadn't taken long to clean the sun-filled room since crime techs had mostly left it alone. Will had called a couple of hours ago and announced that a local company would deliver a mattress for the king-sized bed in Conrad Folger's room. They would take away the old mattress so Emily wouldn't have to see it. Grace had picked up two sets of bed sheets and four pillows for Emily's bed and the bed in Conrad's room.

She spent most of Wednesday at the house, dusting away fingerprint powder, and rolling up crime-scene tape. She hadn't known what to expect when she went upstairs in Emily's house. *It was a beautiful home,* she thought, as she looked out over the banister at the expensive chandelier and the living room downstairs.

That was Wednesday. The carpet cleaning company TJ recommended had come and gone in the afternoon, and now on Thursday the carpet looked normal again and was almost dry. Grace was surprised they could work such magic, and she decided to keep their business card for future wine—not blood—stains at her own house. The Folgers' upstairs no longer displayed any sign of death, and she would just finish up before Emily arrived home in a few hours.

She had washed the new sheets and pillowcases at her house last night and brought them with her. As she made the king-sized bed with deft, quick strokes, she thought about what had happened in court yesterday. Emily had been arrested in the morning for the murder of her husband. TJ broke the news to Grace herself because she knew her old teacher, mentor, and now friend, would be terribly upset. And she was. Emily had been fingerprinted and taken to the city jail and booked. Her lawyer, Aiden O'Malley, was with her, but Emily didn't have to spend more than a few hours in jail. O'Malley accompanied her and the police escort to the Douglas County courthouse, where she was arraigned and charged with second-degree murder. TJ explained to Grace that the DA, Sharon Sorensen, didn't think she could prove intent and planning, so first-degree murder wasn't a feasible choice.

TJ said Judge Cyrus Forrester ruled there was probable cause to hold Emily and try her for the murder. That was when Aiden O'Malley showed his legal experience and talent. Grace was so relieved Will had the money and connections to hire O'Malley. His office was in Woodbury, but people all over the area knew of his legal prowess. He argued successfully that Emily was no threat to her children or the community, and she had no passport. She also didn't have any financial ability to leave because all of the family money was tied up with Conrad's name on the accounts. O'Malley entered a not-guilty plea and asked that a reasonable bond be set since she wasn't a flight risk. He also explained he wanted a forensic psychologist to evaluate Emily's competency to participate in her defense, and to evaluate her mental state at the time of her husband's death.

Fortunately, Judge Forrester ruled in her favor, and he ordered a $500,000 bond and a pretrial release only under the condition she wear an ankle bracelet and check in weekly with the Department of Corrections. He also approved having Emily's mental competency examined. Will put up the bond, and before Emily could be released today, she would have an ankle bracelet attached. Fortunately, the hardware now had GPS so she could leave the house. *Of course,* thought Grace, *she might not want to leave for a while since she doesn't know what people might say.*

It was unfortunate the *Woodbury Sentinel*'s editor was fanning the flames of local opinion. He had worked at other newspapers but was new in Woodbury, a town of thirty thousand just east of Endurance. Grace figured he was intent on upping the readership of his paper. She had picked up Emily and Conrad's edition of the newspaper on their front steps that morning, and also had cleaned up three earlier papers lying in the snow. When she opened the most recent newspaper, the headline was "Alleged Murderess Goes Free." Then it directed readers to the editorial page. Grace's blood pressure shot up, and her scowl could have sunk the thousand ships Helen of Troy launched. "How dare he?" she muttered out loud and sat down in a kitchen chair. She even read the editorial out loud, though no one was around to hear her.

"In a gross miscarriage of justice (according to this humble editor), Judge Cyrus Forrester ruled that a wife who allegedly murdered her husband can go home, scot free. Emily Petersen Folger, wife of Conrad Folger, noted president of the Second National Bank of Endurance, was charged with second-degree murder in the death of her husband. His body was found Saturday, January 7, 2012, at the family residence east of Endurance. While no information has been forthcoming from the police department, this editor has been told Folger's throat was slashed, and he bled to death in his own bed. No one was apprehended at the scene except his wife, who was taken by ambulance to Endurance Hospital's ER. She appears to be in good condition.

"Ms. Folger was arraigned on murder charges and spent only a few hours in jail before she was allowed both bond and house arrest. She is represented by the noted Woodbury attorney Aiden

O'Malley. Riding on the coattails of his recent 'not guilty' verdict for Andrew Stirkes here in Woodbury, he will now take on a huge challenge representing Ms. Folger, especially since she is the widow of a prominent bank president. This editor attended the arraignment and noted that Ms. Folger appeared with her attorney and didn't answer or look around at anyone in the gallery. Mr. O'Malley pleaded her 'not guilty.'

"It has come to the attention of this editor that her husband, the late Conrad Folger, is remembered for many of the philanthropic causes he supported in the small community of Endurance. He spearheaded the drive for United Way, was a major subscriber to the Endurance free concerts at Endurance College, and underwrote costs for the after-school program for boys and girls in the primary grades in the Endurance school district. He will be sorely missed for his good works.

"If this is the case and Ms. Folger alone was apprehended, unharmed, at the murder scene, why is she treated differently from other citizens charged with murder? Why is she free to walk the streets of Endurance, granted, with an ankle bracelet, so she can be monitored? If you or I had been charged with such a murder, fellow citizens, we would be sitting it out in the Endurance jail: No expensive lawyer for us and certainly no pretrial release. What is happening in our legal system that an accused murderess is free to leave jail? Money appears to talk once again."

Finished with her coffee, Grace threw the newspaper down and trudged up the back stairs. "Geez!" yelled Grace out loud. "This makes me sick. How can he write such flagrantly one-sided slop?" *Maybe I can get Jeff to write an editorial that will mute some of this hogwash,* she thought. *Unfortunately, people often believe everything they read in the newspaper, and a lot of people in Endurance take the Woodbury newspaper.*

She finished making the bed, plumped the pillows, and looked at her work. *Good,* she thought. *It didn't look like a room someone had been killed in.* She would hide the newspapers in a bag and take them home with her.

"I could hear you swearing at Editor Shumacher clear downstairs," TJ said, coming into the bedroom.

Grace jumped and turned around. "Oh, TJ, you surprised me. What are you doing here?"

"Just stopped to check and see if you were done. Will should be on his way here in about ten or fifteen minutes with Emily. Passing through the kitchen, I could see you've read Shumacher's trash. Well, not everyone reads it, but with or without it, I have a feeling Emily will not be welcomed back into the bosom of her community, so to speak. I've heard too much talk downtown."

"I was afraid of that," Grace said. "What are people saying?"

"In the coffee shops and at The Depot, the general consensus is she did it. After all, no one else was there. And somehow the story of the alarm and the locked door got out. I think Ms. Simmons has a loose tongue. No one seems to be buying the self-defense idea, and no one seems to be buying Conrad Folger as an abuser, or, if they do believe that, they have no sympathy for a woman who stays with her abusive husband and subjects her children to all that. No, I think there may be hard times to come."

"I'll talk to Jeff and see if he can get some accurate and rational stories in to calm things down. Let's go downstairs. I'm done up here."

TJ took a look around the bedroom, nodded, and started out the door toward the stairway. Then she turned and said, "I know you're sure Emily is innocent, and I'd like to believe that. I'm afraid we have an awful lot of evidence to the contrary."

Grace sighed. "I know. But I'm someone she'll talk to, and maybe, as she remembers what happened, I can help her get to the bottom of the murder. The Emily I knew could never have done this."

"Grace, I keep mentioning, she isn't the Emily you knew 'back when' anymore," said TJ, and she walked on down the stairs.

Grace noted the blue, yellow-ringed eyes staring out of Emily Folger's face. She was pale, bedraggled-looking, and wore some clothes TJ had dropped off at the jail for her. They were at least two sizes bigger than a "small." She sat quietly at the kitchen table, her hands in her lap, waiting for the coffee to finish heating. Grace pulled out cups and saucers from the just-filled cabinets.

"I cleaned while you were—away, and I'm sure I didn't get everything exactly right. At least it's livable now," Grace said.

Emily raised her face and looked at Grace for the first time in days. "Thank you, Ms. Kimball. I'm not sure how I feel about being here even with the house back in order."

Grace poured the coffee, put the cups on the table, and found a sugar bowl and spoons in the cabinets. "Sorry we don't have any cream or milk. I hadn't gotten to groceries yet."

"Will said Darlene would be over later today with some groceries and information about a bank account. I think I won't want to go to the grocery store, at least not yet."

"One day at a time. You have a lot of healing to do."

"I'll be able to talk to Conrad and Caitlin on the phone today." Her face brightened at the thought of her children. "My mom and dad have been doing their homework with them, and the school sent books and assignments."

"That's wonderful. I think it's good they're in a place where they feel safe, and if they can talk to you on the phone, they won't be so worried."

Emily took a sip of coffee and stared out the window straight across from her chair. Finally, she said in a totally flat tone of voice, "I'm so tired, Ms. Kimball. I still can't sleep, and when I do, I see terrible sights."

Grace thought carefully about what she should say. "First, I think you should call me Grace. I know it may be hard at first, but it will get easier. Second, TJ gave me the bottle of sleeping pills the doctor prescribed for you. If it's all right with you, I'll stay here tonight, and if you wake up and are afraid, I'll be here."

Her former student looked straight into Grace's eyes. "You're keeping the pills so I don't take the whole bottle?"

Startled by Emily's frankness and newfound logic, Grace quietly said, "Yes."

Emily moved her upper teeth softly over her lower lip and sighed. A single tear slid down her cheek, and she looked at Grace. When she spoke, her voice was hesitant and slow. "You don't understand." She paused. "I could never leave my children. I've spent my life taking care of them and protecting them." She paused again. "You don't have to worry."

Grace smiled at Emily, rose from her chair, and came back to the table with the coffee pot, warming up each of their cups. It had been a long time since she'd had Emily Petersen in class as a high school student, but now she could see signs of the old Emily she knew. Relieved, she asked, "Any chance you're beginning to remember what happened last weekend?"

"Yes . . . not everything. But bits and pieces come back. I'm to see a psychiatrist Mr. O'Malley got for me." She took a deep breath, stirred more sugar into her coffee, and her shoulders slumped. "I tried for so long—so long to please him. I could never get anything right. I was so worried on Saturday before the dinner and poker game." She bit her lip and looked down at her hands. "He drinks—he drank—too much, and then it was scary. I'm starting to remember feelings. It's not pleasant," Emily whispered, and then she put her head down on her hands on the table.

Grace reached across and touched one of Emily's hands. "I know it will take time to remember and to begin to feel like— like your old self again. I'll help you all I can, and I have friends who will be glad to help."

Emily raised her head and said, "Are you sure you want to do that? Everyone in town will think I murdered Conrad. I'm not even sure myself if I did."

"Since when did I care what everyone else thinks? Listen to me, Emily. People don't change much. What they were in high school is pretty much who they are down the road. You never were, nor are you now, someone who could kill another human being. I know you, and I'm willing to bet on your innocence. We'll get it figured out. I know we will."

Just as Grace offered help, the kitchen door opened, and Darlene Folger came in juggling two large sacks. In the past, Grace had only seen her from a distance. She was tall and very slender, and her dark hair fell to her shoulders. She had the sort of aquiline nose that divided her face in perfect symmetry. Her actions were quick and focused, and Grace thought an air of self-sufficiency surrounded her like a firewall.

She set the sacks down on the kitchen counter nearest the refrigerator. Then she turned and said, "Hi, Emily." Rather than wait for Emily to introduce them, Darlene said, "And you must be the high school teacher."

Grace stood up and extended her hand. "Yes. I'm Grace Kimball. I was Emily's English teacher."

"Nice to meet you." Then she gave Grace a dismissive look and turned back to Emily. "Emily, I brought you groceries and information about a debit account Will set up at the bank until we get things sorted out. See, here is the information." She slid the card across the table, along with some papers Emily would need to sign.

"Thank you." Emily's voice cracked. "I've never had an account at a bank except for when I finished college and was working. Will you help me with this, Grace?"

"Sure," Grace said, and nodded.

Darlene looked at Emily and said, "Now, will you be all right here tonight?"

"Yes," answered Emily. "Ms.—Grace—is going to stay tonight, until I get my bearings."

Darlene looked Grace up and down. "I see. Well, I've spoken to Will, and since you were—indisposed—we've planned Conrad's funeral and luncheon for tomorrow. The funeral arrangements have all been made, and Jessalynn will fly in later today." She turned to Grace. "Jessalynn is Will and Conrad's sister."

"Yes, I know," said Grace.

"Burial will be in the family crypt at St. Rose's, and Will and I will open our home for a light luncheon. I assume all of the bank board will be there, along with other notable people from town."

"But Darlene," said Emily. "Tomorrow? Doesn't that seem—I mean—isn't that a bit quick? How can I get my children and parents back here?"

Darlene sniffed. "The services will be in the afternoon. Your parents should be able to drive back. It's only three hours, after all. Now, do you have something suitable to wear? If not, I can probably find you something."

"Yes, Darlene. That shouldn't be a problem."

"Good. One-thirty at St. Rose's. The funeral home will send a limo for you and your parents and children." She glanced across the kitchen at a blinking light on the counter. "Is that an answering machine for your phone?"

Emily looked in the same direction as Darlene. "Oh, yes."

She lowered her head and bit on her lower lip. "I didn't want to deal with it yet."

"Well, let's check. Could be something important." Darlene examined the knobs and LED screen and finally pushed some buttons.

"You have ten messages," a disembodied voice said in an electronic drone. "First message," and then a man's angry voice came on the recorder and said, "You'll get what's coming to you, you bitch. May you rot in hell." A pause followed and then, "Second message." Again, a pause and then a woman's voice snarled, "You aren't so high and mighty now, are you, Ms. Folger? I can't wait to see—"

Grace saw the stricken look on Emily's face and crossed the room in two strides, pushing the "stop" button decisively. "I think that should do it for today, Darlene. Emily has enough to sort out without listening to such drivel." Her voice was calm, but definite.

Darlene took a deep breath and walked toward Emily, grabbing her coat from the chair where she'd draped it. "Perhaps you're right." She said to Emily, "Might be a good idea not to answer your phone for a few days. You do have a cell phone, too, right?"

"I'm afraid the police confiscated it for evidence," said Grace.

"Oh. I hadn't thought of that. Poor Emily. You have so much to straighten out. If I have to reach you before the funeral tomorrow, I'll have to use your house phone, I guess."

"Yes."

"See you tomorrow." She glanced down at her fingernails and shook her head as if chiding herself. "I'll have to get my nails done quickly. I can get them to squeeze me in." Remembering where she was, Darlene said, "Don't forget to set the alarm as soon as I'm out the door, Emily," and with a flick of her scarf and a toss of two gloves into her right hand, she was out the door, and the kitchen was quiet once again.

Emily glanced at Grace's surprised face. "She's a force of nature, isn't she?"

"I'll say." *And a few other things too,* thought Grace. "Let's put these groceries away, I'll stop at home and pick up some clothes, and come back and stay tonight. While I'm gone you can call your parents about the arrangements." *And I must remember to tell TJ about those phone messages.* She saw Emily glance at the flickering light on the message machine. "And no, do not listen to those messages while I'm gone. That's an order."

CHAPTER EIGHTEEN

Grace glanced at her watch. Three o'clock. Conrad Folger's funeral had been the usual litany of biblical verses, hymns, and recitations, and the minister had done a nice job of making the former bank president and abusive husband sound human. She studied Will and Darlene's dining room, where people still milled around the assortment of catered food and the expensive and well-stocked bar: the board of directors from Conrad's bank, the minister, some assorted church people, Rotary Club members, and a few people Grace remembered from the bank. But the crowd was starting to thin out.

Jeff and TJ walked over to Grace's side. Jeff said, "Emily's out in the kitchen saying good-bye to her parents and kids. They seem to be well-behaved children and very quiet. What a terrible thing for them to have to absorb. You wonder what they've seen and heard in that household."

"I think her parents will take them back to Williamsburg. It's better they have some stability while all this goes on. Also better for Emily to be away from this crowd while saying good-bye. Have you noticed how most people have avoided offering their condolences to the widow? News travels fast and so does judgment." Then she remembered an idea her brain had been formulating. "Jeff, think we could talk to Will about setting up Internet service in Emily's house, along with a laptop? That way she could do a video call with the children," Grace said.

"Sure, I can handle it," he answered, "but we might need to

ask her if her parents have a computer." He looked out toward the dining room at small groups of people who ate and spoke in quiet tones. Occasionally, they heard loud, uproarious laughter, especially from the group around Will Folger. "Somehow I don't think The Depot is catering this luncheon," Jeff remarked with a chuckle.

"Either that or they did cater it for free," said TJ quietly. Jeff smiled.

TJ stared toward the dining room and said, "Darlene seems to be in her element. Maids hired to help with the catering and lots of opportunity to schmooze the bank directors. Of course, she doesn't have to suck up very hard since they named Will interim president yesterday."

"Really? I'm the newspaper editor, and I didn't know about it. On the other hand," said Jeff, "Will has been drinking rather steadily."

"I think we can cut him some slack. After all, it's his brother's funeral," TJ said. "No doubt he has a problem with alcohol, but I guess today, of all days, it's understandable."

At that moment Grace saw Emily walk toward them with Jessalynn Folger in tow. Suddenly, Jessalynn recognized Grace and headed straight over to her.

"Oh, Ms. Kimball. It's so wonderful to see you again." She held out her hand.

"It's certainly been a long time. My condolences over your brother's death."

Jessalynn looked back over her shoulder at the crowd in the dining room. Then she turned back, a neutral look on her face. "Thank you. To tell you the truth, I wouldn't say this to anyone but you." She dropped her voice to a whisper. "I actually came back to make sure he was, indeed, dead." She turned to Emily. "I'm sorry if that shocks you or hurts your feelings, Emily. We didn't know each other very well in high school, but I grew up in that household, and I can guess how difficult your life has been."

Grace admired Jessalynn's candor, as well as her expensive but conservative suit and pumps. She definitely looked like New York City; she wasn't flashy, but her dark brown hair was caught up in a large clip at the back of her head, and her jewelry was sophisticated and expensive. Her body was obviously the work of many hours at a gym. Grace recalled that Emily and Jessalynn had been in the same class at Endurance High School, and she had taught them her first year.

Jessalynn held her hand out to TJ. "I don't remember you from school, but someone pointed you out to me as the police detective. That's quite a feat in conservative, little old Endurance."

TJ shook her hand and smiled. "Thanks. It took some doing. I imagine you won't be here long, but I'd love to hear about the house you grew up in. That is, I'd like to hear about the household. It might help me understand better what happened to your brother."

"Are you sure you want to know? I've spent thousands of dollars in psychiatrist's fees trying to forget it."

Emily patted her shoulder and added quietly, "I don't think you can say much that will shock me."

"Maybe not. But I must leave tomorrow."

"Oh," said Emily, a mildly stricken look on her face at losing a sister-in-law so soon. She struggled to say something foreign to her. "Why—why don't you"—she paused—"come over to our—my—house this evening? I've never had anyone come over to see me—well, except Grace—er, Ms. Kimball. Please, say you will," Emily pleaded. "You come over too, TJ. Grace stayed with me last night and it helped my nightmares. And, Mr. Maitlin, you come too."

Grace smiled at Emily's decision, and she added, "This

sounds like a great opportunity. You're something of a puzzle to all of us, Jessalynn, kind of like the child who got away, as opposed to Will, who was the prodigal son. We could scrape up some food for dinner and light a fire in the fireplace. It will be good for Emily to have some people around."

Jessalynn looked at each of their faces. Then, with a deep sigh, she answered, "All right. Maybe it's time to blow away some of those cobwebs from the past. Perhaps it will help you, Emily, to know you have not been alone in the Folger family curse."

That evening, after the dishes had been cleared away, they sat on various sofas and overstuffed chairs in the late Conrad Folger's living room. The fire crackled in the fireplace, the chandelier's soft light shone down on them, the temperature outside hovered in the low thirties, snow fell intermittently, and Grace distributed coffee.

Jessalynn was the first to speak. "This is always the way I imagined my brother Conrad would be living," she said, glancing up at the ceiling. "Especially the chandelier." She looked at Emily. "I'm sorry. I don't mean to sound so small-minded. But it isn't about you. It *was* about him."

Emily looked down at her hands in her lap. Grace could feel a hush in the room, as if the house itself was waiting for a long-ago story that flowed forward in time into this room, into these lives. The fire crackled and sparked several times, and TJ, Grace, Jeff, and Emily waited for the storyteller to begin.

"I never thought I would ever come back to Endurance," Jessalynn began. "I thought I could live my life in another place and ignore the existence of this little piece of real estate. For a while, that worked. But I guess those deep roots of your earlier life always come back. I spent a great many years trying to understand, and, frankly, forgive my parents for what they were.

At least I could leave, which was more than my mother could do. Will left, too, but he was drawn back here out of necessity, and I can already see his life at the bottom of a bottle is an attempt to forget what is always there, always hovering at the back of both our memories." She paused, leaned over the coffee table, and took a sip of her coffee. Then she dropped her shoes on the floor and sank back into the sofa cushions.

"Growing up in the household with my parents and two brothers was a living hell." She paused for a moment and reconsidered. "I guess my mother loved me, but I'll never know since she was afraid to be demonstrative. She certainly never told me she loved me. Will did care for me, as much as he could. Of the whole group, only Will understood and urged me to leave. By then he was already hopelessly shattered by our father's choices, especially the choice to groom Conrad for the bank and throw the two of us away. If this was the last century, they would have drowned me like a puppy—the runt of the litter—unless my father sold dogs for a living, and then he'd have kept me as a breeder."

Emily gasped at this description and blurted out, "I never knew. I always thought in high school you were so lucky to be born into that family with two brothers and an amazing future."

Jessalynn laughed softly. "Ah, appearances. The Folger family has spin-proofing down to a science. Appearances are everything. Any time we went out, even as children, we had to look perfect. White-glove perfect. My mother lived in fear of her life if our father saw even a strand of hair out of place when we visited him at his bank." At this she shook her head briefly and smiled, perhaps at a long-ago memory. "Sunday dinner at our house was always an epic adventure. After church—we never missed—we would return home, and each of us would have to give our father an account of our sins for the week. He'd go around the table. Then, each meal he'd pick one of us to bully.

Usually it was Will because he fought back. Conrad let it roll off his back. I just looked down at my lap and kept quiet. For anything, the boys were whipped with his belt, a cruel belt with a large, silver buckle. But me, I was a girl. A metal hairbrush did the job on me."

Grace suddenly realized she was holding her breath at this recitation. "Why? Why would he treat you all so terribly?"

"Good question, Ms. Kimball, and one I grappled with for many years. He was an abusive bully, just like our grandfather. I never knew my grandmother. She died before I was born, and it was probably a blessing. Our grandfather was strict and in charge. Because of that, our father grew up in a household where you didn't speak unless you were spoken to. Our grandfather lived to old age, and I can still remember how frail he was, but how his eyes still held a staring, evil gleam. I think he's the source of our father's cruelty.

"And our mother, beaten little mouse that she was, tried to protect us at first. He gave her a money stipend to run the household each week, and heaven help her if she needed more." Grace looked over at Emily and saw tears in her eyes. "No emotion, no love, no hugs, no expression of feelings—oh, except anger. One time he got so angry at Will—and I can't remember why—that he killed his dog right in front of him. Just strangled her with his strong hands and wrists. Unfortunately, Will cried and it made everything worse." She paused and took a deep breath. Then she cleared her throat. "Will didn't go to school for several days because his backside hurt."

"How could this go on in such a small town? Didn't people know it was happening?" asked Grace.

TJ took the opportunity to talk after silently listening to Jessalynn's story. "Goes on all the time, Grace. Even now here in Endurance. Many of our calls are domestic abuse calls."

"Oh," said Grace quietly. She glanced at Emily, who was

looking down at the floor.

Then Jeff spoke up. "So how did you get away? How did you manage to leave all this and become . . . well . . . the normal person you seem to be?"

Jessalynn smiled. "Normal? Now that's an interesting word. To understand how I got away, you'd have to be a witness to the competition."

"Competition?" asked Emily.

"Ah, yes. The race went to the fittest. As far as our father was concerned, Conrad was the one who eventually came out on top. Now, I wasn't stupid, and I was a few years younger than the boys. So I was privy to a great deal. It became obvious Father was grooming Conrad to follow him as president of the bank. It could never have been Will, even though he was the oldest. But Will was not a willing student. He was too weak, too quiet, and too kind. Conrad, on the other hand, was just like the old man: mean, arrogant, and cruel. We had a woods out behind our house, and he used to go out and trap small animals—squirrels, rabbits—and then torture them before he finally killed them."

Emily gasped.

"I'm sorry, Emily. But I'm quite sure you've seen Conrad's cruel proclivities. The sad thing is, Conrad was never as smart as my brother Will. But poor Will. He was always passed over. It was like the story of Cain and Abel in the Bible. Nothing was good enough for my father when it came to Will. But Conrad—he could do no wrong. And it always seemed like every scrape he got in only solidified his tie with our father. I can't recall all the problems he got Conrad out of because my brother had so many, but I do remember before I left for good, it was whispered that Conrad got some poor girl 'with child' in college, and Father had to go buy his way out of that one too."

"It's the perfect setup for what Conrad finally became," TJ

said. Then she looked at Emily and continued. "Only Conrad was really good at keeping up appearances, too, wasn't he, Emily? I checked the hospital records, and he put you in there with a broken arm one time, didn't he?"

Emily bit her lip and hesitated. Then she softly said, "Yes, but I had to lie about it."

Jessalynn's voice said bitterly, "I remember that scene, too, only he didn't break Mother's arm exactly. Mother always had to cook one meal for Father and another for the rest of us. He had to have everything just so. One night—I can't remember what started it—he slapped her right in front of all of us. It shocked me. I ran upstairs and called the police. I think I was in junior high. They came. I thought—I hoped—they would take him away and do something bad to him. But no. They walked him around the block and talked to him, and pretty soon he was right back at the house. After that, I couldn't sit down for a week."

"Doesn't surprise me," said TJ. "Back then, domestic abuse was considered a private situation to be worked out between husband and wife. Rarely were people jailed for it."

Jessalynn's face was serious. "I imagine it still happens in some places, TJ. I decided that as soon as I could get away, I'd leave. I didn't have any money to speak of, but after high school I had saved enough allowance to get a train ticket. I packed my bags and left for Chicago. My father probably thought, 'good riddance,' and I know I felt that way about him."

"But what about an education? What about college?" Grace asked.

"Not for me. Remember: I was a woman. Why would I need an education?" Grace could hear the bitterness in her voice. "I was simply going to marry some man who would have children with me and beat me."

"But how did you live? How did you manage on your own?"

Emily asked, barely disguising her anxiety.

"Wasn't easy. I got a newspaper, checked out the want ads. I began with a clerical position in a bank. Ironic, huh? But I was lucky. An older woman who mentored me thought I was bright and deserved a chance. She helped me, both at work in the bank, and also with my education because I had to save money and find loans and scholarships. I went to night school, off and on, and finally graduated with a BS in 1991. It took me an extra year. That led to a job in New York City because my mentor had some ties to a bank there. Once I got to New York, I was able to pay back some of the loan money, go to school again, and finish an MBA in 1995. Again, it took me a little longer, but I was determined. Now I'm an in-house financial advisor for a corporation in New York City, and I love my job and I'm good at it. Ironic, again. My father would never have put me to work in his bank. But I'm the one who has the head for finance. Conrad barely scraped through his big, Ivy League school."

"That's quite a story," said TJ.

"Oh, I assure you, it's all true," said Jessalynn.

"But what about romance? A husband? Children?" asked Emily.

Jessalynn stared at her for a moment, and then her expression softened as she looked at Emily. "I vowed, quite a long time ago, that I would never let a man have any kind of power over my life or my finances. Never."

For a moment, no one spoke. Then Emily, surprisingly, said, "You know, you do owe your father for one thing."

Jessalynn, curious, looked at the quiet Emily and said, "Really? I can't imagine what."

As Emily looked up, Grace saw, once again, a flicker of the woman she used to know. "Your father gave you the will and the anger to become what you've become in, what I would guess, is a highly masculine world. Look at what you've done with your life, Jessalynn. And look at where I am in mine."

Jessalynn reached over and put her hand on Emily's. "If that's the case—and I hadn't considered the idea—then you have a lot of fighting to do yourself, Emily Petersen Folger. What's more, you have two children to fight for. One is a daughter who needs to grow up strong from your example, starting now, and the other is a son who needs to learn how to treat women with respect. Perhaps you can break the cycle of abuse. They are your life, your legacy, and you have something remarkable I'll never have"—she smiled and added—"little people who love you." She leaned back and said, "And now that I have no one left to hate in this town, perhaps I will keep in touch with you, Emily, and see what happens. I, for one, don't believe you could have killed my brother. I'm a good judge of character, and I don't see you as a murderess. So I hope, TJ, you will hurry up and figure out who did do this deed. I know you'd call it a heinous crime, but I think of it as putting down one more male Folger who has made a life out of beating the hell out of women."

The fire was burning low, and everyone seemed to come to the same conclusion at the same time: it was time to leave. Grace decided to stay with Emily another night, and as she closed the door to the others and listened to the car engines start in the driveway, she turned around and saw a pensive Emily sitting on the sofa, staring at the fire, deep in thought.

CHAPTER NINETEEN

The following morning Grace walked into the *Endurance Register*, intent on transcribing her Lockwood House notes. She unlocked her office door, placed her briefcase on the love seat, and took off multiple layers of winter outer clothing, hanging them in a small closet. The morning was quiet, Jeff wasn't in yet, and Rick Enslow, who was usually at the front desk, was evidently in a back room doing something with the ads. Grace could almost hear the clock ticking, it was so quiet. She opened her laptop and fired it up, clicked on her mouse, and went out to the main room to pick up her mail while her computer loaded. Checking the pigeonhole for two-day-old mail, she glanced at the latest copy of the Woodbury newspaper. She grabbed her mail, studied the outrageous newspaper headline, and shook her head. When would that idiot learn?

After picking up a cup of coffee from the break room, Grace settled into her desk and used her letter opener to slit open the sealed envelopes. She was just placing the first two bills in a pile when she stopped cold at the address on the third envelope. It read "To Ms. Kimball, c/o *Endurance Register*, Endurance, Illinois," but it didn't have a return address. It must have come in the mail yesterday when she wasn't here. She studied the words on the light blue envelope and saw her name was scrawled in childish letters, as if someone had disguised his handwriting.

"Hmm," she said. "This is strange." Then she carefully slit the seal on the envelope and opened it cleanly. Pulling out the matching blue paper, she unfolded it and saw the same childish handwriting, all in capital letters.

EMILY FOLGER IS A MURDERESS.
MIND YOUR OWN BUSINESS OR YOU'LL RE-GRET IT.

Grace dropped the paper on her desk and scowled. *How many stupid people do we have in this town? First, they leave messages on Emily's answering machine and now they leave dumb notes in my mailbox. Well, maybe I shouldn't say "dumb" since everything is spelled and punctuated correctly for a change.* She reread the words and then realized she probably shouldn't have touched the letter because TJ might find fingerprints on it. Pulling a pair of tweezers out of her purse, she grabbed the corner of the paper and laid it on the loveseat. *That doesn't seem at all in character for Emily Folger—TJ's suspect—so it's either the actual murderer (who must be able to spell) or it is some idiot, like the voices on Emily's phone messages.* Just as she was about to call TJ, her phone rang with Cat Stevens's "Morning Has Broken," her generic ringtone. It was a local cell number.

"Grace Kimball," she said, and sat down in her desk chair. She heard the voice of Abbey Parker, talking faster than Grace could hear. "Whoa, slow down a little, Abbey."

"Ms. Kimball. You gotta come over here right away."

"Where is 'here'?"

"The Depot."

"Why? I thought you weren't open yet for lunch. What's going on?"

"TJ Sweeney was just here, and I think she may arrest Camilla." Grace could hear pots and pans banging in the distance.

"Is Camilla destroying the kitchen?"

"Yes. I've never seen her so angry. You gotta come over. She'll listen to you."

"All right, Abbey. Give me five minutes."

A sigh of relief floated through the phone receiver. "Thank you, Ms. Kimball."

"Grace."

"Grace."

By the time Grace reached The Depot, the sky was darkening and another storm appeared to be on the way. Abbey had been sitting at a table just inside the restaurant, and she came to the front door and unlocked it, since they weren't open to the public for two more hours. She pulled her former teacher inside the door, and then shut and relocked it. Grace could hear extremely loud, metallic banging coming from the kitchen.

"Maybe we should get Camilla out here and sit down at a table so we can discuss whatever this is like grown-ups."

"I hate to try to calm her down when she's like this," said Abbey. "She's likely to bean me with a pan. Last time she lost her temper, she ended up punching a hole in our living room wall. That's why I called you."

Grace laughed. "What? So she can throw a pot at me instead of you? I remember her temper in high school. It was legendary."

Abbey shook her head. "I'd like to say it has mellowed over the years, but you can obviously see I'd be lying."

Grace pulled off her coat and scarf and laid them on a table. "All right, Abbey. I'll see what I can do." Walking toward the kitchen, Grace thought, *Well, I didn't really want to do the story on the Lockwood house today, did I?*

Three cups of coffee were sitting on a table in the middle of the restaurant. Abbey was on one end, Camilla on the other, and Grace sat in the middle.

167

First, Grace took a long sip of coffee. "All right. Start at the beginning and tell me what brought on this huge cloud of anger."

"Well," Abbey began. Camilla scowled and looked away. "Sweeney came in this morning early. She knocked on the door and we let her in, of course. Why wouldn't we? She had been at the bank and read a letter *someone* wrote to Conrad Folger." She glared at Camilla. "I told you not to mail that."

Camilla stood up and pointed her finger at Abbey's face. "You always want to just let things go by. 'It will get better,' you say. 'Just wait and things will calm down,' you say. Well, things haven't gotten better, and I won't take that kind of crap from anyone, least of all a rich bastard like Conrad Folger."

"I don't understand," said Grace. "Folger is dead."

"Sit down, Camilla, and stop pointing your finger in my face," Abbey said. She turned to Grace. "She's referring to the letter she sent to him before he was murdered. It was pretty nasty, and TJ found it in Folger's files when she was down at the bank."

"He has no right—especially in this day and age—to tell us we can't borrow money," said Camilla. "I'm so sick of people treating us like we're second-class citizens. We have just as much right to ask for a loan as any straight couple."

Grace put both of her hands out. "It's fine, Camilla. You're talking to the choir here. I don't understand what this has to do with TJ."

Grace looked at Camilla, who appeared to be pouting. "She took my stuff and asked a lot of questions."

"What stuff?" asked Grace. "I know you might regret writing that letter to Conrad, but why would she take things? And what things?"

Camilla laid both her hands on the table, her anger gradually subsiding.

"She took the gloves Camilla uses for her plants," Abbey said, pointing up at the huge planters suspended from the ceiling. "And she also took her bag of potting soil, the one that was open and about half-used."

"That doesn't make sense," said Grace. "Did she say why?"

"No!" said Camilla, her voice rising again. "And then she asked me about the alarm system—you know, the one I put in, that big mouth here"—she pointed at Abbey—"just had to mention when you were in the other day."

"I don't know why you think I shouldn't tell people how proud I am of all the things you've done to make the place work better. Of course I mentioned it," said Abbey. "I know very few people who are that handy: carpentry, plumbing, electricity, and even the alarm system."

Camilla glared at Abbey. "For some reason, TJ was awfully interested in the alarm system, so now I suppose she thinks I could get in the Folger house and do the awesome deed."

"How about a fresh pot of coffee, Abbey?" said Grace.

"Sure."

She watched Abbey head back to the kitchen. "Now," said Grace, moving her hand over to Camilla's arm and patting it softly. "Tell me in a calm, rational, grown-up, Camilla-like manner, why TJ was so concerned about your skills around the restaurant. And quietly," she said, looking toward the kitchen.

"Don't you get it? She read the letter, figured I had a huge motive to kill the scumbag, and realized—thanks to Abbey's big mouth—that I know how to install alarm systems. Didn't people say—right here in the restaurant—that Conrad Folger's house had an alarm system? Sweeney probably thought I knew how to short-circuit it so I could get in. And if I could get in and then reset it, Emily would be off the hook since she was supposedly the only one there."

"And?"

"And what?"

"And do you know how to do that?"

Camilla put her head down and looked away, pausing before she said a word. Then she looked at Grace and answered, "Of course I do."

"So, why the concern about talking to TJ about it? She must know you wouldn't murder someone. Why would she be overly concerned about your alarm system?"

Camilla took a deep breath and then let it out. "I probably acted suspicious when she asked me about it. You see, Ms. Kimball, I didn't exactly get the alarm system we have from ordering it over the Internet. I kind of got it very cheap from someone who had it to sell. He owed me a favor. I didn't mention how I got the alarm system to Abbey because I knew she would be ticked off at me."

Just then Abbey came back from the kitchen, a steaming coffee pot in her hand. She looked down at Grace and Camilla and smiled. "That's better. I knew you could work wonders with her temper, Ms. Kimball."

Grace leaned in and looked directly at Camilla. "You think TJ's got you on her suspect list because she believes you were acting suspiciously, and your letter indicated a strong motive."

"How many times do I have to tell you, Camilla, not to put things in writing?" Abbey said, pouring more coffee. "Your mouth—or, in this case, your pen—seems to get you in trouble these days."

"Well, let's hope this isn't the day. I'll see what I can do. I'll talk to TJ," Grace said. "My guess is she's covering all her bases. Since you didn't have anything to do with the murder, you should just wait, and TJ will come to the right conclusion. But I'm not sure why she took your gloves and potting soil. That's a mystery."

"See," Abbey said. "Listen to Ms. Kimball. She's always right."

"Maybe," said Camilla. She sat silently for a few seconds and then stood up. "You're probably right, Mrs. K. I'd better get back to work. Thanks for coming over. I feel better after listening to you. But I'll never forgive that rotten banker as long as I live."

"I'd better get back to work too," Grace said.

Abbey grabbed Grace's coat and held it out, meanwhile saying to Camilla, "That's something you'd best leave unsaid." She looked at the steaming pot of coffee on the table, confusion on her face. "And now I guess I should put this pot of coffee back."

Grace looked past Abbey at her partner. "Don't worry, Camilla. Time will take care of this. Glad I could help." She turned to Abbey and said, "I'll send you my bill in the morning." They laughed, and Grace walked slowly to the front, where the cash register sat, waiting for the business day to begin. As she passed the table where Abbey had been working before the brouhaha began, Grace glanced over and noticed the light-blue writing paper Abbey had been using, and a black pen lying next to the paper.

She paused momentarily and then thought, *Stop being so suspicious, Grace. Blue paper is very common around here. Anyone can buy it at several stores.*

CHAPTER TWENTY

"Yes, I have been checking in with Emily every so often," TJ said, as she folded up her napkin and pushed away the plate, which had held a warm piece of Lettie's mouth-watering, stomach-filling apple pie. "She is amazingly naïve about many things in this day and age. But, despite the ankle monitor, I am being won over to the Grace Kimball 'we take in orphans and widows' philosophy. Did you ever have students you *wouldn't* defend against the onslaught of the criminal justice system?"

Grace stopped to think a minute, and finished the last bite of her pie. "Well, I'd have to ponder that, TJ. I've already lost a few to the dark forces of the prison system, but—thinking back on their high school years—it's probable, but sad, that they are in the place they were destined to be. My first few years, I thought I could save them all, but I found out I couldn't." She set her fork down on the dessert plate and paused for a moment. "You don't remember Farley Young. He was one of the kids I had early on. When I threw him out of class, he slammed my door so hard I thought the glass would break, and he called me so many awful names that I had to ask another teacher what a few of those words meant. Then he dropped out of school, got married, beat his wife and was jailed for that, robbed a few places and was caught. Next destination: prison. When he got out, he came back and started a meth factory in an old house outside town. It didn't quite turn out like the television show. One night the whole place blew to high heaven with him in it.

Actually, it's the closest to heaven he probably got." She picked up their plates and walked over to the sink. Then she turned. "So, what is winning you over with my Emily?"

"*Your* Emily?"

"I tend to think of her that way. She has quite a hard road ahead of her."

"A few things have happened that should clear the way for Emily, at least financially. How ironic that Conrad's money will now allow her to live as a free woman . . . well, assuming she is not found guilty of his murder. I'm looking at other possible suspects. And," she added, helping Grace with the dishes, "the will was read yesterday—Monday—at the lawyer's office. Emily inherits the estate—the house and his various holdings—and a trust is set up for the children. She also gets the life insurance, with the children as secondary beneficiaries. But should anything happen to Emily, the trustees for the children are Will and Darlene. I have to say, my suspicions of Emily grow weaker as time goes by. This sheds a whole new light on the possibility of Will as a suspect."

"So does this help Emily's case?"

"Somewhat. It gives me additional people to investigate. I am still not leaving Sandra Lansky out of the picture. She's quite a piece of work, and her arrival in town is fortuitous in light of the murder."

"Ah, so the Grace Kimball-trustworthy-albeit-naïve-understanding-of-her-students comes through again."

"Well, let's not get all excited here. Like you said, Emily has a long road to go yet."

"So, who else is on your radar, TJ?"

"I've been working on Abbey and Camilla. Camilla could have been the woman who went into the bank and threatened Conrad."

"Are you kidding? How could anyone disguise Camilla?"

"I have to admit it's a long stretch. But this morning that thought got weaker too. The lab tests came back from the sample of the potting soil she uses in her restaurant. Remember the murder scene had some dirt which could have come off the gloves of the murderer? Unfortunately, it wasn't her potting soil. On the other hand, her letter to Conrad was very specific about him 'cutting his own throat' by not giving them a loan. I stopped in and talked to them."

"And?"

"Camilla's still angry, although I think her desire for revenge has been satisfied with his exceptionally bloody death. She has talents that might lend themselves to the details of the murder scene. She's good with electricity, knows alarm systems, and doesn't lack for nerve."

"Do you think they plotted this somehow together? Abbey and Camilla?"

"Not sure." She sat down at the kitchen table and poured some more wine into each of their glasses. "I might have said so a few days ago, but they have a lot to lose if they did something this stupid when they've just started their business. That's enough anxiety." She drank some wine and added, "Grace, I'm not so sure I understand their relationship with this new employee, Sandra Lansky. They are her alibi. Supposedly they all three got drunk that night, and Lansky stayed over and slept it off at their place. Lansky is a real question mark. Why did she suddenly show up here? Maybe she isn't involved at all? Or, if she is, what's her role in this whole situation?"

"Didn't she say she was visiting a cousin?"

"That's what she said. So far, however, I haven't been able to find any evidence she has any family ties here whatsoever. I'll have a talk with her. Something about her just doesn't quite seem true. Call it my BS detector."

They sat in silence for a moment, drinking the last sips of the wine. Then Grace said, "By the way, after I cleaned Emily's house, I thought I should mention she doesn't do house plants. She says she's good at growing weeds in the garden."

TJ sighed.

"Did you stay at The Depot long enough to hear how the gossips in town look at Emily now? I'd ask Lettie, but she was gone by the time I got home," Grace said.

"The more people pass rumors about Conrad and his spousal abuse, the more the tide seems to go in a positive direction for Emily. Of course, he did make quite a few enemies through his banking practices, and some of those people are starting to remember that. Could be gender-specific—women cheering her on, even if she killed the bastard. But, it seems to be fifty-fifty at the moment. That's considerably better for Emily's sake than it was. I was surprised to hear a few of the comments mentioned by some of the road crew clearing the snow up on the north end of Main Street. They have no love of bankers who beat their wives. The latest I heard was that the folks in town say Emily may be wise to use the 'scumbag defense,' since it's what they think he was."

"Did you listen to the messages on Emily's phone last week?"

"I did. I even recognized a few of the voices, and I had a word with the good folks who left such charming words for her. Don't think she'll get more of those. The word has gone out. I suppose they could disguise their voices next time. But, I think those may stop."

Suddenly, TJ's phone played "Glory Days," and she pulled it from her pocket. "Yes, Myers." Grace watched as TJ listened carefully to what the policeman said. "All right. I'll call her back." Then she listened again. "I've got the number. Thanks."

She looked up at Grace. "Emily called the station looking for me. She isn't paying much attention to what her brother-in-law said about talking to the police only with a lawyer around, is she? Anyway, I have to call her back. Do you mind?"

"No, go right ahead. I'll just stack the dishwasher."

Grace began clearing dishes and rinsing off bits of their supper as TJ walked out to the study to call the Folger home. Her heart was lighter, and she thought, *Thank goodness people in town realize they didn't know the whole story. Just looking at Emily makes a person sure she could never have killed her husband. She couldn't even stand up to him in a good argument.* Wiping off the kitchen counter, or what was left of it after Del had taken most of it away, she began to turn her thoughts to other possible suspects. *Abbey? Camilla? Sandra Lansky? Will Folger? Who stood the most to gain from this murder? Emily, of course, stood to gain financially, but only if she was acquitted. If the motive was revenge, Abbey and Camilla were right up front. But where did Sandra Lansky fit in?*

"Well, that was interesting."

"What? Is Emily all right?"

"Yes. She seems to be more 'all right' every day. Will and Darlene are at her house, and they are helping her clear out Conrad's clothes, plus a few other things. Emily found some receipts in one of Conrad's jacket pockets. They were for expensive lingerie from a pricey boutique in Chicago. They sure weren't a gift for Emily."

"Really?" Grace couldn't hide the shock from her voice. "So Conrad might have had another woman in his life?"

"It appears so. Emily says he had been to Chicago on business trips quite often, but recently those trips had stopped. Will told her to call me immediately. Since Will is a large presence on my list of 'who has to gain from Conrad's death,' it would be to his advantage to push the suspicion away from him. I must admit, however, this does add a new direction to my investigation."

"Were these receipts very recent?"

"Last fall."

"Are you going out to Emily's?"

"Yes. Heading toward the coat closet as we speak."

Grace stopped walking beside TJ, grabbed her shoulder, and looked at her.

"What?" said TJ.

"When did Sandra Lansky come to town?"

"A few weeks ago. Why?"

"Woman in the bank. Threats. Suddenly this waitress shows up with a cousin you haven't traced. Lingerie receipts from the fall. No more business trips . . ."

"*Blond* hair on the woman in the bank, Grace."

"A wig?"

TJ considered. "The red hair would be quite recognizable."

"Want to put some money on it, TJ?"

"Not with you on the other end. Your hunches have been right too often, Grace. Before long, I may have to put you on the payroll."

"Fantastic. Yet another retirement job for me."

She followed TJ to the front hallway, getting ready for the blast from the tundra. As TJ opened the door, Grace said, "Keep up the good work and Emily won't need a 'scumbag defense' after all. Oh, and wait a minute. Come back in. I'm going to put some apple pie on a plate, and you can take it out to her. She needs fattening up."

Grace saw a pained expression cross the detective's face.

"Grace, this does not seem like the thing a detective would do for a chief suspect who is wearing an ankle bracelet."

After TJ left, Grace finished a few tidying-up chores around the house. Then she sat down on the sofa in her den to read another chapter from Olivia's diary.

★ ★ ★ ★ ★

Late August, 1893

The last month has been a whirlwind of activity, going with the judge to the opera house, the theatre in Woodbury, several church socials, and the county fair. Aunt Maud has accompanied us, and the judge has been clever, thoughtful, and well-mannered toward me. He gave me flowers and also a lovely glove box. "Gifts to show his affection and esteem," he said.

I saw Tyler at the library, and even though I have sent several messages to him, he says he has not received them. He asked if I had mentioned his name to the judge and, of course, I had. After all, Tyler was one of the first friends I made in Endurance. A look passed over his face, and he said we should exchange messages only at the library.

I often ride one of the judge's horses, a beautiful mare named Lily. Tyler rides, too, and he said we might meet and talk while I exercise Lily. He is not pleased I am courted by Judge Lockwood, and he says I do not really know what the judge is like. When I told Tyler the judge has been nothing but kind, he got vehement about my seeing him. He could not tell me why, only that he had heard things which were inappropriate for the ears of a lady. Perhaps he is jealous.

I have been invited to the judge's house for dinner next week with Aunt Maud.

I suppose Tyler tries to warn me because he sees that as the office of a friend. I have liked him since I first met him, but about the judge he has only one opinion: I should stay away from him.

I have written to my parents, telling them about Judge Lockwood and also about Tyler. I know Aunt Maud has written to them also, and my mother's return letters urge caution and patience. She and Father will be here soon on a visit and judge for themselves.

When I read the earlier part of my diary, I am surprised my first impression of Judge Lockwood was so negative. Having spent more time with him, I am quite comfortable now in his presence. Perhaps he is the man I was destined to meet since my parents sent me to Endurance to find a husband. See, the eternal plan works out as it should.

2 September, 1893

Aunt Maud and I have now been at Judge Lockwood's home for both tea and luncheon. It is the most amazing place I have ever beheld. The rooms are huge, with vast ceilings, and he has gaslights throughout the house. The parlors are furnished exquisitely, and the walls and woodwork are expensive and ornately decorated.

During our visits I have met his servants. Robert Heaton is his butler, and he is married to Jonalyn, who is a servant and also a lady's maid. She was personal maid to the first Mrs. Lockwood. They look to be thirty-five or forty years old. Then there is the housekeeper, Rose Hernshaw, who is about ten years older. They are all terribly efficient, and do their jobs silently and effectively. I hardly know they are in the room as we eat dinner, and seldom do I see a human emotion cross their countenances. I must confess, however, that I am anxious about navigating a huge house like this with servants. They are all so much older and more knowledgeable than I am. I only learned which fork to use a bare few months ago. It was . . . overwhelming.

The next day I rode out on Lily, determined to think about this courtship and whether or not I truly wanted to live the rest of my life with Judge Lockwood. I know my parents sent me to Endurance to find a husband, and I believe they would approve of the judge. We will find out in a week. I can hardly wait because I have missed them so much. Aunt Maud believes the judge will ask them for my hand. She is filled with excitement at the thought, as if my marriage will raise her value in the eyes of my parents and the town of Endurance.

Riding up to a ridge where I often stop and sit under the trees to think, I was surprised Tyler Quinn was there before me. His horse grazed in the pasture nearby, and Tyler sat on the ground reading a book. He said he thought I might come for a ride today, so he waited to speak with me. As always, it was so easy to talk to him and much less formal than speaking to the judge, and I sat down next to him as we talked. He said his legal reading with Simon Barclay went well, and he felt in the coming year they might become partners in the law firm and work together. Then, he said, he would be able to offer me a life with him, and a small, but growing, salary. He spoke with great earnestness and held my hands as he talked. I listened with dismay, knowing that the judge planned to ask my parents for their blessing. My heart tightened and shrank into a small little ball, and my chest constricted even as it fought against the hated corset.

The longer I listened to his plans for the future, the more I remembered the joy I had when I first met him a mere few months ago. He spoke with such enthusiasm for his job, but also said he wanted to have a future life and children with me. I blushed as he spoke of it. Tears began to form in my eyes, but I brushed them away and tried to be strong. I quietly but firmly explained that the judge planned to speak to my parents about a betrothal between us.

Suddenly, he was a man I did not know. His eyes turned cold, and he rose and used his riding crop to assail the tree behind us. He waited until his anger was spent and then spoke harshly of the judge and his reputation in some quarters of the town. Shaking his head and pacing in front of me, he said Judge Lockwood was not the man I thought him to be. He believed if I knew of the judge's past and some darker elements in his current life, I would not be so quick to say yes to such an engagement. Tyler also claimed the messages I sent to him were intercepted by an office boy who was paid by Judge Lockwood to do so. I was shocked. I asked him what evidence he had of the truth of that statement, and he said the boy had told him so.

I did not know what to say to him. The judge has been generous and mannerly toward me. I do not know where these dark and negative stories come from, and I told Tyler once again the judge has courted me with all kindness. I could not believe he would stoop to the theft of my messages. Tyler started to talk and then closed his mouth. He was angry as he left, and his anger settled in the air around me as I thought about his words.

I feel at ease with Judge Lockwood, and I know he can provide me with a good life. This will be a comfort to my parents. He is, after all, a federal judge and lacks for nothing comfortable and pleasant. He is very formal and, in some ways, courtly. My parents would approve since they sent me to Endurance to find out about how to be a lady and have a man of substance come into my life. On the other hand, when I am with Tyler Quinn, my heart quickens, and I feel a lightness, a happiness, that is so pleasant and familiar. It is the same feeling I have at home in Anthem with my parents, my brothers, and my galloping rides over the hills on Lightning. But he offers not the security and financial future of Judge Lockwood.

My heart feels such a heavy burden, but my intellect

says I am making the correct decision. My parents will be happy, Aunt Maud will be proud, and I will have a prominent position in the town of Endurance. That last thought worries me, but I will learn to be in charge of his household and have children of social standing, whose lives will lack for nothing. My heart does not quicken when I see Judge Lockwood, but my head tells me he is my future.

Grace closed the journal and sighed. She wanted to say, "Stop! Don't marry the judge." *But I have the advantage of knowing what fate has in store for her. Why do we so often think with our heads instead of our hearts when it comes to love? I suppose back then it was important for a woman to marry a man of substance. A woman's life was so circumscribed by the man to whom she was married.*

Grace decided she would go over to Emily Folger's tomorrow and see how she was doing. Each time she saw Emily, her former student seemed stronger and better able to handle things. But she still had the murder charge hanging over her head. *Well, we'll see about that. I almost have TJ won over to the Grace Kimball Cause of the Month.*

CHAPTER TWENTY-ONE

The next afternoon, Grace sat at the Folger kitchen table and looked over Emily's shoulder at the wan, winter sunlight. Then Emily said, "Only in a small town like Endurance would the lead detective, who is trying to prove you're a murderer, deliver you a slice of apple pie and check your ankle monitor at the same time." She smiled, and Grace thought it was the first genuine smile she'd seen on Emily's face . . . well, except for the day her children came home to stay. "Thank you, Ms.— Grace—for the apple pie. It was delicious," said Emily.

Grace, too, smiled at the thought. "I'm working on TJ. Don't worry. She's coming around."

"It seems strange to think TJ and I were in high school together, and here we are now, on opposite sides of a strange situation. What if I could have seen the future back then? Would I be in this spot I'm in now? Could I have changed it with a single decision?" She shook her head. "Each night I go to bed and think maybe tomorrow this nightmare will end. But it doesn't."

Grace reached across the table and put her hand on Emily's. "I have faith in TJ. She'll get to the bottom of this." For a few seconds, a comfortable silence settled on the room.

"What makes you think I'm innocent in all this?" Emily said.

"I know you, Emily Petersen. This—all this—isn't you." Grace studied her former student and was gratified to see the bruises had healed, and her face looked less drawn. Her eyes now had light grayish circles beneath them instead of dark, black rings from sleepless nights. Her hair was clean and pulled back with a clip, and her cheeks weren't quite as pale as they had been. She seemed a little calmer, a little more in control, and a little less vague. "I would have come over sooner, but TJ left for Chicago, I had some columns to finish for the newspaper, and I got Eliot Ness—her cat. You won't believe what Lettie has taught Eliot the cat to do. When he hears 'Stayin' Alive,' the song from the movie *Saturday Night Fever*—you know, John Travolta strutting down the street—Eliot goes crazy, and chases his tail in circles. I have a feeling when TJ finds out, Lettie will be in a lot of trouble. Jeff thought it was hysterical, and I have to agree that I laughed so hard I had a difficult time stopping."

Her voice trailed off as she thought of her last conversation with Jeff at the office. He still acted different, more distant, withdrawn. *What was going on there?* Emily's voice jarred her wandering thoughts back to the present.

"I'm starting to remember more from that night. Some of it is . . . good, well, good because I remember. Some of it comes in strange flashbacks and nightmares. But I take my sleeping pill, and it helps. When I look in the mirror now, I don't see a woman with eyes resembling dark holes in her head."

"How are you doing with the psychiatrist?"

"Well, I think. Much of her practice consists of issues like domestic violence, and she gave me a notebook so I can write down random thoughts. I have to re-frame the way I look at the past." She sat down for a moment, her hands in her lap. "I can't, for example, blame myself for Conrad's behavior. I couldn't control what he did. All I could do was react to it, and I tried to protect the children and me. It was a matter of reading him right and trying to survive day to day. I haven't quite realized down here"—she pointed to her stomach—"that it wasn't my fault . . . what he did."

"You certainly look much better to me, more like the Emily I used to know."

"Thank you, Grace. I'm so glad you called and came over. I still find so many decisions hard to make. I can't always trust my instinct. These last few years, I've been so isolated I've forgotten what it's like to talk with people. And, frankly, right now I don't even know what people are thinking. It still isn't easy. How can I face people? Sitting here like this, just the two of us, works better for me than talking to more than one person at a time."

Grace stood up, brought the coffee carafe over to the table, and poured more in each of their cups. "A step at a time. Wait till you feel more up to it. How are you feeling these days, physically?"

Emily sighed. "I still have flashbacks and nightmares. Some days I have headaches, and I cry easily. But now I take some medications for anxiety and depression, and I think they help. It's strange. I find myself anxious for no reason. Yesterday I was at the grocery store and this redheaded lady looked at me in the strangest way. I don't think I was imagining it." She paused. "Well, maybe I did imagine it. Sometimes my anxiety goes overboard, although I don't notice it as much when the children are home. My mind is more occupied."

Grace glanced up at the drawings and colored papers stuck on the refrigerator with magnets. "It looks like Caitlin and Conrad have made pictures to cheer you up."

Emily smiled and said, "They are the best—the best thing that ever happened to me. But they're so young. We just celebrated Conrad's eleventh birthday, and already his father was grooming him to become a bank president. At age eleven? He's just a child. It's hard on them to comprehend their father's absence. They aren't old enough to absorb or understand, and I certainly hope no one else says anything to them. I have their teachers on alert. I may take them to a pediatric therapist soon."

Grace took a sip of her coffee and paused before she spoke. "I can empathize. My three children were so young when their father died of a heart attack. And I wasn't much help at the time. It seemed like I couldn't make any decisions, like I was in a fog."

"Oh, me too. Me too. I feel better about it, though. The fog isn't there as often as it used to be—in my head, that is."

"You know, it's easy to look back and say, 'If only I'd done this or that, things would be different,' " said Grace, looking out the window and thinking of her own regrets.

"I should have, somehow, seen the signs. I think back to when we first dated. He went out of his way to try to please me and show me what a good life we could have together." Emily smiled at some memory. "Of course, we didn't have a long engagement. I simply thought he was the one. It's weird. Sometimes, the very aspects he loved about me to begin with are the parts he tried to destroy as our marriage went on—my independence, my social life with my friends, or some of the talents I had." She looked at a family photo on the wall near the door to the living room. "Even my relationship with my parents was something he longed for with his own, but then he kept me away from mine.

"And, after we were married, my two miscarriages didn't help. When I got pregnant again, he figured it wouldn't take, but then Conrad was born and he was happy for a while. Of course, I can see that now because I've been talking to the psychiatrist, and I'm only beginning to realize that now, if I make a decision, I can expect no reprisals. He isn't here anymore to hurt me. It's certainly been difficult—the decision-making. What to eat or what to wear—at first, those were really tall mountains. But it is getting easier." Grace watched as Emily nervously wrung her hands. "I have to take it one day at a time.

Re-frame thoughts in the positive. Remind myself of my blessings."

Grace thought carefully about what she wanted to ask next. Emily was opening up considerably, and she didn't want to push too hard. Then, taking a deep breath, Grace asked her a question quietly. "Emily, what are you able to remember about that night when Conrad was killed?" She hoped her question didn't tread down a path filled with rocks and ground glass.

Emily bit her lip for a minute and looked past Grace's shoulder. Then her eyes came down again and focused on her old mentor. "I do remember some things." She dropped her gaze down to her lap. "I don't know how much you know about that night. It comes back to me in flashbacks, and I'm only starting to make sense of it in chronological order. I know when I went to bed the night of his death I took a sedative. I never liked to do that, but I had a feeling something bad was going to happen."

"Really? Why?"

"Oh, signs. Conrad's mood. The children were gone, and he had been drinking way too much, even before I went to bed. Not good. And he had not been himself that week. I think something was going on at the bank. Whatever it was, it made him anxious. I saw him speak in quiet tones with Will in the kitchen on more than one occasion that night. He was angry and impatient in a very controlled way. And he had been coming home from work increasingly late, tense, and short-tempered. But I don't know why. I just know I could always read his behavior and his face. I was a master at reading his moods."

"Do you remember your 9-1-1 call?"

She hesitated. "Yes, although it's foggy since I had taken my sedative, and it always made me groggy in the morning." She paused, and for a few seconds she considered what she would say next. She bit her lip again, a nervous habit which had stayed with her. Then she repeated, "I don't know how much you know about that night." She paused, and Grace waited, holding back any thoughts. Then Emily looked up with hooded eyes and said, "He raped me."

There, Grace thought. *It was out.*

"I mean, I know we were married and all, but what he did was not gentle or loving. I think it's when I got the bruises on my arms. And he—he slapped me several times across the face. I remember that. I thought I was going to stop breathing, but it had happened so many times I had learned to go along with it until he stopped. This time I think I must have fought back. My lawyer said Conrad's DNA was under my fingernails when I went to the emergency room."

"Oh, Emily. I am so sorry. How awful. No one deserves that. I can't imagine how you could deal with it for so long."

Emily looked at Grace with sad eyes, their tears brimming over her lower lids. "Me either. But you see, after he'd do it, it was as if some horrible fury had been spent. The next day he would be the loving Conrad I used to know, the one who sent me roses and was kind and wanted me to forgive him. Trouble was, I never knew which Conrad would show up each day."

Grace looked at her empty coffee cup, decided against more caffeine, and asked, "How are the children *really* doing?"

Emily wiped the tears from her eyes with a tissue from her pocket. "See," she said, smiling. "I still cry for no reason." Then she half-smiled at Grace and said, "They're great. Aside from not understanding where their father is, they're relieved. The house is quiet, and I'm home when they get here from school. I'm so thankful they weren't here that horrible night. Caitlyn asked me about the ankle monitor, and I explained I had to wear it so the police would be able to contact me about their father's death. So far, their teachers haven't reported any hecklers or bullies at school, so it's good, I think."

"Yes. Yes, it is." Suddenly Grace's phone played "If I Had a Hammer." "Oh, hang on. I'd better take this. It's my kitchen contractor." She hit the accept button and listened to an excited Del relay the message. "What? You're at the ER? Is she okay?" Then she listened for a minute and replied, "All right. Hang tight. I'll be there right away. Thanks, Del."

"Trouble?"

Grace stood up and dropped her phone in her purse by her chair. "That was my contractor, and my sister-in-law, Lettie, fell off a ladder and may have broken or sprained her ankle. He's with her at the ER, and I have to get over there now."

Emily was on her feet, and she moved quickly and held out Grace's coat and scarf. "Gosh, I'm so sorry, Grace. If I can do anything to help you, just ask. Please."

Grace smiled and gave Emily a hug. "I'll come see you again. You just get better. It's all I need."

Grace took off her coat and looked around Lettie's hospital room. Del sat by the bed, and a nurse was just leaving, having deposited a syringe in the medical waste bin.

"How did you manage to fall off a ladder? Why were you on a ladder in the first place, Lettie?" Grace asked in a scolding tone that softened as she saw her disabled sister-in-law hooked up to an IV and lying swathed in bed sheets and blankets.

"She was being cussed stubborn, as always," said Del Novak. "She decided to wash the curtains while I had everything torn up, so that's why she was up on the ladder. And, you know how it says on ladders that you shouldn't go above a particular step?"

Grace gave her sister-in-law a skeptical look. "I already understand, Del. You don't need to explain. I've seen decades of this behavior."

Del leaned over the bed and patted Lettie's hand. "Well, I

should go now that your sister-in-law is here. You get better now, Lettie." He turned to leave and added, "Oh, and Ms. Kimball. The nurse gave her some pain meds so she's kind of loopy."

Grace rolled her eyes and laughed. "Loopy?" She thought about it for a moment and added, "This should be interesting."

"Well, okay. I think I'll call it a day and head home. I should rest a little."

"Thanks, Del, for bringing her in and staying with her. That was very kind of you."

"No problem, Ms. Kimball." He leaned over and whispered, "I wouldn't want her to hear this, but I like her."

Grace was still chuckling as he walked out the door. Then she turned to the patient. "Well, Lettisha Kimball. What do you have to say for yourself, climbing up on ladders at your age, and disobeying safety instructions?" She tried to make her voice sound stern.

Lettie's tiny head peeked out from under an enormous sea of white bed sheets and blankets. Grace was startled. She couldn't figure out why Lettie had a bandage on her head when she hurt her ankle. "Oh, Gracie, isn't he wonderful? It was just like the scene from *Gone with the Wind* where Rhett carries Scarlett up a huge flight of stairs. You watch his broad back and massive shoulders strain against his coat, you see him climb the stairs three at a time with no effort, and you know he will take her to his bed and have his way with her." She paused to take a breath, and Grace could swear she saw stars twinkle in Lettie's eyes. Then the stars changed to confusion. "But, of course, with Del, there was more panting on the soundtrack, and more popping of his knees and creaky sounds in his joints as he tried to pick me up off the floor. His face got so red I thought he might have a heart attack, and I'd have to drag myself across the floor and call 9-1-1 for an ambulance for him."

Grace tried hard to keep her composure at the heroic picture of Lettie dragging herself through the sawdust, but her attempt was futile, and she burst into laughter so hard that tears came to her eyes. Lettie seemed totally oblivious and rattled on in her drug-induced delirium.

"He managed to stagger to the car and drop me in the back seat, and I didn't even feel the pain from the tool box on the car seat when I hit my head on it. He had such a concerned look in his eyes." She stopped a moment and reconsidered. "Well, maybe the look was confusion over where he put his car keys. Of course, he had to mop his forehead about that time, and he was sweating considerably, even though it was frigid outside." She sighed. "Oh, what a knight in shining armor!"

By now Grace had stopped laughing, and she noted the rapturous look on Lettie's face. "This is the same Del Novak you tried to kill with your cast-iron skillet?"

Lettie's eyes had closed, her last words fading out into something about Mildred at the bakery. She began to snore in a loud, even solo. Grace watched her for a few seconds and then leaned over and planted a soft kiss on her forehead. She turned and sat down, thinking she'd stay for a little while, talk with the next nurse who came in, and then go to Lettie's and pick up some things her sister-in-law might need. Lettie's snores lent a peaceful backdrop to Grace's vigil, and Grace couldn't stop smiling when she remembered Lettie's comic description of Del's rescue.

It was late afternoon when Grace pulled into Sweetbriar Court. It had become no warmer as the day went on, and the gray and sullen sky cast a pall over everything. But the car was toasty warm, heat blasting out of the vents, so she sat in the driveway for a few minutes, thinking about Emily Folger. She'd come quite a long way from the woman Grace had seen in the hospital; obviously, she had her psychiatrist to thank for that.

But Grace still felt her former student had a fragile core, a lack of self-confidence born from years of being told she was stupid. At this moment Grace really hated Conrad Folger. Why did people like Folger exist? What joy did they get out of destroying women they supposedly loved? Yes, Emily was doing better, but she would need to continue to work hard on rebuilding the person she used to be—the self-confident, smart woman who was comfortable in her own skin.

Going home again was never easy, as author Thomas Wolfe had discovered, nor was it easy to go back to the person you used to be. Too many things had happened to Emily. Actually, maybe it wasn't even possible—to go back, that is. *I should see her more,* thought Grace. *But now with Lettie coming home tomorrow, I'll be tied up considerably with her care.* She sighed and pulled into the garage, turning off the engine. She hadn't collected the newspaper off the porch that morning, so she walked around to the front of the house, going down a narrow, plowed path.

Suddenly, she stopped. *Something wasn't right.* Her front door stood open by at least a foot, and Grace knew it was locked when she left in the morning. *Del Novak? No, he would never leave a door unlocked and open.* She stopped in her tracks and considered what to do. *Someone might still be in there.* She remembered the letter she'd gotten at the newspaper. *What if the writer had been serious?* She felt a lump in her throat and tried to swallow.

What should she do? Go in? What if the intruder had a gun? Call Jake Williams? Then she remembered TJ's cat was inside. *If anything had happened to that animal, TJ would never forgive her.* She took short, anxious breaths and set her briefcase on a snow bank, deciding she would investigate herself. Then she had a better idea. Turning around and marching back to the garage, she grabbed a baseball bat just inside the door. She practiced swinging it and decided it would be better without her mittens. A direct hit was more important than frostbite. *I'm not very threatening with this, but no one else knows that,* she thought. She turned and quietly crunched her way through the snow and back to the front door, leaning over to make a smaller target. She couldn't see any movement inside, but she could hear her breath as well as see it.

CHAPTER TWENTY-TWO

Grace crept up on the porch, baseball bat in both hands. She peered around the open door, but saw and heard nothing. Becoming a trifle bolder, she moved the door a few inches and slid in as quietly as she could. Her coat brushed against the door handle and moved the door still farther, producing a creaking noise. But when the door stopped, all was quiet. No lights were on, so it was like looking into a cave. As she tiptoed down the hallway, she saw small puddles of water on the tile floor, indicating someone had been there or was still there.

If they have guns, they might kill me. Her hands shook on the bat handle, and her heart pounded. She stopped and listened. Nothing.

"Eliot?" She called out softly. "Here, kitty, kitty." Still she heard nothing. She reached over to the wall and flipped the switch. Suddenly, the hallway and living room were flooded with comforting light, and she waited. Nothing. Keeping the bat in front of her, she walked around the corner of the hallway wall and into the living room. She stopped cold and couldn't believe her eyes at the shocking sight. All was in total chaos. Sofa cushions flung hither and yon with huge gashes in them; lamps lying on the floor, glass from their bulbs dashed into pieces; papers and magazines from the coffee table torn into shreds and scattered everywhere; photographs ripped up and the glass from their frames smashed; and a small end table turned upside down, its contents strewn across the floor. Grace's chest tightened, and her breathing came in quick gasps. Her legs shook in a nervous rhythm, and she put the tip of the bat on the floor to steady herself. So far it was totally quiet, and Grace decided whoever had come in was now gone.

"Eliot!" she called out again. She walked slowly into the dining room, which didn't seem to be quite as damaged as the living room since most of the kitchen items were boxed up and stacked in heavy piles. The family room and office were another story. Turning on lights as she went, Grace found most of her family photos destroyed, even the one of Roger which sat on the bookshelf in her office. Her lip quivered, and tears welled up in her eyes. *Why? Why would someone do something so hurtful?* Then tears streamed down her face. She couldn't look any longer, and she turned away, walking forward to the kitchen. It had sustained relatively little damage because Del had already stripped it down to nothing.

"Eliot?" she called out again, in a strangled, weepy voice. Then she stood perfectly still. She could barely hear it, but some soft scratching noises started and stopped. She waited for them to start again so she could figure out where they originated. Then she heard the sound—a soft scraping noise—and she walked over to the pantry. She opened the door and a huge "meow" greeted her. Eliot tore out of the pantry as if the Headless Horseman of Sleepy Hollow were on his tail. Grace saw him race out to the living room and slink under the sofa.

"Oh, thank goodness. I don't think my friendship with TJ would have survived a dead cat," Grace said out loud. "So much for assuming he was a good burglar alarm cat." She walked back to the hallway, studiously avoiding a glance at her office, and picked up the hallway phone. The police station number was in her head since she often called TJ there if she couldn't get her on her cell. When Myers the desk cop answered, she asked for Jake Williams.

★　★　★　★　★

"So, the insurance guy and the cops have come and gone?" said Jeff, as they sat in her dining room, ate Chinese takeout food, and commiserated about Grace's house. "I don't think you should stay here tonight. Whoever did this may return."

"I'll be all right," Grace said, and she used her chopsticks to stuff some shrimp and rice in her mouth. She chewed it slowly, swallowed, and said, "Whoever did this is long gone. It was just like the letter I got at the newspaper. They want to scare me off. This means we are on to something about Folger's death. Besides, I'm all over my sadness and into my anger phase. No one is going to run me out of my house."

"Grace, whoever is doing this is becoming more out of control. This destruction is much worse than an anonymous letter. Maybe we should back off a bit and have TJ deal with everything. I can cover any leads on the story, and we'll distance you from it as far as bylines."

Grace put her chopsticks down, wiped her mouth with her napkin, and looked directly at Jeff. "I'll be fine. The things they destroyed can be replaced. Even Roger's picture and the other ones can be replaced. I have either the negatives or the originals on my computer or on CDs. Besides, Jake Williams said they'd step up patrols around my house this evening. TJ should be back tomorrow, and she'll know what to do."

He put his hand over hers on the table top. "Sorry I've been a little quiet lately. I may have to go on a trip, and I would be gone, possibly, a week—some unfinished business needing to be taken care of."

Grace thought she could cut the stillness with a knife. *He wasn't going to say anything else. What was with this guy and his secrets?* "Who will watch the newspaper?"

"I think between you and the others I've hired, we'll be all right. Unless something big breaks in the murder case, it will be business as usual. TJ isn't exactly moving at the speed of light on this."

"It's only been a couple of weeks. Usually she works meticulously and builds the evidence so she has a tight case."

He nodded thoughtfully. "It will be interesting to hear what she found out when she gets back from Chicago." Again, a silence lay over the table, and Grace felt as if she couldn't breathe.

"Well," he looked at his watch. "You sure you'll be okay here tonight?"

"Yes. I have Eliot the wonder attack cat with me."

"Small good he did in the pantry."

"I'll be fine. I may teach Eliot to dial 9-1-1. Thanks. I really do appreciate your concern, but I'm sure I'll be fine."

They both rose, and Jeff moved toward her and took her in his arms. He planted a firm, but tender kiss on her lips, and Grace wondered if she had imagined his recent preoccupation.

"I'm worried about your safety, Grace, but I have to go. Don't have a choice. I won't be gone long, and I'll call you."

"When are you leaving?"

"Late tomorrow. I'll make sure everything is organized and in good shape at the paper before I go. I'll be back in no time. Meanwhile, don't do anything crazy. Take care of yourself and watch over your shoulder. We don't know who's doing this."

"Yes, Jeff. I won't take any chances. Now, go home and do your packing or whatever you need to do." She walked him to the door, kissed him again, and watched his back as he walked down the sidewalk.

Later, after she cleaned up the food cartons on the dining room table, Grace went upstairs. She changed into her pajamas, climbed into bed, and reviewed the day. She and Jeff had at least cleared up the mess in the family room and the office. Maybe Deb and Jill could help her with the rest tomorrow before Lettie arrived from the hospital. Then she considered Jeff. *Why all the secrecy about where he was going? Deb O'Hara's right. He is a mystery man. I wonder if he has the location set on his phone so I could track him.*

She pulled the covers up and thought about the morning. *Tomorrow's another day, and I have to prepare myself for Lettie's arrival. She'll need someone to watch over her and keep her from overdoing for a few days at least.* Grace turned out the light by her bed and was asleep by the time her head hit the pillow.

Outside on the street, a dark car sat parked, its engine idling in the cold. Jake Williams took another sip of his coffee and settled in for a long, chilly night.

CHAPTER TWENTY-THREE

On Friday morning Grace sat and watched the midday news in her family room, listening for any sign of Lettie needing help. Her mind was only half on the news because her brain kept reviewing the events of the crowded day over and over. She had picked Lettie up at the hospital and brought her back to Sweetbriar Court late in the morning. No way was Lettie able to stay by herself for a while. She was taking pain medicine, and she was on crutches. But no broken bones, just a very painful sprain. Grace made her a bed on the pull-out sofa in the office because trying to walk upstairs to the bedroom would have been exhausting. She started to think about lunch when she suddenly realized with a shock, "Egads! I don't have a cook anymore." It just dawned on her how much Lettie did for her on a daily basis.

Lunch. She considered what to do about the meal and was headed for the kitchen when a knock came at the front door, and she turned back to answer it. Grace opened the door and looked out at a group of about fifteen people, including Del Novak. They carried boxes and bundles of casseroles and all manner of food, and some held buckets, mops, and trash bags.

"Heard you need a bit of help," said Mildred, Lettie's friend from the bakery. "So we're all organized and will fix the damage in no time."

Grace looked at them, her astonishment obvious. In fact, her mouth was open, but no words came out. Then she said, "But how—how did you hear about the break-in?"

"Are you kidding? Lettie texted us as soon as she heard about it. That girl doesn't let any grass grow under her feet. We're all on her speed dial."

"And," said Gladys, who worked at the coffee shop, "we have enough food for the next week or so, but we're organized to deliver up to three weeks after that. People signed for time slots to bring food when they heard Lettie was laid up." She leaned over and whispered in Grace's ear. "Don't worry, hon, your cooking secret is safe with me."

"Well, come in, come in," Grace said, and she smiled as she opened the door wider, relief evident in her voice. At least neither she nor Lettie would starve to death, a fate Grace had worried about when she considered that Lettie wouldn't be able to stand up or move around for some time. She watched as they filed in, Del the last one through the door. They disposed of jackets and hats and scarves, and the elderly contractor carried them upstairs with help from Deb O'Hara. As the coats came off, Grace noticed they all wore light-blue sweatshirts. Jill Cunningham turned around, and Grace could see the message on the front of their shirts: "Lettie's Legions." Grace turned her around and read, "We Work for the Leader of the Pack."

"Don't tell me," Grace said to Gladys. "Someone organized a shirt campaign."

"Jill Cunningham. She's really fast," said Mildred.

"Don't worry," said Gladys. "We'll be out of your hair in no time. We had to check up on the old girl and give her the latest news from around town. And we'll be back with more food once you run out. I'm sure she'll text."

"Well, I don't know what to say," Grace said. "Thank you. I'm so grateful." Suddenly, Grace could hear Lettie's bell—she had given her a bell to ring for help—clanging furiously.

"Who's out there?" Lettie yelled.

Grace shook her head, one eyebrow raised, and said, "She's in the office on the sofa. Through here." Then everyone filed out of the hallway and into Grace's office. Only about half of them could get in at a time, so the other half began to clean up the damage from the break-in. Mildred appeared to be in charge, and she led various people into different rooms to clear away the debris.

Grace waited until the second group was done visiting with Lettie, and then she walked into the office and saw Del on a chair next to her laid-up cook.

"Thought maybe you could use a little help with the cleanup," said Lettie, a smug note in her voice.

"How—?" Grace started to ask.

"Are you kidding? I heard about the break-in from one of my nurses while I was in the hospital. At first I thought it was hallucinations from the pain medicine, but then I decided it was real. So I thought I should organize a little rescue party." Her voice turned to wonder. "Didn't know so many people would turn out, though."

Del patted her hand. "It's a testimony to how popular you are, my girl."

Lettie's face turned red, and she lowered her eyes. Grace noticed she was sitting up on the sofa, her bandaged ankle lying on a pillow—like a potentate reviewing her subjects. Lettie looked at Del Novak and said, "Del, do you think you could be a dear and move this pillow so it's behind my lower back a little better."

"Sure, Lettie. Anything."

"Oh . . . that is perfect. Thank you, Del." Grace watched Lettie look up at him. The stars were still there.

"Well, I'll go along and see how they're doing," said Grace.

Before she even made it through the door, she heard the jarring clang of the bell. "Oh, and Grace, could you bring me some more water? Thanks, dear."

This is going to be a very long rehabilitation, Grace thought.

That was in the afternoon. Now the shadows grew darker, and she wondered what Jeff was doing. *Packing his bags? Finishing up at the office? Surely he'll call before he leaves.* Actually, her mind went in fifteen different directions. She knew TJ was back because she saw her truck slide into the garage across the street, and then, fifteen minutes later, it backed out again. She'd probably stop by the house tonight. Del had been pounding in the kitchen all afternoon, but Lettie's demands slowed him down considerably. At this rate, he might still be sawing and drilling in June.

Grace wasn't used to sitting at home, so she moved restlessly from one window to the other, one eye on the news, but her brain disengaged. It would be easier to type in her office, but Lettie was in there. Now, however, she could hear soft, even snores coming from the doorway. Maybe she should check out the refrigerator and figure out which casserole to warm up.

"Wait a minute," Grace said to TJ, and she tiptoed over to the office door. She could hear the television blasting some *National Geographic* show about bears. She hesitated to close the door completely because Lettie might need her. "We should talk softly. Otherwise, anything you say will be all over town. I had a sample of Lettie's networking power this afternoon."

TJ laughed. "You are so right. That woman has sources I don't know, and she doesn't have to pay them."

"So," said Grace. "What happened in Chicago? How does Lansky figure into all this?"

TJ took a swig of her Guinness and smiled at Grace. "Quite a trip. Interesting information. Nothing I would have guessed."

"When did you get back?"

"Midafternoon. Then I had Sandra Lansky in for questioning. She is one cagey character."

"Don't leave me hanging, TJ. What did you find out?"

"I faxed her picture to a couple of contacts I have up there. She has a Chicago address in a rather exclusive neighborhood and apartment building. Super let me in—all nice stuff, and expensive everything. Not sure she has great taste, but she does have money, and the question is from where? It evidently ran out, because she was behind on her rent by two months, and the super was curious to know her whereabouts."

"So what did your contacts say?"

"She was a call girl for a high-end escort service, but, for several years now, Conrad Folger has paid her bills."

"Wow. Emily didn't know about this."

"No. When I talked to Lansky, I found out Conrad saw her regularly on what he called 'business trips,' but he never let her know how much money he actually had. He took her to expensive restaurants and bought her flowers and lingerie."

"Did he hurt her like Emily?"

"Don't think so. She said the sex was rough—sometimes a little too rough—but the relationship was consensual and the money was good until recently."

"Was she the woman in the bank?"

TJ laughed and nodded her head. "Yes. You were so right on that, Grace."

"Did he think he could just quit seeing her? How many years had this gone on?"

"At least five. She had a lot invested in the relationship. He promised her he would marry her, but the timing had to be right."

"Of course, it never was."

"Correct. I think Will must have known, however. Perhaps after she went to the bank and threatened to expose him, Conrad figured he'd better tell Will. Even though the two of them were competitive, they usually did have each other's backs."

Grace thought about the scene she saw in The Depot's parking lot. *Maybe Will tried to buy her off and get her to go away.* "What brought this all to a head?"

"I think she got tired of waiting, tired of Conrad's promises, and concerned that his marriage promise might never happen. Plus, he'd stopped paying her rent. She did confess she threw a vase at him in his office. But beyond that, she says she didn't kill him."

"Did she give you any information that might point the finger in another direction? Abbey and Camilla? Will? Emily?"

"Her timing is interesting. She says she told him—that day we were at the bank—he could have until Friday, January sixth, or she'd go to his wife and the members of the bank's board of directors. She had nothing to lose since his money had stopped. So I guess she decided to ruin his reputation and hurt his marriage. As you know, he died that Friday night. But we don't know how she got in unless Camilla helped her. Since Abbey and Camilla are her alibi, it is entirely possible. They weren't happy with him either."

"The women are not out of the woods yet."

"No. And, to make things even more interesting, Lansky was unbelievably angry with him. You remember the scene at the bank. I could see her cut his throat. She's a strong woman. If she could get into his house—with Camilla's help—he was a goner."

"But the three of them swear they were together and drunk that night."

"Convenient, huh? Maybe they were, indeed, together at the Folgers'."

"Does this mean you still have the three of them on your list?"

"Definitely. Could have been one or all three or two. But they are viable suspects. You better believe it. Then we have another wild card."

"Really? More?"

"When I had her in at the station today and laid out the cards on the table, she went into a tirade about Will Folger. Evidently, he has been out of sorts, cranky, and angry at his brother. Could be any of a number of reasons, but it was enough that Conrad was increasingly annoyed, and then anxious about whatever was between them. She mentioned some kind of party started it off. But she thought there was more to it than that."

"Oh," said Grace. "Emily Folger said something about it, too. She said Conrad and Will had several tense conversations in the kitchen the night of the murder. Do you think Will has it in him to kill his brother?"

TJ sighed and took another gulp of beer. "Here's the thing. The last two conversations I've had with Will—at the bank— were curious. He was secretive, anxious, and acted furtive, choosing his words with care. Body language said lying. Overall, not the pleasant, kind, non-confrontational guy some people have described to me. Not sure what's going on there, but he's next on my list to check out. I have to do some interviews at the bank anyway."

"You know," Grace said, tapping her lip with her finger, a habit she had whenever she thought hard, "you have at least two people here with serious motives and passions. I always think of killers as people who are moved by passion. Either that, or they are cold-blooded people who simply have no feelings at all and can kill without conscience. But both of those are on either end of a wide spectrum. I keep hearing in my head that Will was passed over again and again by his father. Remember what Jessalynn Folger said? Conrad constantly degraded his older brother and got his job. And then you had some secretive something happening at the bank. You have Will, who screamed at Sandra Lansky in the parking lot behind The Depot. You have Sandra Lansky, who gave Conrad an ultimatum and was increasingly desperate about money. She confronted Conrad and threatened him with disclosure. All of these elements came together about the same time—the night Conrad Folger died. Sounds like some good possibilities to me. And notice—my Emily is not on the list."

"Oh, yeah. 'Your' Emily. I have to admit, the pressure has receded on the wife. Too bad they don't have a butler."

"I suppose the problem is you don't have physical evidence to tie them to the crime."

"True, Grace. I've trained you well. I think I need to go back over the notes from the scene of the crime. But first I'll have Will Folger in for a chat, or, rather, I'll go to the bank and talk to him and a few other people."

"Sounds like a plan."

It was quiet for a moment, and they heard only the loud volume of the television on in the office where Lettie was surprisingly subdued.

"I have to swing around and see Charlie Sims."

"Charlie Sims? What's a retired farmer got to do with this?"

"While I was in Chicago, he left a message for me to stop in. He'd been gone on a vacation after the murder happened, and he's only been back a few days—long enough to hear the details from people. He seems to think he might have some information for me, so this could be a good time to check that out."

"Oh, I wish you could take me with you. In fact, could I go live at your house until Lettie is on her feet again?"

TJ laughed and started to walk toward the front hallway. "Nah, Grace. This is the price you pay for a wonderful sister-in-law who can cover up for your shortcomings in the kitchen. Speaking of cover-up, what is this I hear about Jeff Maitlin possibly leaving town? Did you scare him off? Did he find out you can't cook? I think that would be a deal breaker for me."

"I would love to tell you I have an answer. First he kisses me, then he leaves me. And, he's so secretive about it, I have not a clue what's going on. Deb's right when she says he's a mystery man, and I'm not sure I want to deal with these mysterious goings-on. Why he won't talk to me about whatever it is, I don't know. But I'm tired of it."

"Want my advice?"

"No."

"Well, all right then." She started to walk toward her coat, which hung over the banister of the stairway.

"I may have to run away. Flee back into the Olivia diary," Grace said.

"Somehow I don't see you back in 1893. You wouldn't like corsets, and you'd have to know how to cook."

CHAPTER TWENTY-FOUR

By Sunday afternoon, Grace was restless and still thinking about Jeff. Del had taken Lettie for a car ride to get her out of the house. Grace was so bored, she considered counting suspects for TJ and prioritizing them. Will Folger was near the top of the list; then there was Sandra Lansky, who seemed to have a great motive and a suspicious alibi; Camilla had all the skills and the anger-management problem; Abbey couldn't be dismissed since she had blue paper, black ink, and a motive for hating Conrad; and who else? *Maybe I'd better add Darlene since she and Will are a couple, but she seems more social climber than murderer. Emily brings in the bottom of the list because I don't believe she could murder anyone no matter how much she hated her husband for his abuse.*

Always she came back to two questions: *Where is Jeff and why hasn't he called? Stop it, Grace. He's only been gone a few days.* As usual, patience was not one of Grace's strong points.

After pacing around the kitchen, the living room, the dining room, and the hallway, she threw her hands in the air and went upstairs to get Olivia's diary. Maybe it would take her mind off this boredom. She settled in on the sofa in the living room and tried to remember where she had left off with the diary. *Oh, yes, Olivia finally told Tyler Quinn she was marrying the judge. I have a feeling things are not going to be so happy from now on.*

★ ★ ★ ★ ★

10 September, 1893

My parents have come and gone back to Anthem. They were closeted for some time with Judge Lockwood, and my mother said he assured them he could provide for me with his wealth, and I would want for nothing. My mother explained to the judge that I had been reared out of society in a gentle world, and I might be overwhelmed by his expectations of my housekeeping skills and understanding of my duties in society. He convinced them this would not be a problem. As he had servants who were well trained, I would not be expected to do many of the household duties that women often must perform. He also assured her, with my quick mind and lively nature, I would learn about social duties quickly. And so, my parents spent a day to reflect and discuss his proposal and, in the end, decided my future would be secure with this marriage.

Did they ask me about my feelings? Yes. Everyone seems to believe this is the best offer I could have, and I know my parents would worry less if my future were assured. So it is done. We are to be married later this month. That will not allow me time to go back for a visit to Anthem, a prospect I hoped to do so I could see my brothers, the farm, and my horse. My parents will stay in Endurance a few days so Mother and Aunt Maud can consult about my trousseau. Then Mother and Father will go back to Anthem and return for the wedding on September 26. I am so excited I will be married and have a huge house and a place in society. I am sure once I get to know the judge better, he will be a considerate and pleasing husband.

20 September, 1893

I have heard nothing from Tyler Quinn. Inside my heart is a hollow place, for I am sure he has heard of my betrothal to the judge and is not pleased. I have thought about this for a considerable time. When a person makes a decision, that decision often eliminates other possible thoughts.

The last couple of weeks have been a flurry of activity as we deal with my trousseau. The milliner and the dress-shop owners have had to add additional help to make all the dresses and hats so quickly. The judge, of course, took care of all the bills. Aunt Maud and I made our last social calls and delivered some of the wedding invitations ourselves.

We are to be married at Lockwood House with a dinner and dance afterward. The Rev. Jeremiah Hughes will officiate. My dress is white silk with several flounces, and the veil is all lace and tulle. White roses and orange blossoms make up the wreath for my veil and the bouquet of flowers I will carry. We have already received many gifts—a sugar bowl, cake basket, and several sets of napkin rings. The most beautiful gift, by far, is my engagement ring—a family heirloom with a ruby set between two pearls. My wedding band is a matching gold.

We are to travel by train in a private car to the World's Columbian Exposition in Chicago. Imagine! I will ride on a train, and see that great city I have only read about. I am so excited I can hardly eat or sleep. The judge smiles at my childishness. I am sure this is nothing to him since he has seen so much of the country, but this will be my first trip to a big city. I have read of the Columbian Exposition and World's Fair in the newspaper, but now I will be able to see it.

9 October, 1893

I am writing this entry over several days after we returned from our honeymoon. It was such a beautiful night, and I met so many of the judge's friends. We were married in the front parlor, and only my family was present. It was wonderful to see my brothers and hear of their adventures while I have been away. Then we had dinner with everyone and a dance in the ballroom. The house was decorated with lovely flowers, some of which came all the way from Chicago by train.

My mother talked to me about a wife's duties, beginning with her honeymoon. I suppose I was not surprised since I grew up on the farm and watched the animals in the barn. I dare not write my thoughts about this.

We left for Chicago and the judge—my husband—rented a private Pullman car with electric lighting and even a water closet. We traveled to Chicago in six hours. I am amazed when I consider that my trip to Endurance took four days and was only about sixty miles.

But first, our train trip. We had a parlor car all to ourselves. The walls were filled with landscape paintings, and the woodwork was polished rosewood; the porter said it was hand-carved in Germany's Black Forest. I looked out the windows and watched the various landscapes of Illinois pass by while my husband read the newspapers.

Chicago is the biggest city I have ever seen, and I have only seen a small part of it. We stayed at the elegant Palmer House Hotel. I learned from the information in our room that it was built in 1871, but burned in the Great Chicago Fire. Then it was rebuilt two years later, and it sits at State and Monroe Streets in a district called "the Loop." During our first dinner in at the hotel's dining room, I was delighted by a confection made especially for the hotel during the World's Fair. It is called a "brownie," and it consists of a lovely chocolate cake with an apricot glaze and walnuts. I fell in love and hope I can get our cook to make such a dessert. Each night, if we ate at the Palmer

House, I had a delicious brownie.

Every day we would have breakfast at the hotel and then travel by horse and buggy to the World's Fair. The Columbian Exposition was a sight to behold, and the judge told me it covered 633 acres. Each evening we returned to our hotel exhausted. We could not see all there was to see in only two weeks, but we did observe many displays, which took my breath away. I can only mention a few. The judge knows about the world far beyond my experience, and he explained many of the sights to me.

My first glimpse explains why people call it "the White City." It is filled with huge, neo-classical buildings that house exhibits, and each edifice is painted white. We attended a few of the exhibit halls, and I was astounded by the electrical devices. The judge said someday we will have electricity in our house. We also saw a most amazing projector called a "zoopraxiscope," which shows pictures that move. The Krupp pavilion of artillery had a huge gun from Germany that weighed 122 tons. I cannot envision what something like that would have done in the Civil War, nor what it might do in wars to come. We also walked on a moving walkway, an invention I could never have imagined.

The Midway had attractions and carnival rides and sideshows. It was my favorite part of the World's Fair. We heard many musicians, but my favorite was a black man named Scott Joplin who played the piano. My husband humored me, and we rode on the Ferris wheel, an astonishing ride, which is so high we could see all of Chicago. At first I thought I might faint, but then I got used to the height. How huge Chicago is!

We sat in on a number of lectures, and my favorite was by a man named Frederick Jackson Turner, who talked about the frontier. I liked him best because the frontier is close in description to my rural life in Anthem. After his lecture, we had a box lunch and a new drink called "carbonated soda." We also bought some souvenirs both financial and postal: a quarter and silver half dollar, and picture postcards, a new invention of the post office.

In the late afternoon we often napped and then dressed splendidly for dinner. Some evenings we ate at the Palmer House, and other nights we went to various dining halls in the area. I was overwhelmed by the many foods and places to eat that we have seen and patronized over our two weeks at the Fair. In short, this whole trip—the train, Chicago, the World's Fair—is something I could never have visualized or even foreseen from my little farm in Anthem. Now I know what my mother meant when she said my life in Endurance might lead to further adventures in the greater world. The sights I have seen on this trip leave me breathless for what the world will become in the next century, only seven years away.

I feel I must write about one incident, which has left me puzzled, anxious, and a little fearful. Near the end of our trip, we came across some beggars just before we entered the Exposition. I asked my husband to give them some change, and he said, "Nonsense." He took my arm and pulled me past the poor people who begged on the street, many of them Civil War veterans. When I tried to explain they were hungry and in much worse condition than we are, he gave me a menacing look and did not speak to me most of that day. His silence was fearful.

Later, when I questioned him about those poor people, he seemed irritated, and finally told me I was never again to question him like that in public. I am sure he is right. I should be quieter and more ladylike, and not question his decisions. After dinner at a lovely restaurant, he left me in our hotel room, saying I must be tired, and he thought I should rest. He wanted to go out and see if he could find a game of poker.

I am puzzled and not a little distraught at the events of the past day. The judge has gone down to pay our hotel bill before leaving, so I have a little time to write. I do not know what to think about the judge's actions. Perhaps I have misunderstood the nature of marriage and love.

The last night, after the judge went in search of a poker game, I packed some of our clothing in anticipation of our impending departure. Then I went to bed and fell asleep. Sometime during the night, I was awakened by the judge's return. He had been drinking, heavily I believe, and he tore the covers off the bed and . . . I cannot describe the horror. He was no longer my considerate husband, and he smelled of liquor and tore my nightgown. Afterwards, I was hurt and cried. I sat up much of the night while he snored in a drunken sleep. Why? Before he fell asleep, he did not talk to me except to say I must never, ever contradict him in public again as I did outside the Fair. If I do, I can expect to be subjected to more of these nights.

The following morning I was sore and bruised. The judge acted as if nothing had happened when he woke up. In fact, he whistled as he dealt with his tie and assembled his hat and cane. I simply did not speak, thinking a quiet wife might be his desire. But, on the way to our last day at the Fair, he stopped at an elegant store and bought a fur-lined cape and jewelry for me, having the proprietor wrap and ship them to Endurance. I am bewildered. Why? Why would he hurt me so and then act as if his actions had not happened and shower me with expensive gifts? I do not understand.

Grace closed the diary and thought the life of Olivia Lockwood and her new husband had changed in ways the young girl could

214

never have predicted. The judge seemed to behave like Conrad Folger: abuse followed by gifts. Total disregard for what he had done. Like Emily Folger, Olivia married quickly to a man she believed would love and protect her. Did she recover from his abuse as Emily appeared to be doing? And did that figure into the judge's death somehow, a puzzling and rapidly approaching demise Grace hoped would be explained before the diary ended.

CHAPTER TWENTY-FIVE

It was unusual for Grace to work on a Sunday evening, but Lettie had taken up a great deal of her time so she had to catch up. Fortunately, the aggravating patient now got around well on her crutches with the promise of a walking boot soon. Grace had no compunction about leaving her at home with a cell phone so she could call Grace if she had an emergency.

She looked up from her computer and brooded about Jeff Maitlin. She played over in her mind their last conversation. He was anxious. "I promise I'll tell you all about it when I get back," he had said. "For years I've pursued details of an incident from my past, and, without much resolution, I've been hesitant to talk to anyone about it. But this time it looks like we might have a breakthrough, so I have to be gone for a week—maybe two—but I promise I'll be back, and then I'll explain everything. You understand, right?"

And Grace, being Grace, had said, "Of course, Jeff. It all sounds so cryptic and I'm curious, but I'll be patient and wait until you're comfortable enough to tell me about it. Just be careful if it's dangerous."

"Not dangerous, Grace. You'll see. If I get a chance, while I'm gone, I'll call. But I can't promise. I simply don't know."

Tonight Grace was distracted, thinking about what could be so puzzling. A mysterious something from his past? Maybe a horrible event like a death? Could it be connected to why he was able to buy a huge house and renovate it without any deep breathing over the enormous cost? What was in the past of this mystery man? She sighed, and thought about how few answers she had, and she determined that she would get down to the bottom of the matter when he returned. She'd have to be a bit pushier. She broke off that thought and looked down at her screen again. Then she got back to work setting up an article about the history of Jeff's house.

Grace's phone rang, and she wondered who knew she was at the newspaper office. Lettie. She answered it and heard Emily's voice, actually sounding cheerful. She wanted to stop in and see Grace because she needed to talk to her about some details she remembered from the night of Conrad's death. Lettie told her Grace was at the office. Emily's Conrad and Caitlin had a sleep-over with another family who had children in their classes, so Emily was free. Grace told her to text when she was outside the office, and she'd let her in. After the recent goings-on, Grace was more careful about security.

Ten minutes later they sat in Grace's office. Emily had brought some cookies and a container of fruit punch. "I thought it might be a bit late for coffee," she said. "Since we talked last Tuesday, I've remembered more about the night of Conrad's . . . death."

Grace crossed her legs and sat back more comfortably on the love seat. "So, have you put these flashbacks into some order, and does it seem to work better after we talk?"

"Yes. I think maybe my subconscious brings them out after I sleep on the details my conscious mind considers. Does that make sense?"

"Absolutely."

"I will call Aiden, my attorney, in the morning and tell him we need to speak with TJ Sweeney. I'm sure the reason I remember so little is that I took that sedative. It really zonks me out. Thoughts come back to me in bits and pieces. But now I remember I went into his bedroom that morning. I think I blocked it out before because it was so—so horrifying—and I saw him there all covered in blood. Oh, Grace, I think I almost passed out. But then I thought he might be alive, and I grabbed him by the shoulders and listened to his chest to see if he was breathing. That's when I wobbled to my bedroom and called 9-1-1. I didn't think straight, or I'd have used the phone in his bedroom. As I was talking to the emergency person, I looked down and my nightgown was saturated in his blood. It must have happened when I tried to see if he was breathing. That was when I first screamed because I was shocked at the blood. I went back to his bedroom and looked at him again. I must have cut my foot on that trip because I remember I suddenly realized the pain. We had a glass vase that sat on a table over by the windows. It was gone, so I think the glass on the floor was from the vase."

"It makes sense, Emily. But you don't remember anything after you went to bed and before you woke up and found him the next morning?"

"Well," she said, and looked down. "As I told you, I do remember he—he raped me. I somehow stumbled out of his bedroom and back to my own. I know I must have changed my nightgown before I got into bed because I had a different nightgown on the next morning. I just wanted to destroy the hated memory."

"I still can't figure out how your fingerprints got on the piece of glass."

"Me either. I know I didn't pick it up. I think I would remember that. But maybe not."

Grace recalled TJ telling her about the torn nightgown on the floor, but she said nothing to Emily. Now, however, it made sense. Then she remembered one of the most damaging pieces of evidence. "The alarm system, Emily. What do you remember?

I know it was set when the housekeeper showed up in the morning."

Emily looked over toward the doorway as she thought about Grace's question. She twisted her lips in a grimace, and then relaxed them again. "I'm not sure I can explain that. You only have to set the alarm by pushing a button or pulling this little gadget on the alarm panel in the kitchen. I think my lawyer told me Conrad's fingerprint was on the button to set it. But it makes sense since he would have set it before he came to bed. Well, maybe he did. That's just it. He was really drunk—I know he was because he reeked of scotch when . . . he raped me. But maybe he didn't set it, as drunk as he was. Oh, I don't know. I can't explain the alarm still being on. I didn't kill him, Grace. I couldn't have. Someone has to have come into the house. But how could that be?"

Grace shook her head. "I don't know, Emily. I'm not an expert on those alarm systems. But it's definitely a piece of evidence needing an explanation. I'm sure other people—smarter than I am—can deal with those alarm systems easily," she said, and she thought about Camilla. She didn't want to believe her former student might have murdered Conrad Folger.

Emily drank the last of the fruit punch she'd brought. Grace was glad to see she had an appetite again. She looked so much healthier in the three weeks since Conrad's death. No more bruises or cuts, and her eyes had begun to have some life again. Grace figured her children had put the life back in her eyes. Emily was so much better, Grace decided she'd take a chance.

"You know, Emily, I'm reading a diary we found at Jeff's house. It was written by a woman named Olivia Havelock Lockwood over a hundred years ago."

"Really? Is she somehow related to the house Mr. Maitlin is renovating?"

"Yes." And Grace told Emily some details about the young

woman's life so far. But she also mentioned Olivia Lockwood had an abusive husband, and she, too, fell into a hasty marriage.

"You'll have to let me know how her story ends," said Emily.

"I will. Her story shakes me a bit too," said Grace. She paused and took a deep breath. "No one knows this except my parents, and they're long gone now. But I dated a guy I met my freshman year in college in Indianapolis. I was terribly young and had led a sheltered life. I went to college in my home town with my parents not far away. He was older, quite handsome, and I was smitten. I hadn't dated a great deal in high school. But, as time went by, I began to neglect my college classes, spend all my time with him, and try to be what he wanted me to be. He was a less scary version of your Conrad—he wanted me to spend all my time with him, do what he wanted to do, and arrange my life to suit him. I did less and less with my friends, and after a while he began to get a bit pushier. You know, more physical. I think I lost ten pounds over the weeks we dated, and I worried all the time about pleasing him. Somehow the self-confident me who went off to college had totally disappeared. My grades suffered, and my parents wondered what was going on.

"One day, when I was home on a break, my mother pulled me aside. She gently probed with questions about my happiness, and I caved in and started to cry. That was a turning point for me. She told me—and I'll never forget this—one of her heroines, Eleanor Roosevelt, said, 'No one can make you feel inferior without your consent.' After that we talked and talked. I began to go home on the weekends and managed to get away from Russ—that was his name. But I've never forgotten how deeply I lost myself in that experience. I can understand how easily it happens. And I'm so glad to see you're finding yourself again," Grace said.

Emily smiled, tears brimming in her eyes. "Thank you, Grace. I can't tell you how much you've helped me think this out. And it is true—about allowing someone to crush you. I wasn't strong enough. To know something like that could happen so easily to you makes me feel not quite so stupid."

"Good," said Grace. "Now I believe I'm ready to head home. I think I've done enough work for one Sunday night when I'm supposed to be home anyway."

They both packed up—papers and laptop for Grace and punch container for Emily. Grace locked up the newspaper office and followed Emily to the parking lot. It looked dark and isolated except for their two cars. Tall, overhead lights hardly covered the entire lot. Suddenly, Emily looked down with dismay.

"Darn. It looks like I have a flat tire."

Grace walked over and saw the black rubber flat on the snow. "Well, I'll have to take you home, and we'll deal with this in the morning. You don't have to take the kids to school, right?"

"Right."

"I'll bet Schreiber's would come out and fix it right here. Call them in the morning, and if you need a ride in, just call me."

"Thanks, Grace."

Emily made sure her car was locked and then piled into Grace's car. Grace warmed her engine up for a few minutes, and then she drove out of the lot and down Main Street, heading toward the county road where Emily lived. It was nine, and the streets were practically deserted on a Sunday night in Endurance. The bars closed earlier on Sundays than on week nights, and city streets had been plowed for several days, so she had an easy time. Finally, the car heater was warming up.

They talked cheerfully and were almost to Emily's when Grace first noticed the car lights come up quickly behind her. She had turned onto the county road, which was snow-packed, and they were still a couple of miles from Emily's. Grace glanced in the rearview mirror and anxiously looked around since they were quite alone on this road. Suddenly, the car behind them hit the back bumper of Grace's car, pushing her into a spin on the snow-covered road. Emily screamed, "Oh, my Lord, Grace!" and Grace felt her lip bleed after she bit it hard while trying to concentrate on the road. She fought to gain control of the car, desperately focusing on the feel of the steering wheel, and she had almost succeeded when the car hit her again. Emily squealed and braced herself with her hands on the dashboard. It wasn't a hard crash against the bumper; only a good nudge to make her lose control. In the rearview mirror, Grace could see the vehicle was a dark SUV. She tried to steer into the spin but totally lost control, spun out, went off the road into a ditch, and caught the edge of a tree, causing the air bags to explode and take her breath away. She remembered hearing Emily scream and then she lost consciousness.

CHAPTER TWENTY-SIX

Grace slowly opened her eyes. Everything was hazy, and the light hurt her eyes, so she closed them again. Then she heard TJ's voice, but it sounded all slurry.

"You're okay, Grace. You can open your eyes. You're fine, and you're in the ER at Endurance Hospital."

She opened her eyes again, slowly. Her head hurt, and she could hear her heart pound. The constant throbbing in her head was really painful. Reaching up, she touched her head and decided she had a bandage over her hair. She put her hand down and felt metal railings next to her, and slowly she became aware she was lying in a hospital bed. "What . . . what happened?" she asked. She tried to get up on her elbows, but immediately became dizzy.

Again, she heard TJ's unmistakable voice. "You'll be fine, Grace. Emily, go find a nurse and tell her Grace is conscious."

She could see someone move in the distance, and then her eyes began to clear and objects came into focus. First, she saw TJ. "Oh, TJ. What happened? Why are you here? And where is here?"

TJ put her hand on Grace's arm and said, "We're at the ER. You had an accident on the road when you took Emily home; only, as Emily tells it, you didn't exactly have an accident. Can you remember anything?"

Grace closed her eyes again. She sorted through her head, trying to make sense of what had happened before she passed out. Then TJ turned as a nurse came into the room followed by a young doctor. *John Overmeyer. He was in my class about fifteen years ago. I think I knew he went to medical school. This is good. He aced my Shakespeare final so he's up to the challenge. Very few students in my entire career did that. Geez, even half dead I remember these dumb facts. Too bad Shakespeare wasn't on the medical boards.*

"Ms. Kimball. How do you feel?" asked her former Shakespeare expert.

"I think I've felt better, John. Have I been run over by a truck? Why does my head hurt so much, and how come I have a bandage holding my brain in? I feel like I can't think straight."

"You have a mild concussion," he said. "You were in a car accident, and the air bag went off. You'll be fine; you got hit pretty hard in the head. I think you may have turned sideways and hit your forehead on the driver's-side window." He pulled his stethoscope off his neck and used it to listen to her heart. Then he checked her pulse, and no one talked.

It was so quiet Grace wondered if she hadn't survived the crash. *Maybe I've died and have to do this test to get in to see Roger.* Everything was so confusing.

Dr. Overmeyer looked at TJ and said, "She'll be fine. She may have a little short-term memory loss from the concussion, but in time she may also remember what happened. We'll keep her here overnight for observation, but I'm sure by morning she'll be doing well. I would be more concerned if she had more serious symptoms. She'll just be tired."

"Did you hear that?" TJ said. "No problem. I'll go and check on Lettie. Fate, with a little help, is picking your household off one by one. First, Lettie sprains her ankle, and then you get a concussion. I'd better keep Eliot Ness away from your house for a while."

"I'm so glad you're okay," said Emily Folger, coming up on the other side of Grace's bed. "It was scary."

Grace stared at her, and strained to focus her eyes. "What happened, Emily?"

Emily looked at TJ, who nodded to her. "We were in your car—mine had a flat tire—and you were taking me home. A dark, huge SUV came up behind us, but I couldn't see the driver because it was so dark. The SUV literally knocked us off the road. Of course, that didn't take much of a nudge since the county road's still slick. When we stopped in the ditch and I could think straight, I called 9-1-1, and the police and ambulance came out and brought us here. I'm so thankful you're going to be fine."

Grace looked over at the windows and took a deep breath.

"That does leave a big question," said TJ. "Who was the target here—you or Emily? Or both of you?"

The doctor turned toward TJ and said, "We'll keep an eye on her."

"Thanks, Dr. Overmeyer. I'll be back to pick her up in the morning. I think, Grace, we need to put your household on a strict ration of 9-1-1 calls. You are running us ragged. Come on, Emily, I'll give you a ride home, and I'll call in to have a patrol circle your house several times during the night. We don't know what's happening here yet."

"Thank you, Detective Sweeney. Good night, Grace, and get some rest."

The following morning, TJ rescued Grace from the hospital and drove her home. The detective had arranged for a tow truck, and Grace's car was now at Bert's Collision Shop. TJ looked from the sofa where Grace lay, to the recliner where Lettie sat with her ankle up and her crutches next to her. "I don't know whether to laugh or cry. What should I do with you two? And who will do the cooking now?"

"You don't need to worry," said Lettie. "Lettie's Legions is still on the move and bringing in food daily. Grace wouldn't be any help with that anyway. But I have to say, TJ, you need to get on top of this. How many more heads and ankles can we break around here?"

"I'd say four—Lettie's head and one good ankle, and your ankles, Grace," TJ said.

"Very funny. Now Del will have to take a break because Grace cannot sit there and listen to hammers. She has enough pounding in her own head. I'll just have to try, somehow, to get along without him." Lettie sighed. "I heard from Mildred that Charlie Sims was in to see you, TJ, and he claims a dark SUV was parked outside the Folger house around two-fifteen the morning of Conrad's unfortunate demise. S'pose it was the same person who tried to knock Grace and Emily Folger off the highway?"

TJ glared at Lettie, a look of consternation on her face. "Where do you hear this stuff, Lettie? Do you have some kind of microphone hidden in my office?"

Lettie smiled and chuckled. "My sources are my secret. Doesn't the Declaration of Independence say I don't have to reveal them?"

"I think it's the Constitution, and it usually refers to newspaper reporters, Lettie."

"Well, I'm related to a reporter—at least by marriage."

"You've missed Endurance excitement overnight, Grace," said TJ. "First of all, Emily's tire was slashed, so someone wanted you to be on that road. Perhaps together. Someone is afraid you're closer to the truth, and he wants to scare you off. His tactics must have changed because at first he figured we'd suspect Emily and, of course, we did. But since you and I have begun to dig into the details and interview people, he's decided we don't believe Emily did it, and we're moving closer to him."

"Whoever 'he' is," Grace said.

"A dark SUV narrows the focus to two people we've interviewed," said TJ.

"Will Folger and Sandra Lansky," mused Lettie.

TJ shook her head. "Lettie, we need to have a talk—when you're better—about your jungle telegraph."

"I refuse to testify on the grounds that I have the Second Amendment," Lettie said, her hand in the air.

"I think that's the Fifth Amendment, Lettie," said Grace. "I may have lost some memory, but I do remember that."

They all three jumped when Grace's phone bawled out "Stayin' Alive." Suddenly, Eliot Ness, who had been lying on Lettie's lap, jumped to the floor and began chasing his tail around in circles.

"What is with my cat?" asked TJ, in such disbelief that Grace let the phone ringtone continue playing.

"Oh, just a little trick I taught him when we were at home all day. Grace has that song on a CD, too, and I thought Eliot might get some exercise if I taught him to chase his tail when he heard that song. I think Grace would call it behaving society."

"I think that's 'behavioral psychology,' Lettie."

"Someday, Grace, you must explain to me why that particular song is Myers's ringtone," TJ said.

Grace answered the phone with a "Yes, Myers," all the while smiling at TJ. Then she listened for a long few minutes. "Yes, TJ is here. I'll put her on."

She handed her cell phone to TJ.

The detective listened and said, "Sure, I'll be at the bank shortly. Thanks."

"What's going on?" asked Lettie.

"Really? You don't know?" TJ flippantly responded.

"Hmm," Lettie said with a scowl on her face. "Which bank?"

"The bank examiners have been in town for the last two days, but they've been keeping a low profile. They were called into the Second National—Folger's bank—because of some irregularities. The board of trustees was afraid people might get worried, so the examiners have kept under the radar."

Grace took a deep breath. "What do they think is going on?"

"It's a great deal of legal wrangling. When Conrad died, his will named his brother as executor of his estate. Conrad's lawyer presented information to the court so they could go ahead with settling things. The judge concurred that Conrad's will was in correct form, and Will Folger could proceed. Then, since Conrad's death was violent, the bank examiners got legal papers saying they had just cause to look at the books, and the court gave them permission to go through his financial deals. Evidently, the examiners have questions about some financial management attributed to Conrad and, by extension, Will Folger. It's a mess. We—the police department—are also involved, since the examiners think they might find criminal actions."

Grace was shocked. "Oh, TJ. Not Will, too? He's been so kind to Emily."

"We don't know the whole story yet. I think the board of trustees at the bank may put out a statement today so people won't worry about their money."

"And does this mean Will is in trouble?"

TJ nodded her head. "I wouldn't be surprised."

Lettie picked up one of her crutches and pointed it at TJ. "I knew it! I knew it. My horoscope today in the *Register* said I'd be right about everything—and someone I shouldn't trust would finally be caught in lies." She smiled smugly at TJ and Grace. "Of course, it should say that every day—the 'right about everything' part."

"Do you think Conrad's death is connected to these irregularities?" asked Grace, ignoring Lettie.

"Don't know yet, but they sure muddy the waters, and it's

only going to get worse."

"How could it get worse?" Grace asked.

"Myers said the bank examiners have called in the FBI. It means they suspect serious federal laws have been broken—felonies, I'm sure."

"Well," said Lettie, struggling to her feet on her crutches. "At least this will take the pressure off Emily Folger."

"True," said Grace, "as far as the murder charges. Whoever ran us down might have been after her, you know. But now people will be more worried about their holdings at the bank, wouldn't you say, TJ? That will be the latest news, and Emily might get a rest."

TJ slowly nodded her head. "Somehow I managed to leave my phone in the car, so Myers knew I'd be here. What's with the ringtone for him?"

Grace smiled. "You know how you always complain about how the police department is a testosterone-driven group? You're the only female down there. So I just remembered John Travolta's swagger, and the words of that song when he was walking down the street in the movie. It's all about how he's a ladies' man. Seemed like it would be a good ringtone for Myers."

TJ laughed. "You've got that one right. How clever of you, Grace." She turned and headed toward the hallway and her coat. "I have to leave and head down there." Then she turned. "Will you two be all right here together—one of you with a pounding head, and the other one with a pounding ankle? I feel like I'm escaping from the *Titanic*."

CHAPTER TWENTY-SEVEN

The following evening, Grace could hear Lettie in the office as she watched a reality show called *Senior Couples and Romance: Can Love Last?* The sound was loud enough to be heard three houses away. Grace and TJ were in the kitchen, Grace sitting down and TJ admiring Del Novak's work. Pritchard's Hardware had put in the gray quartz countertops, and a new black granite sink, and Del had finished the sink hardware, painted the ceiling and walls, and added a new light fixture and some recessed lighting under the new cabinets. TJ inspected it all and whistled.

"Wow. Some nice work."

"Hope so," said Grace. "I like it more and more each day. And it's possible for Lettie to cook again, so we won't starve." As TJ turned and sat down, Grace added, "So, how does the accident investigation go? Or Conrad's murder? Or the bank investigation?"

"You'll be happy to know after a long conference with DA Sorensen, I went out to Emily Folger's and removed her ankle bracelet. Of course, the judge had to okay it, and Sorensen has no more plans to pursue charges against Emily."

Grace smiled and clapped her hands. "Oh, that's wonderful, TJ. We have finally won you over to the side of justice and freedom for the innocent."

"You did, I guess. I also sat in on an FBI interrogation of Will this morning. I knew the FBI had found a security tape of him going in and out of the vault area carrying a large briefcase the

Saturday after his brother was murdered. It was after hours and the bank was closed."

"I know the lockboxes are in the vault, but isn't it usually locked over the weekend?"

"Yes. It has three timers—they look like clocks—and each is set so the vault will unlock again at the programmed time."

"Why three?" Grace asked.

"If one or two fail, the third will still work. Everyone saw Will set the timers. He'd told Bev Blackman he'd take care of it. She usually does. Will set the timers so he could still get in that afternoon instead of setting them for the following Monday morning."

"What was he looking for in the vault?"

TJ took a deep breath and then blew it out slowly. "He was moving cash—lots of it—from Conrad's lockbox to his and taking some home with him, Grace."

"Cash from where?"

"Turns out Conrad had a nice little scam going, and he pulled Will into it."

"A scam? What kind of a scam?"

"The fraudulent, go-to-prison-and-don't-pass-go kind of scam. It's a bit complicated and lots of banker terminology, but I think I can sort it out. The bank loans money—large sums sometimes—and has what they call a 'loan-to-value' policy. Say you want to buy a $300,000 house. The bank will loan you eighty percent of the appraised value of the house. It is their policy and they won't loan you more.

"But Conrad set up several larger loans to people he could trust for more than what the borrower needed. Once the loan was funded, the borrower gave him a cash kickback. No one would know because the borrower would agree to the full amount of the loan. Anyone checking would think the balance was correct."

"But what about checks and balances? Wouldn't someone find out?"

"You would think. Unfortunately for Will, Conrad, as the bank president, agreed on the terms, and Will, as loan vice president, signed off on it. No one else was involved. But Gus Hart was beginning to suspect something funny because Will became more anxious about it as time went by. He knew if they were found out, his name was the one on the papers. He didn't have Conrad's nerve."

"That explains why Jeff and I noticed a sizable tension between the two of them the day Jeff signed his loan paper," Grace said.

"Probably. When Conrad died, Will needed enough time to move the cash away from Conrad's lockbox. After all, no one could have explained why it was there and how much was there. This means if Will killed Conrad, he'd do it at a time when he could get into the bank and deal with the money. A Saturday afternoon would give him the weekend."

"Or, conversely, the timing might have been simply opportune if someone else killed Conrad. How did Will get into the lockboxes?"

"He knew where Conrad kept his box key and probably grabbed it early Saturday morning before the office was sealed off. The second key—called a guard key—is kept near the vault by the employee who handles the safety deposit boxes. He could easily use it, move the cash, and reset the vault clocks. But he didn't remember the security camera. Even so, he could have lied about his reason to go into the vault in off-hours, but he's not good at lying."

Grace shook her head. "So both Conrad and Will made money from this, but what about the person getting the loan? Why take the risk?"

"Conrad made sure the borrower got a lower interest rate

and practically nonexistent fees. Right now the FBI is continuing the probe to identify those borrowers."

"Thank goodness Jeff isn't one of them. But poor Will."

"Poor Will? Why would you say that?"

"Conrad's the one who got him into this."

TJ shook her head. "Will thinks he's such a badass. But he fell apart when they questioned him."

"Isn't 'badass' a bad thing?"

"No, Grace."

"Oh." Grace gasped. "What will Darlene do? That's a serious fraud indictment."

"Don't know. The FBI doesn't think she knew about it," TJ said. She checked an incoming text on her phone, decided it wasn't important, and set the phone back down on the table.

"Lots of money is involved here, Grace, and, remember, Conrad gave Will the job years ago. Maybe he attached a few strings. We don't know how long this has been going on."

"Do you really think Will had it in him to kill Conrad?"

"For the right reasons, yes. He knew the alarm code to the Folger house, and we don't know how he felt about being passed over all those times by their father. A great deal of bad blood there. If anything happens to Emily, Will and Darlene are first in line to watch over the children and the money. People have killed for much less."

"Did you ask him about it?" Grace said.

"Yes. He was appalled I would even consider that he might kill Conrad. He gave me a song and a dance about the choice their father had made to have Conrad succeed him. Will said it was the right choice. Besides, Conrad had given him a job at a time in his life when he was down and lost. It made all the difference."

"Did you believe him?"

"No. He had way too much to gain by Conrad's death, and

he was probably unnerved that he signed for those loans if Conrad truly did force him to do it. Didn't you say the brothers had a troubling conversation the day Jeff signed those loan papers?"

"Yes."

TJ paused. "And this brings us to your recent accident on the road."

"And Will? You think he might have been the driver?"

"He has a string of good reasons. First, someone slashed Emily's tire, so whoever it was wanted the two of you together in the car—you for your snooping, and Emily to get her out of the way of the guardianship of her future wealthy children. Will said he was at a Rotary meeting that night, and his story checked out. But after the meeting he said he went to Patsy's Pub for a drink or two, and he got home around eight-thirty. Darlene, of course, agreed. Will also claims he saw the emergency vehicles on the road on the way home, the ones at your accident."

"And we were run off the road around eight."

"Correct. Darlene had volunteer hours at Woodbury's St. Agnes Hospital and said she got home around seven. I checked her shift with the hospital, and she was correct.

"The Folgers actually have not one, but two, dark SUVs. One of them has a small scratch and dented spot on the front bumper. Will said he caused it when he bumped into the back wall of the garage one night. And we did find a similar spot on the garage's back wall. But," TJ said, "and I found this very curious—he glanced at Darlene after he said that, and she gave him a daggers look back. I wonder if they had argued about damaging the car to cover the origin of the dent, and now it turned out Will was right. I can see how Darlene would hate to be wrong."

"It is true that Darlene can be pretty irritating. I've only met her once at Emily's."

"When the FBI arrested Will, she shov
absolutely hysterical. She couldn't believe he w
illegal at the bank. I'm not sure she knew he
loan papers at Conrad's behest. It was someth
action, which struck me as over the top and des

"I think Emily called her a 'force of nature.' "

"We got a warrant for the house, and Darlene, ot
totally uncooperative. Didn't find any guns or blood. N
with bloodstains. We did find some potting soil in a sh
took it along with us. The bag's at the lab, but it will ta
while."

TJ looked out the window for a moment. She turned back to
Grace and said, "I wonder about Will and Darlene's 'lost years'
before they showed up here. I also am curious about where they
got married."

"Marriage," Grace said, thoughtfully. "Conrad Folger and
Emily, Judge Lockwood and Olivia, Will and Darlene. Quite a
trio of marriages."

TJ shook her head. "And you wonder why I keep my options
open."

CHAPTER TWENTY-EIGHT

Grace looked at the most recent copy of the *Endurance Register* on the office counter. She glanced at the front page of the Friday edition. The headline was "Banker Arrested by FBI for Fraud." They had rushed the newspaper out, and she was satisfied that it looked good. Every morning people from each department held a conference, so they could put the newspaper together while Jeff was gone.

Two days. Two days since Jeff had left, and she hadn't heard a word. She turned around and looked at his office door, closed since Monday. Why hadn't he at least called her and told her he was fine? And where was he? She didn't know whether to be worried or angry. *Well, give him another day,* she thought. But there was an empty feeling in the pit of her stomach. She wanted to hear her phone play "A New York State of Mind." His ringtone.

That morning TJ had stopped by the house and asked if she could leave Eliot. With Lettie, Eliot got more attention than TJ could give him while she worked. Grace hated to think what new tricks Lettie was probably teaching the cat. Del still puttered around the kitchen, and Lettie continued to slow him down. Grace shook her head. Lettie still acted like a six-year-old schoolgirl instead of a sixty-nine-year-old around the contractor. Del had finished the biggest projects, except for the floor, and so he was simply doing some finishing work while he waited for the floor tiles to come in.

Since Will had been arrested, TJ had more time to concentrate on Conrad's murder, and she planned to go to the bank today. What a shock it would be if Will had not only signed those illegal loans, but had also killed his brother. Grace suddenly realized she was standing at the counter, totally in la-la land.

"Stop daydreaming, Grace, and decide what's next," she said out loud. Then she took a surreptitious look around to see if anyone had heard her, but she was alone in the front area of the newspaper office. She remembered she had meant to ask Emily about Will and Conrad's relationship, and she glanced at her watch. She texted Emily to ask if she was home and got a definite, "Yes. Stop by if you'd like." She wandered back to her office, grabbed her things, and headed out to the parking lot to make a quick stop at The Depot for a lemon meringue pie. She remembered her mother saying, "You should never go to visit anyone empty-handed."

As she drove toward the county road, she recalled Emily said her children were leaving for a long weekend with their grandparents after school. It was the end of January, and the schools had a three-day weekend because of a teachers' institute day. A thaw had melted much of the snow from the highway so the roads were clear.

Suddenly, the hairs on her neck prickled under her scarf, and her stomach had a rock-and-roll feeling. She looked to her right and it dawned on her she was passing the place where she and Emily had been run off the road. She could see the tire tracks remained in the ditch, and so did the churned-up snow and watery sludge where people had stomped through the ditch to rescue them and study the evidence. Now the remaining snow had turned to slush as it thawed, preparing to freeze up again at night. She hadn't driven by here since the accident. *Well, not exactly an accident,* and Grace bit her lip nervously as she considered how much worse it might have been.

She almost jumped high enough to hit her head on the car ceiling when her phone went off and the Bluetooth picked up the "Wanted Dead or Alive" ringtone. *TJ*. She pushed the button on her steering wheel and said, "What's up, Sheriff?"

Laughter, and then TJ's voice said, "Uh, Detective. Maybe someday."

"I'm almost to Emily Folger's. Anything you want me to ask other than the question of Will and Conrad's relationship?"

"That's exactly what I want from you. And I figured I would bluntly ask if you've heard from the mysterious Editor Maitlin?"

Grace was silent for a moment. "Nope, not a word."

"Hmmm. You don't know whether to send me to bail him out of some horrible foreign prison 'cause you're worried, or whether to kick a few spindles out of his front porch banister because you're so angry. I can hear it in your flat, disinterested voice, Grace."

"You know me so well."

"Patience, woman."

"Sure. I'll give him another five minutes."

"That's the Grace I know."

"Say, I just thought of something I want to mention to you. Before I forget, I took a peek ahead in Olivia's diary. I'll try to read it tonight instead of skimming. Evidently, she went to the library after the honeymoon, and picked up copies of Dickens' *A Tale of Two Cities* and Twain's *Life on the Mississippi*—a book she planned to reread. Remember when you read the Dickens book for a book report in high school?"

"Do I. I think you made me rewrite that report twice. Something about sloppy editing and proofreading. Never could quite put one by you, Grace. Never paid to write it the night before or morning of."

"If my rapidly disintegrating memory serves me right, you

hated that Dickens book. I believe you said something about how ridiculous it was for Sydney Carton to sacrifice his life for true love."

"Yuck. Even now it makes me want to throw up."

Grace shook her head, although TJ couldn't see it. "You were never a romantic, TJ."

She could hear her friend laughing through the phone. "I'm sitting in Emily's driveway, so I have to go. I'll talk to you later."

After removing her winter coat, Grace sat at Emily's kitchen table and watched the coffee drip into the pot. Time to bring up the question of Will and Conrad.

"What do you want to know, exactly?" Emily asked.

"I guess I'm just curious about their relationship over the years. I know you only have Conrad's version before Will and Darlene returned, but what was your take on it all?"

Emily laughed, a low, muffled sound. "Um . . . I liked Will when he first returned to town. I was prepared not to like him from the way Conrad had described him to me. Will was always in trouble in high school—smoking weed and drinking. His grades were quite average, although Conrad said he was way more intelligent than that. I guess Will just didn't care."

"I imagine it did not endear him to Father Folger."

"Not at all." Emily got up and brought the coffeepot over to the table, pouring into each of their cups. "If Conrad had it right, Will and their father had huge arguments about Will's grades and his absences from the house. Conrad always said Will was really arrogant and impossible when he'd been drinking or smoking pot. I guess he had the genetic propensity for addiction. But, still, his father got him into an Ivy League school and pushed him to be a lawyer or go to medical school. Sometimes I think Will's problems stemmed from his father favoring Conrad over him." She thought for a moment. "Maybe things would have been different if Will had simply become the banker instead of Conrad."

Grace finished another bite of her lemon meringue pie. She put her fork down and asked, "So, how did college go for him?"

"As you might imagine, not well. His father could get him into the prestigious school, but he couldn't keep him there. Once in college, Will discovered cocaine. Now this part of the story I know because Will told me. His father pulled him out and paid for a stint in a private rehab facility. To Conrad, he complained bitterly that Will could never do anything right, and he would always be at the mercy of his weaknesses and hedonistic pleasures. I remember the speech by my father-in-law because I had to look up 'hedonistic,' " Emily said, her face reddening.

"Did he finish college?"

"Eventually, but not then. He disappeared one night."

"What? Disappeared?"

"Yes." She wiped her mouth with a napkin and took another sip of coffee before she continued. "No one knew where he was or anything about him for years. They came home, oh, sometime in the early 2000s, maybe 2002 or 2003. He and Darlene, that is. We knew nothing about her until he showed up."

"Amazing. Suddenly, you have a brother-in-law again, as well as a new sister-in-law you didn't know you had."

"Yes. He told us he had gone to Mexico when he left college and almost died of an overdose of bad drugs he'd bought on the street. It changed him. The doctor in the clinic took an interest in his situation and helped him. Eventually, he became stronger as he cleaned out the drugs from his system. I imagine it took a staggering effort." Emily paused, as if thinking what to say next. "When he left Mexico, he decided to search for Darlene, another addict he'd met while he was in rehab during college. He found her, and, fortunately, she was sober too. She already had a job, and he got work to save up and finish college, which he did. But they always scraped for money to pay the bills. Now that I've seen how Darlene spends it, I can understand why. He was determined never to lean on his father or ask him for help. As time went by, his decision caused friction in their marriage, so Darlene suggested they come back here and look up Conrad. By then their father had died, and Will knew he wouldn't have to face him. But he was anxious about Conrad's reception."

"I can't imagine Conrad was all that happy to see his ne'er-do-well brother," Grace said.

Emily took a deep breath. "Actually, I was surprised, Grace. I thought his reaction would be negative. But, you know, his parents had died, and his sister was nowhere to be found. He was an orphan, for all purposes. He saw Will as a companion, a confidant, and someone he could count on, at least at first."

Grace looked up with a puzzled glance. "What do you mean, 'at first'?"

"As time went by," Emily mused, "Will and Darlene's characters became more pronounced. You know, the happy prodigal brother homecoming began to wear thin. First of all, Darlene means well, but she will always be a social climber. Endurance doesn't provide much of a climb, and you saw her schmooze the bank trustees at Conrad's funeral. Disgusting and nauseating." Emily looked down at her hands and seemed to reconsider. "I shouldn't say such things. She means well. I know she volunteers at one of the hospitals in Woodbury. Will, as time went by, still had a drinking problem. He and Conrad would sometimes argue bitterly, especially when Will—or both of them—had had too much to drink."

"I know he has a reputation in town for closing one or two bars."

"Yes. Even I knew that. Conrad gave him the VP job at the bank and figured the responsibility would straighten him out.

241

But I know Conrad. I'm sure he gave Will all the garbage need-ing to be fixed, and no matter what was wrong between the brothers, Darlene always defended her husband. So Conrad didn't spend much time around her. However, I have to admit Will's been kind to me when I needed kindness."

Grace refilled their coffee and then turned and asked, "Em-ily, did you observe anything unusual at young Conrad's birthday party a few weeks ago?"

"Unusual? What do you mean?"

"I had the impression Will was upset at the party. And I've heard from local gossip—not necessarily accurate, of course—that Will was doing decently with the booze until that party. Then he seemed to hit it pretty hard again. Did anything strange happen? Anything that might have set him off?"

Emily thought for a moment. "Nothing really comes to mind." She took her last bite of pie and chewed it slowly as she searched her memory. "Oh, wait. I did notice a rather nasty expression pass between Will and Darlene. Conrad had given his usual rambling speech about how his son was now eleven and soon would head into more responsibility with junior high and high school on the horizon. He declared he planned to send Conrad off to college and have him come back and run the bank for the next generation. As usual, it was Conrad talk-ing crazy about things that might never happen. What if our son didn't want to be a banker? I think after Conrad's long speech, I noticed Will glance at Darlene with some 'I told you so' kind of look. Whatever it was, she briefly shook her head as if to say, 'We'll not discuss this here.' "

"Well," said Grace. "It's something to think about. Will was always the soul of kindness when I had business dealings with him."

Emily considered Grace's remark, paused, and then said quietly, "However, I've seen Will when he's been angry, and I am sure he expected to take over the bank when Conrad retired. Will got a late start in the business, and he believed he could outlast Conrad eventually."

"Quite ambitious of him. Maybe it was the alcohol talking."

"With or without the liquor to give him courage, Will's been quite open about his future at the bank. He just hasn't agreed with Conrad about what it will be."

"And," Grace added, "I hate to think this, but now that Conrad has passed away, if anything happens to you, Will becomes the guardian for the children, including the heir apparent."

"I hadn't thought about it that way. Did it occur to you because of the accident on the road the other night?"

"Possibly. Will doesn't have a great alibi for the time of the accident, and he has a dark SUV. I just don't know how far he'd go."

"I'd like to think not far enough to kill me!" Emily answered, and she chuckled at the thought.

"It might not be as funny as you think, Emily. Someone made sure you would be in my car."

"True," Emily said, and looked out the window, her mood changed.

Grace gave her a moment and then made up her mind. "Say, your children are gone tonight, Lettie is back on her one good foot, and the other one kind of works. She can cook, thank goodness, and she has been slow roasting a turkey all day. Why don't you come over and join us for dinner, say around seven? She's also been watching Eliot Ness, TJ's cat, and she can show you some of the crazy cat tricks she's been teaching him. Eliot keeps Lettie busy, and anything that does that keeps her out of my hair."

Before Emily could answer, the phone rang. She gestured to Grace as if to say, "Hold that thought," and picked up the phone. Grace started to clear the dishes and put them in the dishwasher.

"Oh, hi, Darlene," Emily said. She listened for a long time. "No, I can't. I love Will too, but I can't lie." Then more listening, after which Emily said, "I don't know what you're going to do. I'm sorry. Probably find him a good lawyer would be a start. And Darlene—" She stopped talking and hung the phone up.

"Trouble?"

"Darlene hung up on me. She sounded angry. She says the feds have decided to charge Will with those fraudulent bank loans, and he will go to prison for a long time. And then she said, 'Conrad will get away with this, too'—I suppose she means because he's dead. Then she said, 'He's always gotten away with everything and left Will holding the bag for years.' "

"Oh, my. Did you realize she felt that way?"

Emily shook her head. "No, Grace. I feel really bad for both of them. I wish there were something I could do."

"What did you mean about lying?"

"Oh. She wanted me to lie and say Conrad had forged Will's signature. And then she could bring me some papers showing Conrad had been practicing writing Will's signature. Of course, he hadn't, but she thought it might be a way to get Will out of this serious trouble."

Grace walked over to Emily, who was standing by the sink, her shoulders stooped over and her eyes welling up with tears. She gave her a hug and said, "You are right. You can't lie." She pulled back and looked into Emily's eyes. "If Will's done this, he's going to have to pay the penalty. Maybe it's just my age, but I think parents too often try to get their children out of trouble because they love them, of course. And it usually doesn't come to a good end. Think of those years your father-in-law did that for both Will and Conrad. Eventually, as they say, 'the chickens come home to roost.' "

"I know you're right, Grace, but I still feel bad for Will. Not so much for Darlene," said Emily, and then she laughed, and Grace did too.

"Yes, I've only met Darlene once and she is, as you said, 'a force of nature.' Maybe she'll find a great lawyer and a way to get Will out of this."

"I'll wait for the kids to get home from school and my parents to arrive and take them to Williamsburg. So, I will be at your house by, say, seven tonight, and thank you for the invitation. I'm feeling so much better these days, since I am putting my life back into focus, one step at a time. I still have a hard time making decisions, but it is becoming easier. And you've helped me do that, Grace. Thank you for staying beside me, especially when other people didn't."

Grace hugged Emily again. "No problem. Seven o'clock."

"Yes," said Emily. "See, I will write it on my chalkboard by the phone. '7 p.m. Grace's.' It's part of my new effort at organization. My brain is less fuzzy these days, but I still forget things. See you tonight."

CHAPTER TWENTY-NINE

Only two more months of depressing weather, Grace brooded, and she looked out the window of her bedroom, where dusk was turning on the streetlights. *We're at the end of January and that means it should be possible to suffer through two more months, but survive. The days will start getting longer, and it won't be dark so early. Thaw, freeze, thaw, freeze. This day was a freeze.*

Grace sat on her bed, a pillow behind her back, watching the view out her window. Eliot was curled up on the corner of the afghan, snoozing away. She reached over and pulled Olivia's diary from the end-table drawer, put on her gloves, and planned to resume where she had left off, but as she turned the pages she found her mind wandering to the missing Jeff Maitlin. *Where could he be? And why hasn't he called? I suppose I shouldn't worry. He'll call when he's ready.* She sighed, and looked back down at Olivia's words.

15 November, 1893
We have been back in Endurance for four weeks—the requisite wedding photographs, my parents for dinner, a special ball where I wore my wedding dress, and new "at home" cards. I am well cared for by my personal maid, Jonalyn Heaton, even though it has been strange getting used to someone else performing the offices that will make my life smoother. We do not discuss my bruises, but occasionally I feel her eyes rest upon me as she helps me

dress. The rest of the household runs like a clock due to her husband, Robert, who is the butler and the judge's man, and the housekeeper, Rose Hernshaw. It was difficult at first since they are twice my age, but I believe we will manage. They are well trained and I simply make decisions about menus, dresses, and special occasions. I missed the canning season, when my family and I would be working together over the hot kitchen stove.

I have come to believe this life is all pretense and appearances. The ladies at the social clubs exclaim I have such a generous and well-mannered husband. They do not see the bruises on my arms and on other places I hesitate to name, or worse, the bruises on my heart. My husband still confuses me with his strange behavior. He says he wants children, yet he is so violent about that aspect of our lives. After he has lost his temper and hurt me, he sends me flowers or buys me a bauble to wear. I no longer have tears for the pain.

One of my old girlfriends, from when I first came here, is officially betrothed. I feel as if it is a death sentence. But no one warns a woman before she signs the papers and is locked in marriage. No one warned me. This life is so different from that of my parents. Often I wonder why.

I look in the mirror in my bathing room and can already see my loss of weight. Because I do not sleep well, I have dark circles under my eyes. Yesterday, I found the courage to ask Jonalyn if the judge also hurt his first wife. I would not have dared to ask that question of her when I was first married, but we have become closer since she attends to my needs. As my question hung in the air, I noticed a dark look come over her face. Then quickly it disappeared. She only spoke in vague terms about his treatment of his first wife, Jane, but it is enough. She whispered, "He did not know yet she was with child." I did not know what to say.

My parents will be here for a Christmas Open House. I must look better, more rested, by then.

I went to the library today for the first time since we returned from Chicago, and Mr. Beasley, the librarian, did not recognize me in my thinner version. I have brought home Mr. Dickens's *A Tale of Two Cities* and Mr. Twain's *Life on the Mississippi*. I plan to reread Mr. Twain's book—perhaps it will cheer me up. On the other hand, it may remind me of the first time I read it, just prior to my life changing forever. I wonder if I will laugh as hard at Mr. Twain's antics. Mr. Quinn was at the library, and we conversed briefly. Now that I am a married woman, he is cordial, but distant. I could tell from his facial expression that he is concerned. Do I really look so changed?

I am pleased I have my journal, for this is the best gift my mother could have given me. Sometimes she does not seem so far away when I write. I cannot tell my aunt about my life. After all, I made the decision to marry.

Today I asked Mr. Heaton for tools to fix a buckle on one of my slippers. He offered to help, but I explained that I worked with my brothers on leather goods for the horses. Then I used his tools to pry open a loose floorboard in my bedroom and found a small area in which to hide my journal. Sometimes I wonder if the servants can hear my husband's anger or see my tears. If they can, they do not mention their thoughts. At times I despair when I consider how long this life may be.

Grace closed the diary and thought about the connection she felt with Olivia. She admired her for not complaining about the horrifying situation she was in. In the 1800s, she had no help. Once married, she was in "wedlock." No getting out of it as easily as it happens today.

Perhaps she will find an ally in her personal maid, Jonalyn. It seems as if they are becoming close despite their class distinctions. After all, Olivia was never raised to be an upper-class woman. So much of what she has written about her husband is similar to what I have heard from Emily—over a century apart but experiencing the same symptoms of abuse by their husbands. I guess I'll never know why the judge felt as if he needed to hurt his wives, but, of course, he was a powerful man back then. And often with power comes the feeling you can do anything and get away with it. *How many times have we seen that in this time period?* Grace thought.

How bittersweet that she had met Tyler again, but Endurance was a small town. Yet she never looked back with regret, nor did she pity herself. At least she didn't write about it. Perhaps Emily would find the strength, too, to become a woman who could handle whatever life handed her.

Now Grace knew how the diary came to be in the upstairs bedroom. Jeff said they had enlarged the front bedroom, knocking down a wall to make it a one-room walk-up. It made sense that the diary was found in the north part of the room where Olivia's room would have been.

Too bad Olivia didn't know in a few more months she would no longer have to endure this terrible punishment. That knowledge might have made it easier to get through her long winter and spring.

Grace suddenly remembered Sam had written some thoughts about the town's reactions to the judge's death near the end of his book. The judge's death was still a mystery to be sorted out. Sam's book was sitting on her nightstand, and she picked it up and read the pages where she'd left her bookmark.

Editorial from the *Woodbury Sentinel,* May 25, 1894: "In discussing the untimely death of Judge Charles Lockwood, two theories are prevalent in the community of Endurance. First, his wife poisoned him because of his dalliances outside the marital bond or his treatment of said wife. Speculation is rampant that she was often ill-used by her husband. Within the bonds of matrimony, the wife vows to be obedient. Scripture regards this as a solemn vow, and civil authority considers the role of the husband to be guardian and teacher of his wife, guiding her in the proper path. If this guidance is firm and occasionally harsh, it is still his proper role within wedlock. The second theory prevalent in the community is that of revenge. A released prisoner, upon whom the judge has passed sentence, returned and caused the judge's untimely demise. This editor will take no stand on either theory, but he has observed when wives are left to their own devices and they stray from their appointed tasks, it is an ill wind that blows for the future of the marital bond."

Amazing, thought Grace. *This* Woodbury Sentinel *editor isn't much different from the current idiot. So much for not taking sides. How interesting he totally ignored the "dalliances outside the marital bond" theory.*

Grace glanced down the page and stopped on a diary entry from Rebecca Lynn Hampton, an Endurance resident writing on May 27, 1894. "The Garden Club was all aflutter with highly charged words concerning the death of our member's husband, Judge Charles Lockwood. Mrs. Lockwood is in deep mourning and so did not attend as she observes the customary two years. However, much discussion ensued concerning the confounding and precipitate passing of her husband, the judge. He seemed to be of hardy and salubrious disposition. The cause of his demise is being debated in whispers through many quarters of the community."

The mystery deepens. I wonder if Olivia even knew how her husband died. Back then people often died of food poisoning after lingering for days. I imagine medicine was practiced in a rather primitive fashion, so his death could have been from some kind of illness that had been present all along and no one knew it.

Grace closed Sam's book. She was reaching the end with no answers to the mystery because Sam had no answer to explain. She put Olivia's diary back in her nightstand, maintaining the thought that she didn't really want it to end. She would save the last few entries for later.

She stretched her arms and noticed how dark it was getting outside. She smelled the succulent fragrance of Lettie's turkey wafting up from the kitchen, and her stomach recognized the familiar hunger for Lettie's cooking. *Oh, how wonderful it is to have my cook back,* she thought. The clock next to her bed said 6:15. *Geez, I have to get up and help Lettie with the last-minute stuff.* She smoothed out her slacks, peeked in the mirror at her hair, and headed down to the kitchen. Eliot Ness woke up immediately and followed her, almost causing her to trip over him on the stairway landing. She reached down, picked him up, and stroked his luxurious fur. "Poor Eliot. Has Lettie been mistreating you with all these silly tricks she teaches you?" Carrying the cat with her down the rest of the staircase, she looked at the dark fireplace in the living room and thought they could use a warm, glowing fire. She would start that first.

A couple of hours later, they'd finished Lettie's turkey, mashed potatoes and gravy, dressing, and green beans, and they were still talking in the dining room. Emily had brought a bottle of wine, and they sipped it while they discussed Conrad and Caitlin's progress in adjusting to a one-parent home and going to school again.

"So, what will your next act be?" Lettie asked, looking directly at Emily Folger.

"Next act?"

"Well, you know. Grace works at the newspaper, and I

continue to feed her, give some love to TJ's cat, and"—Lettie's voice grew deeper and she closed her eyes—"bask in a fiery and passionate romance." She put her napkin down on the table and added, "And Grace hasn't considered the future implications of that yet."

Grace looked up at Lettie's smug face. "I think you're a little off the track with your question for Emily," Grace said, and she raised one eyebrow, adding a silent "checkmate" in her head.

"I am just giving some expert examples. So, Emily, what do you plan to do with your time now since you have—well, some control over your own life?"

Emily looked at both Grace and Lettie and pursed her lips. "A good question. I haven't really considered. I still see a therapist, and I need more self-confidence. But I'm better."

"I don't think Emily is quite ready to—"

"Nonsense," Lettie said. "Of course she is. She's young, nice looking—and I like your new haircut, Emily."

"If you're hinting I might need to find another Del Novak somewhere," Emily said, "I don't think that's on my agenda, at least not for a while. But now I feel I have a future." She took a deep breath.

Grace stood up. She thought she might smooth the bluntness of Lettie's questions by redirecting the conversation. "I, for one, am out to get more wine. Anyone else?"

"Sure," said Emily.

When Grace reached the kitchen, Eliot was in the far corner lapping water loudly from his bowl. He followed her back to the dining room, yearning for someone to drop an edible tidbit on the floor.

"I know," Grace said. "You've missed Lettie's cooking too." Trying not to trip on Eliot, Grace sat back down at the table.

In that moment they heard a deafening pounding on the front door, and Eliot once again took off, this time to scramble under the dining-room table next to Lettie's leg. Grace looked at Lettie and said, "What the heck?"

"Beats me," said Lettie. "Obviously, I need to give the cat some lessons in how to guard the house. He didn't give a hint of arriving visitors. I know you said TJ might drop over for dessert and a glass of wine, but she wouldn't beat on the front door. Besides, she always arrives through the kitchen, and I left the light on for her back there."

Grace uncrossed her legs in jerky movements, reacting to the unnerving noise from the front of the house. She moved through the hallway listening for more signs of noise. Her muscles tensed as she reached the front foyer. It was completely dark now outside, only a bit of light shining from the street lamp. She flipped the light switch for the porch lights and saw the familiar face of Darlene Folger through the small window in the upper panel of the door. Breathing a sigh of relief, Grace unlocked the door and pulled it open.

A wool-shrouded apparition, Darlene Folger, stood in the light with a gun in her hand pointed directly at Grace.

CHAPTER THIRTY

TJ Sweeney listened to U2 as she worked in her office. Several darts stuck soundly to her wall calendar, fodder for her thinking process. Her whiteboard, filled with numerous names, motives, and alibis, kept her sagging calendar company. This was all part of the detective's mode of operation for processing a crime. In this case, Conrad Folger's murder details stared at her. Then Myers, the desk sergeant, opened her door, coughed, and dropped some papers on her desk.

"Crime lab info just came in on a fax, TJ," he said, and then he disappeared, silently shutting her door.

She examined the crime scene photos from the banker's murder, and then she opened her desk drawer and took out a magnifying glass. *No, I will not admit to Grace that I use this,* she thought. *I'll never hear the end of it. Grace will never, never, know. Never.* She studied the photos, turning them this way and that, and after she'd reviewed all fifteen of them, she stacked them once again at the corner of her desk and began to look at the itemized evidence list. Sometimes it helped to go over these several times so her subconscious would process the details her conscious mind missed. She checked items off the evidence list with a pencil, leaving the circled ones she wanted to think about and try to connect—dirt, glass, blood, sedatives and water, torn nightgown, the unfired Glock, pieces of thread or yarn, some torn pages from a book, tissues, broken eyeglasses, and some minor details that seemed insignificant. After fifteen minutes, she had settled on only a handful of details that might be relevant.

Then she remembered the faxes. Turning them over and reading each one, she realized she knew the owner of the potting soil left at the scene and on Conrad Folger. She stared again at the list of items and sat back in her chair. Her heart raced, and she got that fluttery feeling of intuition in her belly. "Well, I'll be damned. It was there all the time, and I didn't see it." She dropped her pencil on the list, pushed her chair back from the desk, and put her hands on her cheeks, her breath coming faster and her fingers pressing on her face. "Yes, Grace, I did hate that book, but at least I remember it—and Madame Defarge. It was Madame Defarge all along." Suddenly, she rose from her chair, left her office, and found Myers.

"Get Jake Williams in here, ASAP. Tell him it's an emergency."

"Sure," Myers said. "Uh. Why?"

She grabbed his arm. "Never mind the why. Just get him here!"

"Yes, ma'am." The desk sergeant hurriedly punched numbers on his phone while TJ charged back to her office. She pulled her gun out of her drawer, grabbed an extra cartridge, and was out the door. "Tell him I'll wait in my car out back," she yelled to Myers. "Meanwhile, get on the computer and give me a couple of license plates from the DMV for Will and Darlene Folger. And call in whoever we've got as backup. We'll be at Will Folger's house."

"Yeah. Got it, and Jake'll be here in ten."

"Good."

Williams was actually a minute early. "What's up? I've got the license plate numbers from Myers."

TJ turned the heat up to counteract the car door opening. "It's an interesting story, Jake. Ever read Charles Dickens's *A Tale of Two Cities*?"

"Sounds familiar. High school?"

"Yeah." She began to turn the car around.

"I think I read the Cliffs Notes. Why are you asking me this?"

" 'Cause I missed it, and I could kick myself. Remember Madame Defarge?"

"No."

"Next time you need to read the whole book, Jake. She was the owner of a wine shop during the French Revolution, and she was bitter about the past and her poverty. She was a ruthless, unmerciful monster, like Conrad Folger's murderer, and she was organized and calculating. During the beheading of aristocrats, her knitting recorded the destruction of their lives and families—class warfare against the wealthy." She put the car in forward gear and coasted silently out of the parking lot behind the station.

"Seriously? A literature lesson?"

"I was taught by the best, Jakie."

Williams's eyes narrowed and he gave her a blank look. "I don't follow, TJ. What does this have to do with Conrad Folger?"

"It was his sister-in-law, Darlene. Like Madame Defarge, she's often called 'a force of nature' by Grace and Emily Folger. She did it. Madame Defarge sat and knitted the story of the beheading of aristocrats as she watched them die. We found yarn at the murder scene and Darlene was knitting that night. She must have caught some loose yarn on her clothes. We have to get to her house. Fastest way is down Primrose Street to Seventh Avenue. A few minutes and we'll be there."

She continued to explain to Jake while she drove down Main Street and east toward Primrose. As they rolled past Sweetbriar Court, TJ glanced down at her house and saw Emily Folger's car parked on the street. Then she pulled in her breath and felt her back stiffen. She saw another car—a black SUV parked directly in Grace's driveway. She hit the brakes—almost sliding off the street—and her heart began to race as adrenaline surged through her veins.

"She's at Grace's. Got those two license plates? Bring them and your gun and ammo. This could be ugly. I don't know how far ahead of us Darlene is. Let's hope we can talk some sense into her if it isn't too late. Call Myers and send backup here. 1036 Sweetbriar Court. Tell them to come in lights off."

While Jake got on the radio, TJ reversed the car carefully, shut off her headlights, and crept quietly into Sweetbriar Court.

"And I was so looking forward to a glass of wine and a piece of Lettie's pie," she whispered.

Jake touched her shoulder. "You'll still have them, but first it may take a little more work than we figured."

CHAPTER THIRTY-ONE

"Time to invite me in for dinner, Grace," Darlene said in a quiet, restrained voice. She smiled. "Lead the way."

"Darlene. I don't understand."

"Move, Grace," Darlene said more emphatically, and she turned Grace around and pushed the gun barrel into her back. Grace walked back toward the dining room, and she heard the front door close behind her and footsteps follow her. *How to call 9-1-1 and get TJ over here sooner,* she thought, and she walked as slowly as possible. They reached the dining room and Emily saw them first. She stood up as if to come over to Darlene, her sister-in-law, but then she saw the looks on Grace's and Darlene's faces, so she stopped and sat down again. Lettie sat across from Emily, her back to the hallway, but when she saw the look on Emily's face, she turned in her chair, almost knocking over the crutches she had leaned on the table edge.

"Hi, Darlene," said Lettie, attempting to be pleasant. Grace moved toward the side, and Lettie and Emily could see the gun in Darlene's hand. "Darlene! What the heck?"

"Shut up, Lettisha," said Darlene, a snarl in her voice. "Your gossiping days are over tonight, you bantering bitch."

"Hmm. I like the alliteration," Lettie said thoughtfully. Then she remembered the gun. "Now you see here—" Lettie started, but Darlene pushed the gun forward in a menacing way, and Lettie didn't finish her sentence.

"What are you doing, Darlene?" Emily said.

"You can shut up, too, my soon-to-be-dead sister-in-law."
She pushed Grace forward, toward her chair. "Dear Grace, why
couldn't you just leave it alone? Now you force me to kill you
and Emily, plus this busybody."

Lettie started to rise, grabbing her crutches as if to run away,
but Darlene waved the gun at her and she sat back down. Grace
looked at Darlene's crazed eyes and wild hair, touched in spots
by snowflakes. *It must have been snowing sporadically,* she thought,
and then wondered why she was worried about the weather.
How can I slow her down, maybe play for time so TJ will show up?

Lettie said, "Why don't you take off your coat, Darlene, and
have some pie and coffee with us? We have more than enough,
and you can do your killing on a full stomach."

Grace rolled her eyes at Emily, and Darlene prodded her to
sit down at the head of the table, a safe spot when she had left
it a few minutes ago.

"Darlene! Why?" asked Emily, her voice pleading on the last
notes.

Darlene's voice segued into sarcasm. "Oh, Emily, you sweet
thing. Can't you figure out why? No, you always were the naïve,
little, small-town girl, so eager to please Conrad and so stupid
about your own existence. In fact, so stupid you wrote down
where you'd be tonight right next to your phone."

"Darlene, please, if you'd just—"

"You should be happy I killed Conrad, Emily. And it was so
easy. The alarm system was a piece of cake. Gloves on the
outside, and a small lever to reset it on the inside. It meant only
Conrad's prints were left on the inside security pad, since he
wasn't so drunk he left the house without an alarm on. Last
thing he told me in a drunken slur was that he'd set it."

Grace thought, *Maybe if we appeal to how smart her plan was
we can keep her talking.* She glanced over at Emily, catching her
eye. Then she turned toward Darlene.

"Darlene, you had me fooled. I figured it might have been Will."

"Will?" Darlene's face changed again, this time into a look of disdain. "How could Will pull something like this off? It was always, 'Yes, Conrad,' and 'No, Conrad.' He thought if he waited he could get the bank." She stopped and thought for a moment. "Actually, for a while we both thought that. But no, Emily, your little brat will get it all. Conrad made it very clear at our beloved nephew's birthday party. And that was it, Emily, the point where I knew I would have to take the plans in my hands, step-by-step, and execute the details. Will was too wasted most of the time to keep a clear head."

Grace looked at Lettie from the corner of her eye, and she could see her sister-in-law look down at her crutches, sitting next to her chair and right in front of Darlene. Lettie's back had been toward Darlene in the doorway, but now she swiveled in her chair so she could see the ghostly apparition.

"Tell us this perfect plan," Grace said, and she tried to keep her voice from wobbling. "I bet I can poke holes in it. What have you got to lose? You're going to kill us anyway."

Darlene moved a little closer to the table, and Grace saw her hand wavered not a bit.

She smiled and said, "Sure, Grace. After all, no one will miss a sniveling schoolteacher, a small-town nobody." Her voice became more matter-of-fact, and her face visibly relaxed. "I waited, you know, for Will to fall asleep that night. As always—an alcoholic stupor. Ever since we came back here, Emily and Conrad have lorded over him, and Conrad made sure Will had every menial job he could find for him. How many nights did I watch him drink himself into oblivion because he knew how smart he was, but he was stuck under Conrad's thumb—Conrad, a man who was so stupid he had to constantly ask Will about any issue that came up at the bank."

"But Darlene—"

"Didn't I say 'shut up,' Emily? Don't you want to hear the details you slept through or not?"

"I don't think—"

"Again, just shut your mouth. And you're right. You don't think. Otherwise, you'd have grabbed those kids and left Conrad long ago. Now, where was I? See, Emily, what happens when you interrupt me?"

She stared straight at Emily, while Grace watched Lettie and then looked down at her phone on the table. Lettie suddenly smiled. *Fortunately, Darlene couldn't see her smile,* thought Grace.

"And how did Conrad repay Will? He put him in prison, probably for the rest of his life. And you, Emily. You could have gotten him out of that fate. But you're too selfish and self-centered to do it. So you destroy my only hope of happiness, you selfish bitch."

"Darlene, how could I destroy Conrad's reputation by swearing he forged those papers?"

Suddenly, Darlene threw her head back and let out a huge laugh. Then she suddenly became calm again, looked at Emily, and said in slow, measured tones, "Why should you worry about the reputation of a man who constantly beat you and told you how stupid you are? You should be glad I killed him. You could have had some kind of wonderful life after his death. But now you won't live to see that. You were too much of a wimp to do what had to be done, but at least you can take the blame for this debacle. Who wouldn't believe you went crazy and killed Grace and busybody here?"

"How did you manufacture Emily's prints on the murder weapon, Darlene?" Grace pushed, hoping to bring her back to a less hysterical, more rational state.

"Ha! The glass and fingerprints were easy. I knew Emily took sleeping pills, which zonked her out. No reason she'd wake up.

I had gloves on, but she was out like a light, and I simply walked into her bedroom, put the glass piece in her hand, and held the edge of it before I took it back to Conrad's room. Perfect. And I planned. Oh, so carefully. I wore a plastic raincoat the blood would slide down, and disposed of the coat in Woodbury. Booties from the hospital where I work kept the bloody prints from any shoes showing up. I carefully put them on after killing him. Of course, they're gone too. Disposed of."

"But Darlene," Emily said. "You'll never have Will again. He'll go to prison for a long time."

"Not if I can help it. With you gone, Emily, and you, too, Grace, no one will know Will is guilty because I'll use the story I already made up. Conrad forged Will's signatures on those loans, and I can make up a paper where he practiced."

Grace felt a furry ball sit on her foot and rub against her leg. Eliot was under the table. She remembered she had her phone within a hand's-length on the table. Maybe she could sneak it down to her lap while Darlene was enthralled in her own story.

"What about us?" Lettie asked, directing Darlene's attention to her instead of Grace or Emily. "How will you explain our deaths?"

"Easy," Darlene said. "Emily went crazy, and she shot both of you and then herself. I can make it look like that. She was in despair because of her husband's death, and you tried to stop her, but she shot you and Grace in the struggle. Then, of course, she'll shoot herself. Too bad the kids aren't here tonight. I'll have to dispose of them down the road." She stopped a moment and caught her breath. Then she began to laugh again, first quietly, and then more shrilly. "At least you can all three go together!"

Grace had slipped her phone onto her lap during Darlene's monologue, and she looked at Lettie. Lettie caught Grace's stare and struggled to rise and say, "Darlene, you don't want to do this—"

Then all hell broke loose. Grace tapped Myers's ringtone from her list, the "Stayin' Alive" ringtone came on, and Eliot jumped out toward Darlene and began chasing his tail in a circle as Darlene—startled—screamed and moved backward. Lettie raised her crutch and smashed Darlene's arm, and the stunned woman dropped her gun, but it discharged once when Lettie's crutch hit it. Suddenly, the swinging door into the kitchen flew open, and TJ rushed in, her gun leveled at Darlene.

"It's over," TJ said, as Jake Williams and two other officers followed her in from the kitchen, and one kicked Darlene's gun out of reach.

"Nope, not over—not by a long shot, or a short shot," said Lettie grimly. Grace Kimball lay on the floor in a spreading pool of blood.

Chapter Thirty-Two

"Grace, we have to stop meeting in the ER."

Grace Kimball looked at TJ standing in the doorway of the ER patient room. She started laughing and so did Emily, who was sitting on a chair while the doctor wrapped Grace's arm. "Not so bad this time, TJ. Just a flesh wound, bleeding but no damage to nerves. I was lucky. When Lettie hit the gun with her crutch, it spun Darlene in my direction."

"Otherwise, she would have shot me," Emily said. "So thanks, Grace, for taking the bullet."

"And do you know where the other witness to the crime is?" TJ said.

"Lettie?" said Grace. "Well, no. They brought me in here by ambulance, so I don't know what you and the police have been doing . . . probably making a huge mess in my house. I'll bet Lettie is right on top of them, too, giving directions about what the police can and can't do."

"I'm sure she would be yelling at them. Actually, by now she's at her house holding Eliot and petting him because he's traumatized. She called Del to come over and help."

"How did you know, TJ?" asked Emily.

"Know to come to Grace's house?"

"Yes."

"We weren't going to Sweetbriar Court. Actually, we were heading to Darlene's house, and I happened to look down the court as we passed and saw Darlene's car."

"How did you figure out it was Darlene?" Grace asked.

"Yarn."

"Yarn?"

TJ looked at Grace and laughed. "It's your fault. You forced me to read *A Tale of Two Cities* in high school. Remember Madame Defarge? The night of Conrad's death, Darlene knit in the family room while she waited for the poker game to end. The yarn—which I thought might have come from the killer brushing up against a sweater, was in the list of trace evidence. I remembered you mentioned to me, Grace, that Jeff said Darlene had stayed that evening. I imagine when we check her house we'll find the yarn and it will be a match. A small piece of it was evidently on her clothes. Then the potting soil cinched it. Her house has been on the garden walk in the summer, and she has a shed full of gardening equipment. She just happened to have left the potting soil in the shed, but I believe she disposed of the gardening gloves she used. When she killed Conrad, some of the soil from her gardening gloves came off on the bed. It's a match," TJ said. "Oh, and by the way, just before I took her to the public safety office, Darlene admitted to running you two off the road and sending Grace the warning letter. She also broke into your house, Grace, to scare you."

"I find it so hard to believe," Emily said. "Now Will may end up in prison and so will Darlene—the last adults, except for Jessalynn and me, in the Folger families."

"Sure looks that way," TJ said. "Maybe you can have a clean start with Caitlin and Conrad. I suppose the bank will pass into different hands. The board of directors will elect someone. What an amazing end to a four-generation history with the bank and the town."

"Well, that should do it, young lady," said the doctor. "I think, just to be safe, you should take a course of antibiotics. Here's the prescription, and also I'm sending some pain pills with you.

Otherwise, just get a lot of rest and let the stitches heal up in your arm."

The weary women walked out of the ER arm in arm—one a cop, one a retired teacher, and one a healing abuse victim. TJ took them back to Grace's, and Emily headed home.

Later that evening in Grace's living room, TJ stoked the fire and made sure the flames burned brightly. The remaining police had left, and most of the mess was cleaned up.

TJ sat back down and took a sip of wine. "It's pretty ironic when you think about it."

"Think about what?"

"Darlene. Here she thought if she murdered Conrad she'd advance her husband's career. Instead, Folger's murder kicked off an investigation into his finances, which led to the discovery of the kickbacks. Darlene claims she didn't know about the money they were getting under the table so, essentially, she ended up putting her own husband in prison and herself too." TJ looked at the flames burning brightly and shook her head. "Amazing."

"Greed and envy. They'll get you every time." Grace paused. "I think I can see now how Emily might have fallen into the trap of abuse. It makes sense, especially as I read Olivia Havelock's diary. She had no protection from abuse back then. Even today, it's hard to escape from that cycle of self-doubt and fear you'll die."

"At the risk of sounding like a textbook, Grace, the women who leave battering partners are seventy-five percent more likely to be murdered than those who stay. And that murder usually happens about the time the woman tries to leave. Unlike those women who left, Emily is at least lucky in a sense because Conrad's death took away his possibility of killing her or even stalking her."

"I don't think Olivia Havelock ever had a peaceful day once her husband began abusing her. The laws, courts, and police departments were run by men. Women's shelters didn't exist."

"So true. Today we have the Violence Against Women Act, and it does give some protections. But it's still tough. I think the last statistic I read was that women who stay in a shelter have a fifty-fifty chance of getting permanently away from their abusers."

They were both silent for several minutes. Then Grace said, "Emily is a stronger person now than she was just a month ago. With the support of her parents and the help of her children, she'll be able to make a life for herself. She won't ever be the woman she was, but she will be stronger."

"I agree," said TJ. "And she has the financial resources, along with the family support. Most abuse victims don't have that."

The logs in the fireplace moved and the fire crackled. Both TJ and Grace sank back a little deeper into their chairs, and Grace took a long, deep breath.

TJ felt the warm glow from the wine. "You know, Grace, this will never end."

"What will never end?"

"Me pulling you out of catastrophes of your own making."

"What do you mean, 'of my own making'? Sounds rather accusatory."

TJ shook her head slowly. "You are sitting here with your arm bandaged up, and you just got over a concussion."

"So? What's your point?" Grace said, a tiny smile on her face.

"It's just second nature to you. You've never met a stray kitten, dog, or former student you didn't believe in."

"So?"

"Well, I was just thinking. It doesn't look good. How many students do you suppose you've had over twenty-five years?"

Grace counted in her head. "Hmmm. Maybe between twenty-five hundred and three thousand."

"I don't think my career will cover them all. I rest my case."

The two friends watched a log move and sparks fly up the chimney. Then, after seeing Grace wince, TJ said, "I don't suppose you're going to take one of those pain pills."

"You know how I hate to take pills."

"Yeah. I figured. Here, let me pour you some more wine. So, what are you going to do about the diary you found from— what's-her-name? Olive?"

"Olivia. I will show it to Sam and let him read it, and then I will try to trace whether she had any children or grandchildren. If she had any descendants, they should have it."

"And how did it end? Happily ever after, as in a fairy tale?"

"I'm going to read the end tonight. Stay tuned." She paused and then added a thought. "You know, if Jeff hadn't bought Lockwood House and asked me to research it, I wouldn't have learned so much about domestic abuse. And it will enable me to keep helping Emily. The house has such a sad past, but maybe Jeff can turn it around. It looks so dark and gloomy now, but with the right restoration he can turn it into something special. Maybe that will banish the mysteries and remove the presence of whatever unhappy ghosts still haunt it."

They stared into the fire, a comfortable warmth filling the room.

"And what about Jeff Maitlin?" TJ said, breaking the silence.

"Oh, he'll show up again. I'm sure. He said he'd be back and he will be. The only question is when, and whether or not the demons that pulled him away have been destroyed. I haven't a clue what his business is, but I think it must be about his past— just like everything else."

"Will you tell him you've been shot?"

"Are you kidding?" Grace paused. "If things get serious, he may want to check on my medical and life insurance before he makes a commitment," she said.

"You know, Grace, you've lived an unusually exciting life for a retired English teacher in a small town in the boring Midwest."

"You think?"

"You've been tied up and almost died, threatened, run off the road, and shot. I'm a homicide detective and my life isn't even close to that dangerous."

"Maybe I should write a book."

"I think it sounds more like what a small-town, retired English teacher in the Midwest would do."

"Well, that settles it. I can't do that. I'd hate to give people what they expect."

CHAPTER THIRTY-THREE

Grace walked TJ to the door and watched her slip and slide across the icy street to her house. She smiled as she heard her swear a few times, attempting to stay on her feet. Then she went back to her sofa in front of the fire and thought about the events of the past month. Was it only a month? It seemed like years. She took a sip of her wine and looked at the bandage on her arm. Her arm was sore, and the local anesthetic was wearing off, but she had felt worse. Tonight she should sleep well, knowing Emily and her children were safe, and Darlene was behind bars where she couldn't hurt anyone else.

And then there was Lettie to consider. She would be losing her crutches tomorrow and have some kind of walking hardware so she could get around better. And although she was at her own house tonight, she planned to be back tomorrow with Eliot in tow. *TJ has probably lost her cat,* Grace thought. Lettie will be telling her "legion" that she and Eliot Ness were the heroes of the day, and, in fact, they were. This time, Grace had to give Lettie credit. But she wasn't sure it was going to make her sister-in-law any easier to be around. *And what if she and Del Novak become an item? And what if they marry? Arghh! What will I do for a cook?*

She stared into the fireplace, and the flames burned down to embers. From there, her mind wandered to the Will Folger family and how avarice and envy changed their lives forever. On the other hand, what might Will's life have been like if his father hadn't favored one son over the other? It was an age-old story, wasn't it?

And Conrad. She remembered looking at the pictures in his bank office—was that only a month ago?—and thinking about the generations of despair on the faces of the women in those families. She sighed. There were better laws these days to help abused spouses, but what good was an order of protection if a former spouse could stalk his victim and kill her? The prisons were filled with victims who murdered their abusers. *I must remember,* Grace thought, *that men are abused too. But I think the statistics of victims weigh heavily in the female direction.* Emily would most likely still be in the cycle of abuse if Darlene hadn't killed her husband. *And she is working so hard to get better and take care of her children.*

Darlene as Madame Defarge? Grace had thought of her more as Lady Macbeth—but she was a little more sanitary about the blood spatter. *Hmmm . . . she had the ambition and the weak husband.*

Well, it's about time to go to bed and hope for sleep with this bandage on my arm and a bit of pain. She paused for a moment with her thoughts, and then she started to cry. She didn't know if it was the close calls of almost losing her life lately—in a ditch on the road, or in her own dining room from a gun—but it finally all came too close to home. She grabbed a box of tissues and just let it all out, everything, from the threats to Emily and herself, to the departure of Jeff Maitlin. It was all too much to take in, and she knew she needed to sleep. Finally, her waterlogged eyes began to slow, and the flood turned into sniffles, and she knew she would be able to go on.

Damn that Jeff Maitlin, she thought, in a rare instance of swearing. *How could he leave me at a time like this? And why does he never call to let me know he's all right?* She glanced at her phone, checked to see if she'd missed any calls while she was at the ER, and laid it back down on the table. *Well, that's it.* The fire was down to ashes, and she walked over to make sure the fire screen was safely in place. Then she turned off lights throughout the house, especially the front porch, double-checked the locks on the doors, and went to the kitchen for a glass of water to take upstairs. She took one last look around the living room and had just put her foot on the first step, when she heard the ringtone go off on her phone.

"A New York State of Mind."

Suddenly all the anger of the evening disappeared, and she turned and walked back over to the sofa and stared at her phone. His picture smiled up at her, and she couldn't help but smile back. She studied her phone display with the "Accept" and "Decline" buttons. *Let's see. Which one should I choose?* Then, she quickly tapped her screen.

EPILOGUE

25 April, 1894

The spring is upon us and it gives one reason to hope. But that is difficult for my own life. The judge sent me to Dr. Brown to make a determination of why I have not conceived. The physician looked at me with concern, but did not inquire about the bruises on my back. He can find nothing wrong with my ability to bear children, so perhaps I should be thankful fate has kept me from bringing a child into this miserable existence.

My parents were here at Christmas and my mother asked if I were happy. I had to think quickly and invent a disingenuous answer for my current state. I could not tell her the truth. If she could see me now, she would take me in her arms and flee from this house. I have lost so much weight, and now I have spent little time outside the house because the judge prefers I not speak with my friends—at least the ones I had last year. Aunt Maud has not returned my inquiries. I believe that she would, so I now wonder if she even got my messages.

The last time I went riding was in March when it was still cold. But today I decided to ride, so I slipped out and Lily and I went to my old, favorite haunt. Sometimes I think about simply running away like Jane Eyre, but I know the judge would find me.

While I rested from my ride, I heard another horse approaching. It was Mr. Quinn. Somehow he knew I was on my favorite hillside ride once again. We spoke of many things, but I could not find the inner strength to tell him of my plight. After all, I agreed to this marriage. He looked at me with concern, took my hands, and told me he had never stopped loving me.

So, my diary, I can never go back there again. My husband might kill him, and I believe he has friends who could make Mr. Quinn disappear forever. I have no hope and no one to help me. How different my life would be if I had waited for Mr. Quinn to make his way in the world.

30 April, 1894

I have not had the strength to write in my diary since the judge found out Mr. Quinn was talking to me on my ride. I do not know who told him, but I believe he has eyes and ears everywhere. That evening he consumed a great deal of brandy and began to make remarks that caused me to believe he knew about Mr. Quinn. Afterward, it took me four days to rise from my bed. Jonalyn has attended to me and worried about me since I was not conscious for the first day. She told me he forbade her to send for a doctor. I fear the judge may kill me the next time he becomes angry. By then, perhaps, I shall not care.

Several days later, Jonalyn came to my room before dinner was announced. She said the judge wanted me to appear at the table instead of taking sustenance in my room. I bathed with Jonalyn's help and dressed for dinner. Then she had me sit down on my bed, and she told me I must claim not to feel well—that will not be difficult—and eat nothing of the beef and mushroom gravy that she is preparing for dinner. When I asked her why, she simply said I must do so and ask no questions. The judge loves morel mushrooms, and this is the time of year they grow wild in the forests. Jonalyn was out all morning collecting them.

I did as she asked. I had difficulty walking down the stairs, but I somehow managed to reach the dining room and have dinner with my husband, who was looking hale and hearty. How ironic that he who should be so evil to me and to his first wife should look so happy and contented with his own life. Mrs. Hernshaw went to see an ailing sister this week, so Jonalyn had prepared our dinner.

As I watched him eat his food and ask for seconds, I could only guess what kind of morels were in the gravy— the kind my mother warned me about. She found them near fallen logs, and showed me when you cut a good morel in half, the inside is hollow. But the morels beside the fallen logs in the forest are often filled with toxin, and the inside is a dense filling unsafe for the human anatomy. The judge inquired about my lack of appetite, and I explained that I did not feel well and so would take a little tea and soup. "All the more for me," he exclaimed, and put another helping on his plate.

I ask God's forgiveness and will do so every day of my life, just as I will ask a blessing on Jonalyn Heaton. As I watched my husband's gluttonous nature compel him to ravish two plates of roast beef and mushrooms, I knew in a few weeks I would be free of this locked prison.

23 May, 1894

This will be my last entry in my journal, and then I will hide it away in this house which I will leave forever. Perhaps someday, long after I am gone, another human hand will find this book. But it is more likely the house will perish in the future—as all material goods must end—and my thoughts and longings will go with it.

Over the past two weeks I have remained by my husband's side—appearances and pretenses—so all of

Endurance believes me to be the grieving wife. The judge was quite healthy for a week or so, and then the toxins began to destroy his stomach. It commenced with vomiting and stomach pain, which led to seizures, a coma, and, finally, death. Dr. Brown attended him daily, but could find no reason for his sudden decline. He dosed him with medicine, but it had no effect. And finally, three days ago, my husband, the judge, went to meet the Judge we shall all face. While I know I should not condemn, I believe my husband must have found that a most distressing meeting.

The judge's will was read two days ago, and, as I am the only surviving relative, I will inherit a vast fortune. Each of the servants will also receive a stipend. This has caused me to make many decisions. I have found new employment for Mrs. Hernshaw and the Heatons, and I plan to close up the house until I decide what to do with it. My good-byes to the servants were laced with tears, especially for Jonalyn. I will try to stay in communication with them if I can. I will hire Tyler Quinn's mentor, Simon Barclay, to manage the businesses, and it will give him quite a substantial living. I believe Mr. Barclay to be a good and honest man. He will keep my financial business quiet and continue to watch the accumulation of wealth which I can leave to my children, should I have any. Otherwise, I have designated charities as the recipients of my late husband's wealth.

I have given a great deal of thought as to what I shall do with the life I have left. I am but eighteen years of age, so I hope to see many years to come. I do not imagine myself going back to the tiny town of Anthem to live; that life, as well as that naïve girl, is gone. They died the day I left and came to Endurance. But I will love and visit my parents and brothers, and now I will be able to help them financially.

Yesterday, Mr. Tyler Quinn called on me with his official calling card. We sat in the front parlor and had many words to say, words we could not say during this dark period of my life.

And so I take my leave from Endurance, a town that held such hope, but also such pain. I plan to visit the many cities on the East Coast of America. I would like to see New York City and Boston and Philadelphia—and even Buzzards Bay—places I have simply read about. Now that I am a widow, I may visit them in a widow's black clothing, and none will question my unaccompanied travel. And I hope to try a balloon ascension ride, the most wondrous thing I saw when I first came to Endurance. I believe I will take this trip to the East Coast to heal myself and consider the next part of my life.

The Heatons and Rose Hernshaw will accompany me to the railroad station and make sure my belongings are put on the train with me. When I leave Lockwood House, I will turn and look one last time at the turrets, walls, and windows of the mansion, and I will remember the rich mahogany staircases and the thick stained-glass windows. Such beauty. Then I will turn my back on it forever. What a different journey this will be from the one I made last October. Perhaps I shall wave at the White City as I head toward the East.

And my diary—you that has sustained me throughout this ordeal—I will leave you here in this house of sadness. The Lockwood name I will never answer to again, nor will I ever use it, since I must work hard at forgetting this period of my life. But my locket, with the pictures of my parents, I will wear forever, a reminder of their love for me.

In two years, when my time of mourning is over, if all goes as planned and God is willing, I will meet Tyler Quinn somewhere far from the town of Endurance. We will marry and live in mutual respect, a bond I once hoped to find. I now know that he was in my heart all along.

And, despite the anger and sorrow and tears I shed here, I will continue to have an abiding memory and fondness for that library and reading room, the public square, my Aunt Maud, the Fourth of July picnics, and the wondrous feeling in my heart when I first laid eyes on the astonishing town that is Endurance.

ABOUT THE AUTHOR

Susan Van Kirk lives in a small town very much like her fictional Endurance. Educated at Knox College and the University of Illinois, she taught high school English for thirty-four years in the small town of Monmouth, Illinois. She taught an additional ten years at Monmouth College. Her short story "War and Remembrance" was published by *Teacher Magazine* and became one of the chapters in her 2010 creative nonfiction memoir, *The Education of a Teacher (Including Dirty Books and Pointed Looks)*. *Marry in Haste* is her second Endurance mystery. The first, *Three May Keep a Secret,* was published in 2014. She divides her time between Illinois and Phoenix, Arizona, where her three children and nine grandchildren live. Visit her website at www.susanvankirk.com.

DEC   2016

ORANGE COUNTY MAIN LIBRARY
137 W. MARGARET LANE
HILLSBOROUGH, NC 27278